She coul...... and the gent...... nce.

She wanted to look at him. She really did. She wanted to gaze into his eyes and feel that click of closeness to him. To let him look deeper and let herself dream of having handsome Lorenzo Davis fall in mad love with her.

It wasn't going to happen.

"Next harvest will be better," he promised. "I'll put it in my prayers."

His smile drew her once again. Unable to resist, her eyes met his and the world faded. The jarring of the sleigh ceased. The cold vanished and there was only his sincerity, his caring and the quiet wish in her soul she could not give in to.

"We're here."

Books by Jillian Hart

Love Inspired Historical

*Homespun Bride
*High Country Bride
In a Mother's Arms
  "Finally a Family"

**Gingham Bride
**Patchwork Bride
**Calico Bride
**Snowflake Bride

Love Inspired

*A Soldier for Christmas
*Precious Blessings
*Every Kind of Heaven
*Everyday Blessings
*A McKaslin Homecoming
A Holiday to Remember
*Her Wedding Wish
*Her Perfect Man
Homefront Holiday
*A Soldier for Keeps
*Blind-Date Bride

†The Soldier's Holiday Vow
†The Rancher's Promise
Klondike Hero
†His Holiday Bride
†His Country Girl
†Wyoming Sweethearts

*The McKaslin Clan
†The Granger Family Ranch
**Buttons & Bobbins

JILLIAN HART

grew up on her family's homestead, where she helped raise cattle, rode horses and scribbled stories in her spare time. After earning her English degree from Whitman College, she worked in travel and advertising before selling her first novel. When Jillian isn't working on her next story, she can be found puttering in her rose garden, curled up with a good book or spending quiet evenings at home with her family.

Snowflake Bride

JILLIAN HART

Love Inspired

Recycling programs
for this product may
not exist in your area.

LOVE INSPIRED BOOKS

ISBN-13: 978-0-373-82891-3

SNOWFLAKE BRIDE

www.LoveInspiredBooks.com

Printed in U.S.A.

Therefore...put on tender mercies,
kindness, humility, meekness, longsuffering;
bearing with one another and forgiving one
another...but above all these things put on love.
—*Colossians* 3:12–14

Chapter One

December 1884
Angel County, Montana Territory

Snowflakes hovered like airy dreams, too fragile to touch the ground. They floated on gentle winds and twirled on icy gusts. Not that she should be noticing.

"How long have you been standing here, staring?" Ruby Ballard asked herself. Her words were too small to disturb the vast, lonely silence of the high Montana prairie or to roust her from watching the beauty of white-gray sky and dainty flakes. They reminded her of the crocheted stitches of the doily she was learning to make.

"Your interview. Remember?" She blinked the snowflakes off her lashes and hiked up the skirts of her best wool dress. Time to give up admiring the loveliness and get her head in the real world. Pa often told her that was her biggest problem. Could she help it that God's world was so lovely she was mesmerized into noticing it all the time?

"Focus, Ruby. You need this job. Badly." Enough that she'd hardly prayed about anything else for days, ever since her dear friend Scarlet had told her about the opening. She quickened her pace up the Davis's long, sweeping drive because Pa hadn't been able to get any work in town so far this winter and her family was desperate.

Ping! The faint sound was at odds with the hush of the flakes plopping gently and the crunch of her shoes in the snow. A very suspicious sound. She glanced around, but there was nothing aside from fence posts and trees. The wind gusted and knifed through her shoe with the precision of a blade. Fearing the worst, she looked down.

A spot of her white stocking clearly peeked between the gaping leather tongue of her black left shoe. Her stomach dropped in an *oh-no!* way. She had lost a button. What kind of an impression was she going to make when Mrs. Davis, one of the wealthiest women in the county, noticed?

Ruby hung her head. She would look like the poor country girl she was. Not that she was ashamed of that, but she didn't think it would help her get the job.

"Don't panic. Stay calm." First things first. She needed to find the button. How hard could it be to locate in all this white snow? It would surely stand out; she could pluck it up and sew it back on her shoe. Since this wasn't the first time this sort of thing had happened, she carried thread and a needle in her reticule for emergencies. Problem solved. Job interview saved.

Except she couldn't see the button—only pure, white snow in every direction. There was no sign of a hole where it had fallen through. Nothing. Now it was time to panic. If she couldn't sew it back on, she needed to come up with another plan.

"Looking for something?" A warm baritone broke into her panic.

Ruby froze. She knew that voice. She'd heard it before when she'd overheard him talking with his family before or after church. She remembered that deep, kind timbre from the previous school year as he would answer the teacher's questions or chat with his friends during recess.

Lorenzo Davis. Her heart stopped beating. Her palms broke out in a sweat. The panic fluttering behind her ribs increased until it felt as if a hundred hummingbirds were trapped there, desperate to escape. What did she do? She straightened, realizing she must look like an idiot.

A snow-covered idiot. She swiped the damp stuff off her face and spun to him. *Try to be calm, Ruby,* she told herself. *Be dignified.*

"Ilostashoebutton," she said, the words tumbling off her tongue as if she were no more than a dummy. Honestly. The words had sounded just fine in her mind, but the instant they hit her tongue, they bunched together like overcooked oatmeal, and now she looked twice as stupid to the most handsome man in the territory.

Brilliant, Ruby. Just perfectly brilliant.

"Sorry, I missed that." Lorenzo tipped his hat cordially, disturbing a slight layer of snowflakes that had accumulated on the brim. He looked like seven kinds of dashing as he rose from his sleigh. He had a classic, square-cut face, impressively wide shoulders and enough quiet charm to send every single young lady in town to dreaming.

That was one thing she was *not* dreaming about—

Lorenzo Davis. She might not be as well-schooled as her friend Meredith or as well-read as her friend Lila, but she knew a man like him would never be interested in a plain girl like her or one who could embarrass herself so easily. Not only did she have a button missing, but she had to explain it to him—again—and pray this time she regained the power of speech, or he would think she had something terribly wrong with her.

"Oh, you have a button missing." He strode toward her, a mountain of powerful male concern. She'd never realized how tall he was before, as she'd never been this close to him before or alone with him. She swallowed hard, realizing there was just the two of them and the veil of the falling snow for as far as she could see.

"Do you have any idea where you lost it?" His deep blue gaze speared hers with something that could have been friendly, but it was far too intense. "It's a long way between here and your farm."

"Ah, over here." Thankful her command of the English language had returned, she felt silly pointing in front of her, where she had been looking when he'd driven up. His horse watched them curiously, blowing air out his nose and sending snowflakes whirling. "I'm afraid it's gone for good."

"I'm afraid you're right. You may have to wait until spring to find it." A slow grin accompanied his words. There was a reason most of the young ladies in Angel Falls had a crush on the man. When he smiled, good humor warmed a face that was already perfection and gave heart to his intense, dark blue eyes, the straight, strong blade of his nose and the hard, lean line of his mouth. His cheekbones were sharp enough to cut glass, and the uncompromising angle of his square jaw spoke of strength and character. He didn't need his heart-stopping dimples, but they made him mesmerizing. Incomparable. The most handsome man ever.

"I better not wait until April for a button," she quipped. "I should be going. Thanks for stopping."

"Sure." He tilted his head slightly to one side, as if he was studying her or trying to make up his mind about her.

So far, so good, she thought. She hadn't said anything that she considered inane enough that it would haunt her for days. She tightened her grip on her reticule, nodded good day and set out like the dignified young lady she wished she could be.

Ping! Ping! Shoe buttons went flying and plunked into the snow right in front of Lorenzo.

How embarrassing. Now her stockings were really showing, plus she looked like someone who couldn't afford sturdy shoes. Mrs. Davis was never going to hire her now. If she did, the woman might worry what other part of her new maid's attire would fail next. And as for Lorenzo, he had to be thinking she was the most backward country girl he'd ever seen.

"Got one." He bent quickly and neatly plucked something out of the snow. "Let's see if I can hunt down the other."

Mortified, she watched in horror. Dreamy Lorenzo Davis dug his leather-gloved fingers through the snow in search of her battered shoe button with the patience and care he would spend looking for a fallen gold nugget.

Don't think about the patch in your shoes, she told herself. She'd carefully repaired the hole on her handed-down shoes from the church donation barrel and had oiled the leather carefully. At a distance, they could have been new, but up close, they had clearly seen better days. She feared she looked as secondhand as her shoes. Definitely not in Lorenzo's class.

"Found it." Triumphant, Lorenzo stood, all six feet of impressive male towering over her, and held out his hand. There, on his gloved palm, sat her buttons. "Are you interviewing with my mother this morning?"

"Yes. Thank you." She plucked the buttons from him quickly, because she'd made her own mittens and they were a sad sight. She was only learning to knit and the uneven gage showed more than just a tad.

He didn't seem to notice. "I know she's looking for someone dependable. Her last kitchen maid eloped with the neighbor's farmhand without giving notice, so Ma is particularly miffed about that. Mention you are as dependable as the sun, and she'll hire you."

She slipped the buttons into her coat pocket. His advice was nice, but why would he bother? "You're giving me an advantage."

"Guilty. It would be nice to see a friendly face around the house. I miss everyone from school. Don't get me wrong, I love working on the ranch, but I spend more time with cows and horses than people." Those dimples deepened and held her captive.

Surely a sign of impending doom. She could not let a handsome man's dimples draw her in like that. What was wrong with her? She tried to hide her smile and stared at the toes of her shoes. She needed to repair her shoe in time for her interview. How could she do that while he watched? Surely, as nice and kind as he was, Lorenzo couldn't help drawing conclusions.

Well, she was never going to be as stylish as her friend Scarlet, endearing like Earlee or poised like Kate. She couldn't pretend otherwise. She could only loosen her reticule strings and fish around for the packet of needles and bobbin of thread.

"Let me drive you up to the house." His warm offer startled her.

"D-drive me?" She nearly dropped the buttons.

"It will give you time to sew everything on. My mother will never suspect." Kindly, he held out his hand, palm up, as an invitation. "You can sew while I drive."

Did his unguarded blue eyes have to be so compelling? Veiled in the snow, he could have been a western legend come to life, too dreamy to be real and too incredible to be actually speaking to her.

Don't do it, she decided. Her pa had raised her to be self-reliant. She was perfectly capable of walking the rest of the way. Besides, she was too shy to think of a thing to say to him on the drive. She should simply say no.

"C'mon. I'm not leaving without you. If you walk, I walk. Not that I mind, but Poncho might take offense."

As if on cue, the beautiful bay blew out his breath like a raspberry, making his lips vibrate disparagingly.

"See?" Lorenzo chuckled, and the sound was warm and homey, like melting butter on a stove. "If Poncho is upset, he will take it out on me all day long. You don't want that for me, do you?"

"No, as Poncho looks like a terror." The terror in question reached over to lip his master's hat brim affectionately. Even the horse adored him. "I suppose one short, little ride won't hurt. It's only so I can sew."

"Of course. That's the reason I asked." Lorenzo's assurance came quick and light.

He must offer rides to stranded young ladies all the time. He was a gentleman. It was nothing personal, which made it easier to lay her palm on his.

A current of awareness telegraphed through her with the suddenness of lightning striking. The sweet wash of sensation was like a hymn on a Sunday morning. A sweetness she had no business feeling, though it brought her a gentle peace. She didn't remember stepping forward or climbing into the sleigh. Suddenly, she was on the seat with him settled next to her and the steel of his arm pressed against hers.

How was she going to concentrate enough to sew?

"What happened to the horse you usually ride?" He snapped the reins gently. Poncho stepped forward, although the gelding swiveled his ears back, as if he wanted to hear the answer, too.

"Solomon threw a shoe, and I didn't dare ride him." She leaned forward to work on loosening her laces.

"It's a long way to walk. Three miles or more."

"I don't mind. It's a beautiful morning." Soft, platinum curls, fallen loose from her plaits, framed her heart-shaped face and fluttered in the wind.

"It's a cold morning," he corrected gently, but she didn't seem to see his point as she tugged off her shoe, shook off any melting pieces of snow and set it on her lap. He tried to think of a woman he knew who would walk three miles on a morning like this because it was better for her old horse. "You must really want the chance at the kitchen job."

"Yes. I'm sure I'm not the only one. Work is hard to find these days. Pa is always talking about the poor economy." She unwound a length of thread from a small wooden spool, her long, slender fingers graceful and careful.

Wishing swept through him as he studied her profile. Long lashes framed her light blue eyes. Her nose had a sweet little slope, and her gentle, rosebud mouth seemed to always hold the hint of a smile. The way her chin curved, so delicate and cute, made him want to run the pad of his thumb along the angle to see if her skin felt as soft as it looked. Every time he gazed upon her, tenderness wrapped around him in ever-strengthening layers. He had a fondness for Ruby Ballard, but he suspected she did not have one for him.

The sting pierced him, but he tried not to let it show. Never, not once, had he caught her glancing his way. A few times, he'd spotted her in town, but she was busily chatting with her friends or running her errands and did not notice him.

Then again, he had never been alone with her, and she was fairly new to town. She'd arrived late in the school year last year. He remembered the day. How quiet she'd been, settling onto her seat in the back of the school room. She hadn't made a sound, but he'd turned in his seat toward her, unable to stop himself. To him, she was like the first light of dawn, like the first gentle notes of a song and he'd been captivated.

"Everyone is talking about the poor economy," he agreed. The low prices of corn and wheat this last harvest had been a disappointment to his family and a hardship to many others. He didn't have to ask to know her family had been hard hit, too. "Did your father find work in town?"

"How did you know he was looking?" She glanced up from threading her needle. Wide, honest eyes met his with surprise. "How do you know my father?"

"He came by during the harvest, looking for work. We had already filled our positions, or I would have made sure he had a job." He knew how fortunate his family was with their plentiful material blessings. He had learned a long time ago wealth did not equate to the goodness inside a person and that everyone was equal in God's eyes. Having money and privilege did not make someone better than those without. God looked at the heart of a person, and he tried hard to do the same. When Jon Ballard had come to ask for employment with hat in hand, Lorenzo had seen a decent, honest, hardworking man. "I gave him a few good recommendations around town. I had hoped it helped."

"It didn't, but that was nice of you, Lorenzo."

"It was no problem." The way she said his name tugged at his heart. He couldn't deny he was sweet on the woman, couldn't deny he cared. He liked everything about her—the way she drew her bottom lip between her teeth when she concentrated, the care she took with everything, including the way she set the button to the shoe leather and started the first, hesitant stitch.

Snow clung to her in big, fat flakes of fragility, turning the knit hat she wore into a tiara and decorating her light, gossamer curls framing her face. Snowflakes dappled her eyelashes and cheeks until he had to fight to resist the urge to brush them away for her.

"In other words, you are in serious need of employment." He kept his tone light but determination burned in his chest.

"Yes." She squinted to draw her needle through the buttonhole a second time. "My brother has found work in Wyoming. Pa is considering moving there."

"Moving?" Alarm beat through him. "Is there work for him there?"

"No, but he has the hope for it." Her rosebud mouth downturned, she fastened all her attention on knotting her thread. "I would have to go with him."

"I see." His throat constricted making it hard to speak, harder to breathe. "You don't want to go?"

Please, say no, he thought. His pulse leaped, galloping as if he'd run a mile full out. It seemed an eternity until she answered, her voice as sweet as the morning.

"I'm happy here. I wish to stay." She bit off the thread and bent her head to re-knot it.

I wish that, too. It wasn't exactly a prayer, he did not believe in praying for himself, so it was for her happiness he prayed. *Give her the best solution, Lord,* he asked. *Please.* He had no time to add any thoughts because a shadow appeared through the gray veil of the storm, which had grown thick, blotting out all sign of the countryside and of the lamp-lit windows of the house that should have been in sight.

Poncho gave a short neigh, already anticipating the command before it happened. Lorenzo tugged briefly on the right rein anyway as the gelding guided the sleigh neatly around the figure. A woman walked up the lane,

her head covered with a hood and her coat shrouded
with snow. She glanced briefly at them, but he could not
recognize her in the downfall. His first inclination was
to stop and offer her a ride, too, but then he wouldn't be
alone with Ruby. He felt Poncho hesitate, as if the horse
was wondering why he hadn't been pulled to a stop.

Out of the corner of his eye, he saw Ruby, head down,
intent on sewing the final button as fast as she could
go. This was his one chance, his one shot to be alone
with her. He hoped that she might see something in him
she liked, something that might lead her to say hello to
him on the street the next time they met or to smile at
him across the church sanctuary on Sunday. He gave
the reins a sharp snap so Poncho would keep going. Up
ahead, another shadow rose out of the ever-thickening
curtain as the storm closed in.

"There. Done," Ruby said with a rush and stowed
away her needle and thread. "Just in time, too. There's
the house."

"It was good timing," he agreed as he slowed the
gelding in front of the portico. The tall, overhead roof
served as a shelter from the downfall. While she leaned
forward to slip on her shoe, he drank in the sight of her
until his heart ached. He didn't know why she opened a
place inside of him, a deep and vulnerable room he had
not known was there.

"That will have to do." She shrugged, for a glimpse of
her stocking still showed between the gap in the buttons.
Her eyes had darkened a shade, perhaps with worry. She
didn't wait for him to offer his hand to help her from the
sleigh but bounded out on her own.

That stung. He steeled his spine and straightened his

shoulders, determined not to let the hurt show. She made a pretty picture circling around the back of the vehicle, her skirt snapping with her hurried gait. Snow sprinkled over her like powdered sugar. She couldn't look any sweeter. His heart tugged, still opening up to her when he knew he ought to step back and respect that she didn't feel a thing for him.

"Thank you, Lorenzo." She stared down at her toes.

Was it his imagination, or did her soft voice warm just a tad when she said his name? The wind gusted, driving snow between them, and he couldn't be sure. He cleared his throat, hoping to keep the emotion from his voice. "Glad I could help you out, Ruby."

"Help me? You saved me. This way, your mother won't see me sewing on my buttons in her entry." She bobbed a little on her feet and lifted her eyes briefly to him. "Thank Poncho for me, too."

"I will." He rocked back on his heels, shocked by the impact of her gaze. Quick, gentle and timid, but his heart opened wider.

She was shy, he realized, which was different from not being interested in him. Her chin went back down, and she swept away like a waltz without music, like a song only he could hear.

Chapter Two

Ruby stared at the marble floor beneath her, where the snow melting from her shoes had left a puddle. A stern housekeeper in a black dress and crisp apron had taken her mittens, coat and hat and left her clutching her reticule by the strings and staring in wonder at her surroundings. The columns rising up to the high ceiling were marble, too, she suspected. Ornate, golden-framed paintings marched along the walls, which were wainscoted and coved and decorated with a craftsmanship she'd never seen before. She felt very plain in her best wool dress, which was new to her, being handed down from her older cousin. Very plain, indeed.

"Lucia tells me you are quite early." A tall, lovely woman came into sight. Her sapphire-blue dress of the latest fashion rustled pleasantly as she drew near. "With this storm, I expected everyone to be a bit behind."

"My pa has a gift for judging the weather, and he thought a storm might be coming, so I left home early." Ruby grasped her reticule strings more tightly, wondering what she should do. Did she stand? Did she remain seated? What about the puddle beneath her shoes?

"Over an entire hour early." Mrs. Davis smiled, and there was a hint of Lorenzo in the friendly upturned corners. She had warm eyes, too, although they were dark as her hair, which was coiled and coiffed in a beautiful sweeping-up knot. "Why don't you come with me now, since everyone else is late? We can talk. Would you like some tea? You look as if you could use some warming up."

"Yes, ma'am." She stood, feeling the squish of her soles in the wetness. "But first, should I borrow something? The snow stuck in my shoe treads melted. I don't want to make a mess."

"Lucia will see to it. Don't worry, dear. Come along." Mrs. Davis gestured gently with one elegant hand. Diamonds sparkled and gold gleamed in the lamplight. "Come into the parlor."

"Thank you." Her interview was now? That couldn't be good. She wasn't prepared. She hadn't recovered from being with Lorenzo. Her mind remained scrambled and his handsome face was all she could think of—the strong line of his shoulders, the capable way he held the reins and his kindness to her over the button disaster.

Pay attention, Ruby. She set out after Mrs. Davis. *Squeak,* went her right shoe. *Creak,* went her left. Oh, no. She stopped in her tracks but the woman ahead of her continued on and disappeared around a corner. She had to follow. *Squeak, creak. Squeak, creak.* She hesitated at a wide archway leading into the finest room she'd ever seen.

"Come sit across from me," Mrs. Davis invited kindly, near to a hearth where a warm fire roared. "I hear you know my dear friend's daughter."

"Scarlet." *Squeak, creak.* She was thankful when she reached the fringed edges of a finely woven rug. Her wet shoes were much quieter as she padded around a beautiful sofa. *Squish, squish.* She hesitated. Mrs. Davis was busy pouring tea from an exquisite china pot. The matching cups looked too fragile to actually drink from.

"I hear you girls went to school together."

"Yes, although Scarlet graduated last May." She knew the question would come sooner or later, so she might as well speak of it up front. "I haven't graduated. I wasn't ready."

"Yes, I heard you did not have the chance for formal schooling before you moved to our town." Mrs. Davis eased onto one sofa and gestured to the one across from her. "Do you like sugar, dear?"

"Please." Her skirts were still damp from the snow, so she eased gingerly onto the edge of the cushion. She had to set her reticule down and stop her hands from shaking as she reached for the tea handed to her. *Clink, clink.* The cup rattled against the saucer. She didn't know if she was still shaky with nerves over her encounter with Lorenzo or over her interview with his mother.

A little help please, Lord. She thought of her pa, who was such a good father. She thought of her brother, who worked so hard to send money home. *For them.*

"You must know my Lorenzo." Mrs. Davis stirred sugar into the second cup. "You two are about the same age."

"Yes, although we were not in the same crowd at school." She didn't know how to say the first time she'd ever spoken to the handsome young man had been today.

He'd been terribly gallant, just as she'd always known he would be. He treated everyone that way.

She knew better than to read anything into it.

"Tell me what kind of kitchen experience you have." The older woman settled against the cushions, ready to listen.

"None." Already she could see failure descending. She took a small sip of the hot tea and it strengthened her. "I've never held a job before, but I am a hard worker. I've cooked and cleaned for my pa and my brother since I was small."

"And your mother?"

"She passed away when I was born." She tried to keep the wistfulness out of her voice, the wish for a mother she'd never known.

"And your father never remarried, even with young children?" Concern, not censure, pinched in the corners of the lovely woman's dark eyes.

"No. He said his love for Ma was too great. I don't think he's ever stopped loving her." Ruby shrugged. Did she turn the conversation back to her kitchen skills? She wasn't sure exactly what a kitchen maid was required to do.

"The same thing happened to my father when I was born." Mrs. Davis looked sad for a moment. She was striking and exotic, with her olive complexion and dark brown, almost-black eyes. Ruby thought she'd never seen anyone more beautiful. The older woman set her cup on her saucer with a tiny clink. "He raised me the best he could. In our home there were maids to do the work and a nanny to help, but nothing can replace the hole left behind when someone is lost. You prepare meals, then?"

"Yes." Her anxiety ebbed. She'd seen the great lady in town and, of course, at church, and Mrs. Davis had always seemed so regal and distant. Ruby hadn't expected to feel welcome in her presence. Hopeful, she found herself smiling. "I'm not sure what you are looking for, but I know how to clean, I know how to do what I'm told, and I follow directions very well."

"That's exactly what Scarlet told me." Mrs. Davis smiled. "Whomever I hire will be expected to assist the cook, to help do all the cleaning of the pots and pans and the entire kitchen. Do you know how to serve?"

"No." She wilted. "I've never done anything as fancy as that."

"I see." Mrs. Davis paused a moment, studying her carefully from head to toe. It was an assessing look and not an unkind one, but Ruby felt every inch of the inspection.

What did the lady see? The gap in her shoe buttons? The made-over, handed-down dress?

"What about your schooling?" The older lady broke the silence.

Ruby hung her head. She tried not to, but her chin bobbed downward of its own accord. "I am still attending this year. I had hoped to catch up and be able to graduate in the spring, but my home circumstances have changed."

"And you need to work," Mrs. Davis said with understanding.

"Yes." She was not the best candidate for the job. She was probably not the type of young woman right for the

position. It hurt, and she tried not to let it show. A blur
of color caught the corner of her eye. She turned just an
inch to see beyond the wide windows. Outside, a man
made his way through the thick curtains of snow, a familiar man.

Lorenzo.

Don't look, Ruby. But did her eyes obey?

Not a chance.

He lifted a leather-gloved hand in a brief wave, and
the snap of connection roared through her like the crackling and cozy heat from the fireplace. Hard not to remember his kind advice to her.

"I am very reliable, Mrs. Davis." She was content
with who she was, and she let the fine lady see it. "I
have good values, I know the importance of keeping
promises, and I will do my best never to let you down.
If you hire me, I will arrive early, I will stay late, and I
will work harder than anyone else. I would never leave
you in a lurch by not showing up when expected."

"That's nice to hear, dear." Mrs. Davis smiled fully,
and it was Lorenzo's smile she saw, honest and good-
hearted and kind. "Now, tell me a little more about your
background."

He'd timed it perfectly, he thought, grateful as he
seized Poncho's reins, thanked the horse for standing
so long in his traces and gave the leather lines a snap.
His heart twisted hard at the sight of Ruby slipping out
of the front door and into the snow. Was he in love with
her? He feared love was too small a word.

He loved a woman who hardly knew he existed. He'd
pined after her whenever he'd seen her in town and long

before that, during their final year of school together. Not once had she ever looked his way. Until today. She'd accepted a ride from him, she'd smiled at him, she'd given him the faintest ghost of a hope.

Time to put his heart on the line and see if the lady rejected him or if he had a chance with her.

That was one chance he wanted more than anything on this earth. The marrow of his bones ached with it, the depth of his soul longed for it. He snapped the reins, sending Poncho out of the shelter of the barn and into the fierce beat of snow and wind. But did he feel the cold? Not a bit. Not when he kept Ruby in sight, slim, petite, as sweet as those snowflakes falling.

"C'mon, Poncho," he urged. "Don't lose her."

She walked at a good clip, bent into the wind. Her blue dress flashed beneath the hem of her coat and twisted around her ankles, trying to hamper her. But she kept on going without looking back. He saw nothing more of her as the gusts shifted, stealing her from his sight. The storm couldn't stop the longing in his soul to see her again.

This was his chance to be with her. To try to get past her shyness and see if she could like him. His stomach knotted up with nerves as he snapped Poncho's reins, urging him to hurry, although he could barely see his horse's rump in the whiteout conditions. Surely Ruby couldn't have gotten far.

Poncho seemed to understand the importance of the mission, for the mighty gelding pushed into the storm, parting the thickly falling snow. He walked right up to Ruby and stopped of his own accord. Lorenzo grinned. It was nice having his horse's support.

"Poncho? Is that you?" Ruby's whimsical alto drifted to him through the storm. He could see the faint outline of her, already flocked white. "It *is* you. So that means…" She hesitated. "Lorenzo? What are you doing out in this weather again?"

Her words may be muffled from the wind and snow, but they carried a note of surprise. As if she truly had no idea what he was up to.

"I have an errand, which will take me by your place." He pulled aside the buffalo robe he'd taken from the tack room. "Would you like a ride?"

"Well…" She wavered, considering.

"It will be an awfully difficult walk with this drifting snow." He'd tried over and over to stop his feelings for Ruby. An impossible endeavor. He braced himself for her refusal and tried one more time. "You may as well let Poncho do the hard work."

She edged closer, debating, her bottom lip caught beneath her front teeth.

"I appreciate Poncho's offer." The hint of a smile tucked in the corners of her mouth deepened. "I suppose his feelings would be hurt if I turned him down?"

"Very. He's the one who insisted on stopping. Apparently he's taken a shine to you."

"Well, I think he's a very nice horse. He's as gentlemanly as my Solomon." She disappeared, perhaps believing it was the horse who cared for her and not the driver. Although he could no longer see her, the faint murmur of her voice as she spoke with the gelding carried on the wind. Just a syllable and a scrap of a sentence, and then she reappeared at his side. "Poncho talked me into accepting."

"He can be persuasive." Lorenzo held out his hand to help her settle onto the seat beside him. Her hand felt small against his own, and the bolt of awareness that rushed through him went straight to his soul. He wasn't used to feeling anything this strongly. "Besides, a storm like this can turn into a blizzard, something you don't want to be out walking in."

"It would be no less dangerous to a horse and sleigh." She settled against the cushioned seat back. "I wonder why you would venture out. Surely there isn't much ranching work this time of year?"

"I never said it was ranch work." He tucked the buffalo robe around her, leaning close enough to catch the scent of honeysuckle. The vulnerable places within him tugged, defenseless against her nearness. He didn't know why his heart moved so fast, determined to pull him along. He could not stop it as he gathered the reins, sending Poncho forward.

"In my worry over my shoe and my interview, I forgot to ask you. I heard your father was injured a while back. How is he?"

"He's still recovering." Lorenzo did his best not to let his anger take hold at the outlaws who had taken up residence west of town last summer and stolen a hundred head of cattle in a gun battle. "My father wasn't as fortunate as the others the outlaw gang shot. He was hit in the leg bone and the back. He's still struggling to walk with a cane."

"I'm so sorry." Sympathy polished her, making her inner beauty shine. Her outer beauty became breathtaking, so compelling he could not look away. Soft platinum locks breezed against the curving slope of her cheeks and the dainty cut of her jaw. "I noticed he wasn't coming to church, but I didn't know he was still struggling with his injuries. I don't get to town much."

"It's not something Pa wants everyone to know. He's a private man." He adored his father. Gerard Davis was a proud and stubborn Welshman who could have lived leisurely on his inherited wealth but chose to put his life to good use by ranching on the Montana frontier. Lorenzo hoped he took after his pa.

"I won't mention it, but I do intend to pray for him." Her hands clasped together within the rather lumpy mittens made of uneven stitches. They looked twisted somehow, as if they had not faired well through a washing. But her earnest concern shone in her voice. "I hope he has a full recovery. I know how difficult it is for a man used to providing for his family when he is too injured to work."

"It is tough on a man's pride."

"When I was little, Pa had an accident on our farm. A hay wagon overturned on him, and he was crushed. He was working alone and no one found him until my brother came with the mid-afternoon water jug. Rupert was too young to help free him. All he could do was run to the neighbors over a mile away."

"I didn't know. I'm sorry." Interesting that they had this in common. He thought of the humble, quiet man who had begged him for a job. "He obviously recovered."

"It took many years. We feared losing him at first. The doctor didn't know how he survived. A true proof of grace," she added, staring down at her misshapen mittens. "God was very good in letting us keep our pa.

I don't know what Rupert and I would have done if we'd lost him, too, so I understand what you might have gone through."

"Worry, mostly. For a while we feared Pa might not walk again. Doc Frost said it was grace, too, that he's up on his feet."

"Grace is everywhere, when you look for it."

"And when you need it most." It was so easy to talk to her about what really mattered. Did she feel the same way? "How long ago was your pa injured?"

"I was five years old." The sleigh bounced in a rut as Poncho turned onto the country road. She lifted a mittened hand to swipe snow out of her eyes. She felt closer somehow. Like they were no longer strangers.

"You were five? That must have been hard on your family."

"Yes. Pa was laid up so long, we lost our crop. We couldn't pay the doctor bills. Then we lost our land and our house, and we couldn't pay any of the other bills, either. The bank took everything but Solomon. Rupert worked long days in a neighbor's field to earn the money to keep him."

"Did you have any other family to help?"

"My uncle and his wife finally took us in. It was a long spell until Pa was able to work again, and he was determined to pay back every cent of his debts still outstanding."

"Most folks would have walked away. So your family was never able to get ahead?"

"It was a hardship paying off the debts, but it was the right thing."

"Doing the right thing matters." His dark blue eyes

deepened with understanding. "It's worth whatever the cost."

"Exactly." When her gaze met his, her heart beat as fast as a hummingbird's wings. It mattered that he understood honor. So many hadn't. Probably because he had honor of his own. She blushed, because it would be so easy to like him, to really like him. Just as it would be to read more into his act of kindness in offering her this ride.

"Your family owns land now, so your father must have paid off his debts." He broke his gaze away to rein Poncho to keep him on the hard-to-see road. Even speckled with snow, Lorenzo's handsomeness shone through.

Not that she should be noticing.

"Yes. Pa managed to save up enough for a mortgage, although we had to pay a lot of money down." She picked at a too-tight stitch in her right mitten to keep from looking at him again. Not looking at him was for the best. "It is good to have our own land, but it's only a hundred acres."

"A hundred acres of untilled land. Let me guess. Your first harvest wasn't as good as it could have been. A first crop on new land is always a small one."

"And on top of that, most of our crop was damaged by a summer storm." She blushed, still picking at the stitch. She could feel the tug of his gaze, the gentle insistence of his presence, and she wanted to look at him. But she was afraid of coming to care too much.

"Next harvest will be better," he promised. "As long as there isn't a drought or a twister or a flash flood."

"Or another hailstorm," she chimed in lightly. "Farming doesn't come with a guarantee, but it would be a great blessing to have a good harvest, if we manage to stay on. My pa and brother work so hard. It would be a comfort for them."

"Then I'll put it in my prayers."

His smile drew her gaze. Unable to resist, her eyes met his, and the world faded. The jarring of the sleigh ceased. The cold vanished, and there was only his sincerity, his caring and the quiet wish in her soul.

Don't give in to it, Ruby. Don't start dreaming.

"Here we are." He tugged on the reins, Poncho drew to a stop. How had three miles passed so quickly?

"Why, young Mr. Davis." Pa's voice came from far away, stupefied. He gripped a pitchfork in one gloved hand, emerging from the small barn. "Ruby, is that you?"

"Yes, Pa." Reality set in. She pushed off the buffalo robe and grabbed up her reticule. Snow slapped her cheeks as she tried to scramble out of the sleigh.

"Allow me." Lorenzo caught her hand. His warmth, his size, his presence overwhelmed her. Her breath caught. She forgot every word of the English langage. Her knees wobbled when she tried to stand on them. Little flashes of wishes filled her, but she tamped them down as he withdrew his hand.

"What are you doing on this side of the county?" Pa asked, curiously. "Looking at the property for sale down the way?"

"Not in this weather." Lorenzo released her hand. "I wanted to make sure Ruby got home safe in this storm. I hear you have a horse with a shoe problem. I happen to have my tools in the back of the sleigh. If you wouldn't mind, I can take care of that problem for you."

Her jaw dropped. She stared, stunned, as Pa led the way to the barn, taking Poncho by the bridle bits. All she could see was the straight strong line of Lorenzo's wide shoulders through the storm until the thick curtain of snow closed around him, leaving her standing alone on the rickety, front doorstep of their lopsided shanty. That Lorenzo Davis. He was being charitable, that was all, but her heart would never forget.

Chapter Three

"And he went into the barn with your father?" Kate peered through dark lashes, astonished as she sorted through her embroidery floss.

"And he re-shod Solomon for you?" Newlywed Lila looked up from stitching on a new shirt for her husband. "Out of the blue, just like that?"

"Without being asked." The tea kettle rumbled, so Ruby set aside her crocheting. The wooden chair scraped against the wood floor as she rose. It was a tight squeeze to have all seven of them in the front room, but it was warm and cozy, and she loved having the chance to host their sewing circle. "You could have knocked me down with a feather, I was so shocked. I guess this proves the rumors true. Young Mr. Davis is as nice as a man can be."

"That's what we have been trying to tell you." Red-headed Scarlet set down her tatting to get up to help with the tea. "He's amazing. That's why we have all been in love with him at one time or another."

"Not all of us," Fiona corrected as she stitched on baby clothes. Her wedding ring winked in the lamplight as her needle slipped into a seam. The pleats of her dress hid the small bowl of her pregnant stomach. "I've always thought Lorenzo was nice, but I was never smitten."

"Not even a little?" Ruby set the tea to steeping in the old ironware pot. "Lorenzo is terribly handsome. Are you sure you didn't like him at all?"

"I'm positive." Fiona's smile came so easily.

"He adored you from afar. We all saw it," Scarlet added, taking a knife to the johnnycake cooling on the nearby table.

"You broke his heart when you married Ian. Don't deny it." Earlee gave her golden curls a toss as she looked up from basting an apron ruffle. When she smiled, the whole world smiled, too. "If I were penning a story about him, I would have him fall in love with one of you three. A sweet, gentle love with lots of longing and a perfect happily-ever-after."

A perfect happily-ever-after. Didn't that sound romantic? She tamped down her sigh right along with the memory of riding alongside Lorenzo in the sleigh. Her hands shook as she carried the pot and the stack of battered, mismatched tin cups to the circle of chairs in the sitting area.

"It sounds like a story I would read," Lila quipped, the voracious reader of the group. "So, Earlee, who would you match up with Lorenzo?"

"Me!" Kate spoke up before Earlee could as she separated a thin strand of embroidery floss from a green skein. "I would be perfect for him."

"True," Meredith agreed, head bent over her latest patchwork quilt block. "Except doesn't he spend a lot of time with Narcissa Bell?"

"Oh," they all sighed together. Narcissa had been their arch nemesis for as long as anyone could remember.

"I suppose it's only a matter of time before we hear of their engagement." Kate licked the end of the floss and threaded it through the eye of her needle. "It's inevitable."

"It's expected," Lila agreed. "To hear my stepmother talk, their engagement party will be any day now."

"They are both from wealthy families." Ruby couldn't explain why pain hitched through her ribs.

"And their mothers are close friends," Earlee chimed in.

"But so are Scarlet and his mother." She lowered the pot to rest on the short end table Pa had made, which now sat in the center of their circle, a coffee table of sorts. Her hands shook inexplicably. She wasn't disappointed, so no way could that be disappointment weighing like a lead brick on her heart.

"Yes, but Lorenzo and I don't keep the same friends." Scarlet bent over her work, knife in hand. "Did you see Narcissa and Lorenzo at church on Sunday?"

"Sitting side by side." Kate gave a long-suffering sigh. "Right there in the middle of their families."

Ruby hadn't noticed because she didn't have a crush on the man. She couldn't afford to have one. Romance was not in her plans. She didn't have time for it. She wasn't free to pursue her own life. Her father and brother needed her to help save the farm. And besides, if their efforts failed, she would have to leave town.

She wasn't exactly the best candidate for romance. Not for any man. As for Lorenzo, he was a dream she didn't dare have. So why did she ache down to the marrow of her bones as she crossed the room? She couldn't focus on the conversation surging around her, the laughter and friendly banter ringing like merry bells. She lifted down a stack of mismatched plates.

"How did the interview go?" Scarlet lowered her voice, so the others wouldn't hear. She cut the final slice of johnnycake.

"Good, but I'm not right for the position. Mrs. Davis is awful fancy. Nice, but fancy." She set the butter dish next to the plates on the table. She tried to tell herself it didn't matter that she wouldn't get the job. "I would be totally uncomfortable in that house. I'd worry about everything—leaving dirt from my shoes on the floor, turning around and knocking some expensive doodad to the ground, spilling something on those beautiful carpets. What a relief I'm not suitable."

"That's too bad. I thought you would be perfect. My mother said so right to Mrs. Davis. I heard her."

"Thanks, Scarlet. I appreciate it more than you know."

"So, does this mean your family will have to move?"

"I think so, since I won't be getting that job."

"I'm so sorry, Ruby."

"Me, too." She wished she felt comfortable saying more, but she wasn't good at expressing her feelings. They made her feel awkward and exposed, but she knew Scarlet understood. Best friends had that ability.

The cornmeal's sweet, warm scent and aroma of melting butter had her mouth watering. She'd been too nervous to eat all of her breakfast, fearing the interview and too unsettled to eat lunch afterwards. Leftover nerves from meeting Mrs. Davis and not because of her encounter with Lorenzo.

At least, that's what she told herself.

"So, what happened after he fixed Solomon's shoe?" Earlee asked, setting down her work to come help distribute the cake. "Did you offer him a nice, hot cup of tea?"

"And then lunch?" Lila inquired.

"And afterwards, a nice, long chat around the table?" Kate knotted the end of her thread.

"You *did* invite him in, didn't you?" Scarlet asked, two plates of cake in hand.

"Well, no. It wasn't like that. He and Pa were visiting in the barn."

"Did you even go out there?" Fiona set her sewing aside to accept a plate of cake.

All eyes turned on her.

"No. Why would I? I'm not as brazen as the bunch of you."

Laughter flourished, echoing off the walls cheerfully. She couldn't very well admit that she'd kept an eye on the window, glancing out from time to time, straining to see a glimpse of Lorenzo through the snow. She hadn't. She'd only spotted her father stomping the wet off his boots on the lean-to steps. He'd been alone.

"Next time, go out with a nice hot cup of tea for him," Meredith advised.

"And some of this cake," Earlee added. "If he takes one bite of this, he just might propose."

"Oh, I doubt that." She retrieved the last plate from the table, but her stomach had bunched in knots. She was no longer hungry. "He drove off without a word to me, but Pa was mighty pleased with the shoeing job. I'm surprised Pa accepted his charity."

"Maybe he did it for you, Ruby." Scarlet sounded thoughtful as she brought the last plates of cake into the sitting area.

"For me? No. Don't even start thinking that." She had best forget the snap of connection when Lorenzo had taken her hand. Wishful thinking on her part, that was all it could be. "I have Pa to care for. He's the only man in my life. Besides, Lorenzo has Narcissa. Who can compete with that?"

"I wouldn't mind trying," Scarlet spoke up, making everyone laugh.

Ruby settled into a chair, laughing with her friends. How much time would they have together? She didn't know. That question haunted her as talk turned to other handsome bachelors in town. If one particular bachelor lingered in her thoughts, she didn't have to admit it.

Lorenzo leaned back against the chair cushion, grateful to be sitting in front of a warm fire at the end of a tough afternoon. Half frozen, he soaked in the fire's blazing heat, hoping to thaw. After returning from Ruby's home, he'd saddled up and resumed his afternoon shift in the fields, checking cattle, hauling feed and taking a pickax to the animals' water supply, which had frozen up solid.

Ruby. Thoughts of her could chase away the cold. He stretched his feet toward the fire. He still didn't know what his chances were, but she'd been easy to talk to. He would like to talk with her some more. But what were the chances of that if she didn't get the maid's position?

She kept to herself, she lived on the other side of town, and their paths rarely crossed. He didn't want to go back to sneaking gazes at her in church because his mother or one of her friends were going to catch him at it, and then his secret love for Ruby would no longer be private.

"Hot tea for you." The upstairs maid was doubling her duties and slid a tray onto the table at his elbow with a bobbing curtsy. "Cook added some of those scones you like."

"Thank you." He didn't wait for her footsteps tapping on the polished oak floor to fade before he wrapped his hand around the scalding hot cup. He was so cold, he could barely feel the warmth. He blew on the steaming brew before he sipped it. Hot liquid slid down his throat, warming him from the inside. The first step to thawing out.

Ruby. His thoughts boomeranged right back to her. Why her? Her big, blue eyes, her rosebud smile, her sweetness had snared him the instant he'd laid eyes on her. He didn't want to feel this way, he wasn't ready to feel this way. He had a lot to learn about ranching, he had a lot to prove as his father's foreman. And responsibility? That was a huge burden on his shoulders these days. He was in charge of providing for the family and preserving the Davis legacy. No, this wasn't the time to be smitten with anyone.

But his heart kept falling in love with Ruby a little more day by day, taking him with it. He couldn't stop it. He wouldn't if he could. He wanted Ruby to be his fate, the destiny God had in store for him.

"Lorenzo." His mother swept into the room. "Look at you. You were out in that weather too long."

"I'm tough." He'd learned from his father not to let excuses stand in the way. "Work needed to be done, so I did it."

"Yes, but you've gotten frostbite." She hauled a footstool close and tried to look at his hands.

"Nothing serious." He refused to surrender his teacup. "No fussing, Ma. I'm not twelve anymore."

"You are my only son." She smiled, attempting to hide her weariness.

"How did the interviewing go?"

"So many women showed up for one opening. My heart goes out to them all. Every one of them was in sincere need of employment." She swept a strand of black hair from her eyes, troubled and worried as she always was for other people. "I can only choose one. I feel bad for all the others. What will they do?"

He thought of Ruby, of her very humble home, her unreliable shoes and her situation. Her family clearly needed the income her employment would bring. He suspected many of the others who had come during a brisk, winter storm were in as much need. "I don't have an answer. I've had the same worries ever since I took over the hiring for the ranch. Have you decided on anyone yet?"

"I've narrowed it down to a short list, but how to decide from there? I do not know." She stole a corner off one of his scones and popped it into her mouth. "One of them was a young lady about your age. You went to school with her."

"Ruby." His mother didn't miss much. He tried to hide his reaction by taking a quick swallow of tea. The scalding liquid rolled over his tongue, nearly blistering him. He coughed, sputtering.

"Oh, I see." His mother paused thoughtfully. "She seemed like a nice girl."

"Nice? I suppose." As if he was going to tell his mother what he really thought. Fortunately, he had a burning tongue to distract him. "She would be a reliable worker."

"Yes. I thought she was very earnest, but she has no experience."

"She could learn." He hoped he sounded casual, not like a man hoping. He wanted Mother to hire her and make a difference in her life. "She takes care of her family. She does the cooking and cleaning. That's experience, right?"

"I suppose." His mother rose. "I have some pondering to do. So, have you thought about who you want to invite to our pre-Christmas ball? It's getting closer, and I have yet to get out the last of my invitations."

"And you're mentioning this to me why, exactly?" He sipped more tea, taking refuge behind the cup. Had he made a strong enough case for Ruby's sake? He couldn't tell by the look on his mother's face.

"Because I'll want to know so I can send the young lady an invitation. It's time you started thinking about a wife. I'm looking forward to the next Davis generation."

"You mean grandchildren?"

"Of course." His mother laughed, delighted. "I see that blush. It's as I thought. You have your eye on someone, and I know who."

"You do?" Tea sloshed over the rim. His heart

slammed to a stop. Fine, so he'd been a little obvious. "I admit, I do have someone in mind."

"Excellent. You know the Bells are on my guest list anyway, but I wanted to send a special one to Narcissa." Poor, misguided Ma. She'd leaped to the wrong conclusion.

"I'm not escorting Narcissa." Not again. "Normally I let you do what you want, but not this time, Ma."

"Why?" Confused, his mother slipped onto the chair across from him. "I thought all that time you two spend together meant something."

"Mostly arranged by you or her mother. It's very hard to say no to either one of you."

"Yes, but she sits beside you in church every Sunday."

"Coincidence on my part. I'm thinking intentionally on hers and her mother's."

"I'm terribly disappointed."

"Of course you want me to marry your best friend's daughter, Ma, but that's not going to happen. We're just friends."

"I see. Well then, who? There's plenty of suitable young women in town. Surely her family is on my list?"

"I'll take care of inviting her myself." Just as he'd suspected. This was going to be a disappointment to his mother. He was sorry for it. He hated letting her down. He thought of Ruby. How would his parents handle it if they knew the truth?

"I think I hear your father coming. Oh, Jerry, it's you."

"Selma, there you are." Pa's cane tapped on the hardwood, and although he winced in pain with every step, he transformed when he saw his wife. "I see you are keeping our boy company. You did great work today, Renzo."

"I did my best."

"Can't ask for anything more than that. You're doing a fine job. Better than your old man can do." His father's chest puffed out, full of pride, as he slowly limped across the room. "I'm obsolete."

"Never you, Pa. I can't wait to hand you back the reins." Even as he said the words, they all knew they were only a wish. Gerard Davis had been injured far too badly to ever return to the rigors of ranching work. In deference to his father's hopes, he shrugged lightly. "I miss being bossed around by you."

"I miss doing the bossing. But I get my fill on a daily basis. What's this I overheard about your escorting a young gal to our ball? Selma, I thought we agreed you wouldn't push the boy."

"I wasn't pushing, merely suggesting." His mother sounded confused as she held out her arms and wrapped them around her husband. The pair cuddled, glad to see each other after being separated for much of the day. "I want to see Lorenzo settled."

"Yes, dear, but he has enough new responsibility to manage. This ranch is the largest in the county. Renzo ought to be concentrating on learning all there is to know about our land, crops and animals."

"He's doing a fine job. Goodness." Ma's gentle amusement rang in her chuckle as she gave her husband one final hug. She swept backward, love lighting her eyes. "Gerard, I don't see why Lorenzo needs to hold off. You managed to run a ranch and court me at the same time."

"Yes, but I wasn't barely twenty years old. Renzo's mature for his age, but I don't want him distracted. I know how distracting a pretty lady can be." Pa winked, always the charmer, and Ma blushed prettily.

Ruby was definitely distracting. She was all he could see—snowflakes sifting over her to catch in her hair, big, blueberry eyes shyly looking away, the blush on her heart-shaped face when he'd taken her hand in his to help her from the sleigh.

This wasn't the right time in his life, and his parents wouldn't like it, but his heart was set. Nothing could stop it.

"Renzo? Where did you take off to this morning?" Pa leaned heavily on his cane, tapping closer. "Was there a problem I didn't know about?"

"My trip wasn't ranch related." His pulse skipped a beat. What else had his father seen?

"He drove past the window and picked up one of the applicants. He must have taken her home." Pa's tone gentled. "She looked like a dear. That Ballard girl, I think. I know her father from church. He's a good man."

"The poor girl." Ma settled onto the sofa, compassionate as always. "My heart aches for her. Being both daughter and woman of the house. They must be as poor as church mice. I've seen her getting clothes out of the church's donation barrel. It was all I could do not to rush up and give her a big hug when she was here."

Please, he thought. *Please give her a chance.* A job would mean she could stay in town. That he would have a hope of winning her.

"Selma, I know that look." Pa chuckled as he eased

painfully onto the cushion beside his wife. "Son, something tells me your mother has just made up her mind about the new maid."

"Those friends of yours are sure nice girls." Pa knocked snow off his boots on the doorstep. "You all seemed to have a good time."

"We did." She doused the last tin cup in the rinse water, glad to see her father back safely from town. Since Solomon's shoe was fixed, there had been errands needing to be done. "We always have great fun together, and I got a lot of help with my crocheting."

"That's nice, Ruby-bug." He shouldered the door closed against the whirling flakes, and the cold followed him in as he unloaded the groceries he'd bought on the far end of the table. It wasn't much—a bag of beans, a package of tea, small sacks of cornmeal and oatmeal— but she was grateful for it. When Pa swept off his hat, he looked more tired than usual. "I'm glad you made friends here."

"Me, too." She rubbed the dishtowel over the mug, drying it carefully. With each swipe, she felt her stomach fall a notch. Had her father stopped by the post office? Was there a letter from Rupert? Her brother had been hoping to send news of a job.

Sorrow crept into Pa's eyes, and he sat down heavily on a kitchen chair. "I didn't want to say anything to you earlier, but I had chance for work in town, unloading cargo at the depot. It went to someone else. A younger man."

"Oh, Papa." She set down the towel and the cup and circled around to his side. He was a proud man, a strong man, but hardship wore on him. He fought so hard to provide for them, and had struggled for so long. Just when it looked as if life was going to get easier, the storm had hit. Without a crop, there had been no income, and they were back to desperation again.

How little of their meager savings remained? She placed a hand on his brawny shoulder. He was such a good man, and love for him filled her up. They did not have much, but they had what they needed. They had what mattered most.

"I got a letter from Rupert." Her father rubbed his face, where worry dug deep lines. "He sent money."

That explained the groceries. She hated seeing Pa like this. He'd always been invincible, always a fighter, even when he'd been injured. Every memory she had of him was one of strength and determination. He'd always been a rock, the foundation of their family, who never wavered.

Not tonight. He looked heart-worn and hopeless. Like a man who was too weary to fight. The shadows crept visibly over him as the daylight dimmed. Sunset came early this time of year, and she needed to light a candle, to save on precious kerosene, but she could not leave her father's side, not when he bowed his head, looking beaten.

Was their situation far worse than he'd told her? She bit her bottom lip, knotted up with worry. Pa did have a habit of protecting her. If only she could have gotten the job. She winced at the dismal interview she'd had, the squeaky shoes, the rattling teacup, her lack of experience and polish. "I will scour the town tomorrow,

Pa. There has to be something I can do. Sweep floors, do laundry at the hotel, muck stalls at Foster's Dairy."

She would beg if she had to. Her father and brother had been carrying too much burden for way too long. She ached for them, struggling so hard against odds that turned out to be impossible. The dream of owning their own land and being farmers again was fading. At this point in Pa's life, it would likely be gone forever. She knelt before him and laid her hand on his. "I can be persuasive. I will talk someone into hiring me. Please don't worry so much."

"Oh, my Ruby." Pa cupped her face with both of his big, callused hands, making her feel safe. "You are a good girl. I'm afraid the news in Roop's letter wasn't good."

"He found you a job, and we have to leave after all." She squeezed her eyes shut for just one brief moment to hide the stab of pain ripping through her. It was selfish to want to stay when it was a burden for her family, so she firmed her chin. "This will be better for you. A job. Think what this will mean."

"No, honey, there isn't a job. Roop lost his. The mill closed down. It's gone out of business. He's coming home without his last two paychecks. The company promised but in the end couldn't pay him." Pa looked far too old for his years as he squared his shoulders, fighting to find enough internal strength to keep going. "It's a blow, but I don't want you worrying, Ruby. You must stay in school."

"I won't do it." She brushed a kiss on her father's stubbled cheek. "You know me. When I set my mind to something, nothing but God can stop me."

"And even He would give pause before trying," Pa quipped, the love in his eyes unmistakable. "We have to trust Him to see us through this. He's watching over us."

"I know, Pa." She whirled away to light a candle or two, thankful for the bountiful summer garden she'd been able to grow. Selling extra vegetables to the stores in town had given her enough pocket money to make plenty of candles and soap to see them through the winter. It was a small thing to have contributed, but she'd been proud to do it. The warmth of her friends' laughter lingered in the home, making it less bleak as she struck a match.

Encouraged, she watched the wick flare, and the light chased back the shadows. She shook out the match, shivering as the wind blew cold through the walls. Faith was like a candle dispelling the darkness, and she lit another, determined to believe they could make their upcoming mortgage payment, that they would not be homeless by Christmas.

Chapter Four

The snow whirled on a bitter night's wind as Lorenzo guided his horse and sleigh down the drift-covered driveway. Lanterns mounted on the dashboard of the sleigh cast just enough light to see the dark yard and front step of the shanty. Poncho drew to a stop before the doorway. Ruby's doorway.

Her adorable presence stayed with him like a melody, and a smile stretched the corners of his mouth as he climbed from beneath the robes. His boots crunched in the snow, icy flakes stung his face, but he kept going, untouched, seeing Ruby through a crack between the curtains.

She sat in a wooden chair, holding a crochet needle and thread up to a single candle's light to make a slow, careful stitch. Her platinum hair gleamed golden-silver. Her heart-shaped face, flushed from the heat of the fire and caressed by the candlelight could have belonged to a princess in a fairy tale. Wholesome and good, she was the most beautiful woman he'd ever seen. Captivated, he knocked snow off his hat as it continued to fall.

The muffled tap of footsteps tore his attention away

from Ruby. Jon Ballard ambled into sight inside the house, reminding Lorenzo of his mission. He had a message for Ruby, one that would make her life easier. He took the few snowy steps to the front door and knocked. His pulse rattled against his rib cage. He was suddenly nervous, anxious with the anticipation of seeing her again.

The door swung open, and her father stood inside the threshold, surprise marking his lined face, proof of how hard the last few months had been for the family. "Young Mr. Davis, is that you again? What are you doing out on these roads this time of evening?"

"I'm on another errand. My father wanted to send one of the hired men, but I volunteered." His gaze arrowed straight to her. Her crochet work had fallen to her lap. She stared at him with worry crinkling her forehead. Worry. He hated it. He squared his shoulders, glad he could fix that. He pulled the folded parchment from his pocket. "I have a letter for Ruby. From my mother."

"For me?" She set aside her needle and thread, rose to her feet, and every movement she made was endearing—the pad of her stockinged feet on the floor, the rustle of her skirt, the twist of her bottom lip as she swept closer. The place she had opened within him opened more, widening his heart.

Vaguely, he was aware of Jon stepping back, disappearing from sight. Ruby remained at the center of his senses. Ruby, wringing her slender hands. Ruby, in a very old, calico work dress, the color faded from so many washings. The careful patches sewed with tiny, even stitches were too numerous to count. As she stepped into the puddle of nearby candlelight, her beauty and goodness outshone everything.

"It was nice of you to come so far in this cold." Shy, she lowered her gaze from his. "Just to tell me I didn't get the job."

"Why would you say that?"

"Because the interview was a disaster. The missing button, my wet shoes, I dripped all over the floor, I was completely wrong for the position." Pink flushed her cheeks and her nose, making her twice as sweet. "I'm sorry you had to drive so far in this weather. Your mother could have posted the letter."

"I suppose." This was why he'd come so far in frigid temperatures. So he could see the happiness chase away the worry from her big, beautiful eyes. "Ma wants you to start working for her first thing Monday morning. Will that be a problem?"

"What?" Her jaw dropped. Disbelief pinched adorably across her sweetheart face. "I couldn't have gotten the job. I have no experience."

"My mother liked you, so she's hired you." He held out the envelope. "Here are the specifics."

"Really? Oh, Pa, did you hear?" She took the parchment. Delight chased away the worry lines, put blue sparkles into her irises and drew a beautiful smile. "I got the job. I got it."

"I'm mighty proud of you, Ruby-bug." Jon Ballard's love shone in his voice, love for his precious daughter.

Lorenzo thought she was precious, too.

"Oh, thank your mother for me. I mean, I will thank her on Monday, too, when I see her. But, oh, just *thank* you." She clutched the letter tight until it crinkled.

"I will tell her. Your interview went better than you thought."

"But how? It's a complete and total mystery."

"No mystery." His reassurance held notes of humor and kindness. "You deserve this, Ruby. My mother wants you to start at six o'clock sharp."

"I'll be there early, just like I promised." This was too good to be true. She'd been so sure she had failed, that it was impossible, and yet here she was, an employee. She had her first job, she would be earning a wage. A real wage. Joy bubbled through her, impossible to contain. She had a job! "I hope I don't break anything. Or spill something. I don't know anything about serving."

Good going, Ruby. Point out to your employer's son exactly how much of a mistake his mother had made. She laughed. "I'm so happy and anxious and everything."

"I understand." The deep shine of his dark blue gaze met hers, sincere and powerful enough to knock the beat out of her heart. Her happiness dimmed, her soul stilled as he tipped his hat, and she could not look away. She could see the shadow of day's growth on his strong, square jaw. His masculine strength shrank the shanty and made every bit of air vanish. No man on earth could be as amazing as Lorenzo

Candlelight flickered over him, caressing the powerful angles of his face and gleaming darkly on the thick, dark fall of his hair. She lost the ability to breathe as he took a step backward into the darkness. Snow sifted over him like spun sugar.

Don't start wishing, Ruby.

"I shouldn't leave my horse standing in this cold. Good night, Ruby. I will see you on Monday."

"On Monday." The words stuttered over her tongue, her legs went weak, and she grasped the door frame before she tumbled face-first onto the snowy step. Monday. A different kind of panic clutched her, cinching tight around her middle.

She would see Lorenzo every day. She would be in his house, be in proximity with his family and washing his dishes. The warm place in her heart remembered his touch, his gallantry, his kindness. It made a girl want to dream.

Focus, Ruby. She no longer had time for schoolgirl wishes. Pa's tired gait drummed on the floorboards behind her, coming closer. In the dying storm, Lorenzo was a shadow, then a hint of a shadow and finally nothing more. The beat of Poncho's hooves faded until there was only the whispering hush of falling snow and the winter's cold.

She closed the door firmly against the darkness. Discarded wishes followed her like snowflakes in the air as she headed toward the stove to make a cup of tea for her father. She had the chance to make a real difference for her family. Monday was what she ought to think about. Monday, when she started her new job.

In the predawn light, Ruby slid off of Solomon in the shelter of the Davis's barn. Breathing in the scents of hay and warm horse, she glanced around. Stalls were filled with animals eating out of their troughs. What did she do with Solomon? Where did she take him?

Something tugged at her hat, knocking it askew on

her head. Dear old Solomon's whiskery lips nibbled the brim and the side of her face in comfortable adoration. They had been friends for a long time. She patted his neck and leaned against him, her sweet boy. "I'm sure I'm supposed to put you somewhere, but I didn't think to ask when Lorenzo delivered the letter."

Solomon's nicker rumbled low in his throat, a comforting answer of sorts. Fortunately, she did not have to wonder for long as footsteps tapped her way, echoing in the dark aisle. She couldn't see his face, but she would know those mile-wide shoulders anywhere.

"Good morning, Ruby." Lorenzo Davis ambled out of the shadows. Two huge buckets of water sloshed at his sides as he made his way to the end stall. "You are early."

"Only twenty minutes." She'd meant to be earlier, but the roads had been slow going with a thick layer of ice. It had been all Solomon could do to keep his footing. "I'm surprised to see you packing water. Isn't that the stable boy's job?"

"Sure, but I help with the barn work." His answer came lightly as he hefted one of the buckets over the wooden rail. Water splashed into a washtub. "Stay back, Sombrero, or you'll get wet again."

Inside the stall, a horse neighed his opinion. A hoof stomped as if in a protest or a demand to hurry up with the water. The man had a way with animals, she had to give him credit for that. His powerful stance, his rugged masculinity and his ease as he lifted the second ten-gallon bucket and emptied it etched a picture into her mind. That picture took on life and color, and when she blinked, it remained. Another image of the man she could not forget. Her soul sighed just a little. She couldn't help it.

Solomon nudged her a second time, gently reminding her she was doing it again—staring off into thin air when there was work to be done. She shook her head, cleared her thoughts and gently patted her gelding's shoulder. "Where can I put up my boy?"

"I'll take him." Lorenzo set down the bucket and held out a hand to Solomon. "You remember me, don't you, old fella?"

The swaybacked animal snorted in answer. His ears pricked, he snuffled Lorenzo's palm with his muzzle, gray with age. His low-noted nicker was clearly a horsy greeting. Did every living creature adore the man?

"Are you nervous about starting your new job?" He caught Solomon's reins. If he noticed the leather straps were wearing thin, he didn't comment.

"Just a tad." That was an understatement, but she wasn't about to admit it. All she could see was doom. So much could go wrong to cause Mrs. Davis to change her mind or for the stern-looking Lucia to fire her. Anxiety clawed behind her rib cage like a trapped rodent.

Just breathe, she told herself. No need to panic.

Lorenzo's intensely dark blue eyes glowed softly as if he cared. While his gaze searched hers, she felt as if she were the only woman on earth. His slow smile spread wonderfully across his mouth. Like the sun dawning, his smile could light up her life if she let it.

"Everything will be just fine." Lorenzo's hand settled on her shoulder, a pleasantly heavy weight meant to be comforting.

It wasn't. Why was he touching her? The panic clawing inside her chest doubled. Maybe he was trying to soothe her, but it unnerved her. Air squeezed through her too-tight throat in a little hiccup.

His hand didn't move, his touch remained like out of a dream. Was she really smiling up at him, so close she could see the nearly black threads in his irises and the smooth-shaven texture of his square jaw? Good thing she was independent, because a woman less confident might be tempted to lay her cheek on the powerful plane of his chest.

Not her, but some other woman might let herself dream what it would be like when he folded his iron-hewn arms around her and held her tightly.

It was a good thing she had her feet firmly on the ground. Because that wasn't what she wanted. Nope, not at all. What she wanted was to save her family's farm. To lessen her father's burden.

Solomon blew out his breath, drawing her out of her thoughts. Lorenzo moved away, rubbed the gelding's nose. "Go in the back door. Just follow the path around the side of the house."

"Take good care of my boy." She lifted her chin, trying to shake away the effects from being too near to the man. He was an absolute hazard.

"I'll treat him like my own. Right, Solomon?" That irresistible kindness rumbled in the low notes of his voice.

Her heart fluttered against her will as she watched both horse and man head down the dim aisle.

A little strength, Lord, please. Strength to resist the man's warmth and decency, strength to put one foot in front of the other and face the grim Lucia, strength to make it through the day without making any mistakes. It was a lot to ask for, but she thought of her father's burdens and added, *for my pa.*

Horse hooves clomped behind her, and she spun around. A roan horse flared his nostrils at her, bared his teeth and careened to a stop. On his back sat a woman she did not know, who was a few years older.

"So you are the new girl." Her tone was not friendly. Her green eyes squinted with a hint of disdain. "You must have been a pity hire."

A pity hire? Heat stained her face. Lorenzo heard that. He might have been gracious enough to disregard her patched shoes and secondhand dress, but this woman was not. Ruby lifted her chin higher. This job mattered to her. That's why she was here. Not to compete with another maid for his attention.

"Lorenzo." The newcomer brightened when she spotted the boss's son. She swung down from her horse with the air of a princess leaving her throne. Her attention riveted to the man stroking Solomon's cheek. Her smile was breathtaking. "I didn't know you would be in the barn this morning. This is my lucky day."

"Not mine, as I've been packing water." His smile had vanished, but his kindness had not. "I'll have Thacker see to your roan. Mae, this is Ruby."

The moment between them had broken. With the gelding's reins in hand, he took a step backward and tipped his hat in farewell. A tiny pain clutched behind her sternum as he withdrew into the shadows. She was *not* smitten with the man. She was utterly in charge of her heart.

"You won't last the day." Mae shook her head as if

she were an experienced judge of such things. "Whatever happens, don't think I will do any of your work."

"No, of course not, I—" But the woman took off, leaving her alone in the barn. A horse stretched his neck over the top of his railing and tried to catch the hem of her scarf with his teeth.

That could have gone better, she thought as she tucked the scarf around her throat. She squared her shoulders and took a deep breath. At least there would be no shoe disasters today. Last night, she'd spent an hour and a half tightening and repairing all the threads holding her shoe buttons in place. Confidently, she launched out of the barn and into the snow.

That was the key. To be confident. To visualize a good outcome instead of disaster. This would be her new attitude. She breathed the wintry air deep into her lungs until they burned and breathed out great, white clouds of fog. Her shoes crunched on the path, her skirts rustled and swirled with her gait. She had to concentrate on her work and not on Lorenzo. Forget how handsome he'd looked. Forget how kind. Make her heart stop fluttering because he'd smiled at her.

Her family's livelihood hung in the balance.

The sky began to change to a lighter shade of gray. The beauty of the still plains, sleeping snow and amazing world buoyed her spirits. The enormous house rose up in front of her with bright windows and smoke curling from numerous chimneys. Far up ahead, Mae yanked open a door. A few moments later, Lucia appeared on the threshold, gesturing impatiently. "Let's get you in a uniform. You can't work for the mistress wearing that."

"Yes, ma'am." The panic returned, clawing her with a vengeance. She hurried up the steps and the minute her wet shoes hit the floor, *squeak. Creak.*

Great, Ruby. Just great. She slipped out of her coat and hung it on a nearby wall peg.

"Definitely a pity hire," Mae whispered from the far side of the foyer.

Not knowing what to say, Ruby dutifully followed the head housekeeper. *Squeak, creak.*

It was going to be a very long day.

A weak sun filtered through a thin blanket of quick-moving clouds. Although at its zenith, the bright disc gave no warmth. The arctic winds dominated, burning the high Montana prairie with its bitter chill. In his warmest coat, Lorenzo's teeth chattered as he trudged the snow-covered path to the house. He could tell himself he hurried along the path at a breakneck speed because he couldn't wait to unthaw in front of a fire with a cup of tea and a hot meal, but that would be a lie.

His gaze searched through the main-floor windows. His toe caught on a snow clump. His right foot skidded on a patch of ice. Did he watch where he was going? No, he didn't lift his eyes from the house. He spotted his mother in the parlor, working at her embroidery. Lucia bustled around the dining room table, checking that everything was ready for the family's meal. He spotted Mae at a window above the kitchen's water pump but saw no sign of Ruby.

He had thought of nothing else all morning. He'd finished his barn work, hauled hay and taken a pick once again to the cattle's water supply. He'd spread out bags of feed corn and stopped to doctor a cow who had a painful run-in with a coyote, but Ruby stayed front and center in his mind, a beautiful song he could not forget.

"Renzo!" Boots pounded on the path behind him. His cousin, Mateo, fell in stride beside him. Mateo was a few years older, a few inches shorter and a dedicated cattleman. "You spent a lot of time in the horse barn this morning."

"Not much more than usual." Snow scudded across the pathway ahead of him as he debated slowing down or speeding up. His cousin had a sharp eye; he didn't miss much. Not ready to have a member of his family aware that he was sweet on Ruby, he launched forward, faster. If Mateo wanted to give him a hard time, let him at least have to work for it.

"Sure, you do your fair share with the horses, but did I see you tending one of the maids' horses?" Mateo caught up, breathing hard. "Don't tell me you have an interest in that ancient, swayback horse she was riding."

"Sure I do. Solomon and I are old friends." Maybe humor would distract his cousin, because the back door loomed closer and this was not a conversation he wanted anyone in the house to overhear. "I wanted to check on his shoe. I re-shod him yesterday."

"Oh, so that was the errand you went on." Mateo didn't look fooled. "Whoever the young woman is, she's awful pretty. She's easy on the eyes."

"Maybe you should stop looking." A furious power radiated through him as strong as iron, and he heard the growl in his words. Jealousy wasn't his style, so it surprised him.

"Sorry, man. I wasn't interested, really." Mateo's smile flashed. "But you are."

Couldn't he hide it better than that? He stomped the snow off his boots on the step and grasped the doorknob. "Let's keep it quiet. Ruby doesn't know."

"Sure. But when she rejects you, I'm next in line to beau her." Mateo probably wasn't serious, but his words were like an arrow to a target.

Would Ruby reject him if she knew about his feelings? She hadn't done one thing to confirm any affection on her part. Shy smiles, gentle humor, yes. But did she feel drawn to him? A weight settled on his chest as he turned the knob. The warmth of the kitchen pulled him in, but his knees knocked as he shrugged out of his coat. What he felt for Ruby was powerfully rare. It was gentle as a December sun dawning, as everlasting as the stars in the sky and so true it came from the deepest places in his soul.

He still did not know if he had a chance with her. Would she want him for a beau? What would he do if she didn't?

He shouldered into the kitchen doorway, searching for her in the ordered chaos. Cook sliced a roast chicken, steam billowed from a potato pot while workers scurried around putting food on platters and finding a colander for the boiling potatoes. Everything faded when he spied Ruby at the farthest worktable, transferring piping hot dinner rolls into a cloth-lined basket.

Gossamer tendrils of her platinum hair curled around her face as she bent over her work. He took in the long, lean curve of her arm, the straight line of her back and the way her every movement was graceful. She plopped the last roll into the basket and covered the baked goods to keep in the heat. How dear she looked in her dove-gray maid's dress and white apron. She spun around, holding the baking sheet with a hot pad in one hand and their gazes collided.

The chaos vanished, the clatter silenced and time froze. In the stillness, he saw her unguarded, with her feelings exposed. A lasso of emotion lashed around him and roped his heart to hers. For one perfect moment, they were bound and tied together in an immeasurable way, and he could see something he hadn't before. Her heart. Tenderness washed over him like grace.

"Hey, Romeo." Mateo lightly punched him in the shoulder. "Didn't you hear your pa? He's calling you."

He heard nothing but Ruby. When she shyly broke away, hope took root in his soul for what could be.

Chapter Five

Crocheting was harder than it looked, at least for her, but it gave her something to focus on aside from the fact that she had been forced to sit at one of the worktables crammed into the corner of the kitchen for her midday meal. When she'd gone to join the others at the table near the warm stove, all the chairs had suddenly become mysteriously saved for someone else.

No matter. She suspected her knowing Lorenzo might have something to do with it. Lorenzo. She hoped a sigh hadn't escaped her as she unhooked her crochet needle from the loop of white thread and gave it a tug. Hard-won stitches disappeared before her eyes, unraveling as she counted backwards to the place where she'd made the error.

She'd decided to learn to crochet because she figured working with one crochet hook instead of two knitting needles had to be easier, but she had been sorely mistaken. She inserted the hook, checked the pattern Scarlet had copied down for her and looped the thread three times. Concentrating, the morning's troubles slipped away.

"How is it going?" A man's voice sounded close to her ear, and she startled. The needle tumbled from her grip, more stitches unraveled and the ball of thread rolled across the floor.

"Lorenzo." She gaped up at him like a fish out of water. Dashing in a dark, blue flannel shirt and black trousers, he knelt to retrieve the ball. "What are you doing here?"

"Scaring you, apparently." He handed over the thread, kneeling before her like a knight of old, so gallant every head in the room was turned toward him. Apparently she wasn't the only young woman on the staff who couldn't keep her eyes off him. His dimples framed his perfect smile as she took the ball. Her fingers bumped his, and the shock trailed up her arm like a lightning strike.

"You were right." She dropped the skein onto her lap. "Everything has gone fine. I'm trying to learn all I can."

"Good to hear. Do you mind if I join you?" He unfolded his big frame, rising to his six-foot height. His hand rested on the back of the chair beside her. "I thought we could catch up."

"But we talked a lot on the sleigh ride, and we aren't exactly friends."

"We can change that." He pulled out the chair, turning it sideways so that when he settled on the cushion, he faced her.

Not a good thing. How could she think with his handsomeness distracting her? Worse, the women at the other table had fallen silent, openly staring.

"What are you making?" He lowered his voice, perhaps hoping to keep the conversation just between the two of them.

"It's supposed to be a snowflake. For Christmas ornaments." She held up the poor misshapen mess of stitches. So far, her greatest aptitude in the needle arts was crocheting, but she couldn't bring herself to admit that to Lorenzo. His nearness tied her in knots, and she wondered what he really saw when he looked at her. Although she wore a uniform just like the other maids, she could still feel her patches. A world separated her and Lorenzo. So, why was he really talking to her?

"It does look like a snowflake." He tilted his head to one side, studying the rows of stitching. "You were working on this when I came by the other night."

"Yes, although I already finished that one. I'm making them for Christmas gifts and to add to my hope chest." She blushed, aware of how that must sound. "Not that I'm hopeful or anything. It's just something girls do."

"I'm aware. My sister has one, too." He relaxed comfortably against the chair back and planted his elbow on the table. A shaft of watery sunshine tumbled through the window, bronzing the copper highlights in his dark hair and worshiping the angled artistry of his face. "Bella and my mother do a lot of sewing for her hope chest. They have been at it for years now."

"That sounds nice. It must be wonderful to have a ma." She tried not to think of all the ways she missed the mother she'd never known. She fingered the half-made snowflake, trying to imagine what it would have been like to sew alongside a mother. "Yours is especially nice."

"I'll keep her. Who taught you to sew? Your aunt?"

"No, my Aunt June didn't have the time to spare." She bit her bottom lip, remembering those hard times when her father had been injured. "I'm mostly self-taught. After Pa was well and we moved out of our uncle's house, I had to figure out how to mend everyone's clothes. I wasn't that good, but when we moved here to Angel Falls, my new friends took pity on me."

"Not pity." His dark eyes grew darker with interest. "I'm sure they couldn't help adoring you on that first day you came to school."

"Me? No." Shyness gripped her, and she bowed her head, breaking away from the power of his gaze. She didn't want him to see too much or to know how sorely her feelings had been hurt on her first day of school. "I was the new girl and didn't know anyone. I think they felt sorry for me."

"I know I did."

Mortified, time flashed backward, and in memory, she was at her desk in the back row. Sunshine warmed the classroom and open windows let in the fresh smells of growing grass and the Montana wind. Shouts and shoes drummed as kids rushed toward the door for lunch break, but Narcissa Bell's voice rose above every sound. "Does it look as if I want to be friends with you? What is your name?"

"R-Ruby." She bowed her head, miserable beyond description. Her first day of school. She'd come with hopes of making friends.

"I'm going to call you Rags. Look at that dress."

Girls had laughed as they pranced by in their tailored frocks in the latest fabrics and styles, in their shining new shoes and hair ribbons and bows. She'd felt her face blaze tomato red as her dreams of making friends shattered.

She hadn't realized Lorenzo had witnessed the whole thing. What had he thought at the time? He was friends with Narcissa. They were in the same circle of friends. Had he gazed at her that first day with pity, too?

"I remember you wound up eating lunch with Meredith and her group." No sign of pity marked his chiseled, lean face. "You were hard not to notice, being the new girl and the prettiest."

"Not the prettiest, not by far." How could he say such a thing? She squirmed in her chair, uncomfortable but grateful, because his generous compliment took the sting out of the memory of Narcissa's taunting. "But I could be the most blessed. I got a new circle of friends that day. The best friends anyone could have."

"That is a great blessing," he agreed, so sincere, she found herself leaning in a little closer, drawn to him in a way she could not control.

"God was watching over me." She would never forget how it had felt when Fiona, Meredith, Lila, Kate, Scarlet and Earlee had approached her with friendly smiles and asked her to eat with them. "They asked me to join their sewing circle. We try to meet every week."

"And so they have helped you with your sewing."

"And my kitting and crocheting." She gestured to the delicate circle of stitching cradled in the folds of her apron. "They are like family to me."

"It had to be rough, thinking you might have to leave them." Understanding arced between them, and aware of the women sipping their after-lunch tea at the nearby table, he lowered his voice further. "With this job, will you be able to stay in Angel Falls?"

"I don't know, but right now I have a job, and I'm grateful for it. Thanks to you."

"Me? I didn't do a thing."

"You said something to your mother, didn't you? You were the reason she chose me."

"She did the choosing all on her own. It was my father, actually, who influenced her."

"Your father? I've never met him." Bewilderment crinkled her porcelain forehead and adorably twisted the corners of her rosebud mouth. "Why would he do that for me?"

"He's met your father and liked him." Tenderness became like an ailment that afflicted him more every time his gaze found hers. He could not forget what he'd seen her in her eyes. Encouraged, he tried not to think of all the ways she could still reject him. "Tell me about your family. Surely now your father still isn't planning to move?"

"It's hard to say." She bowed her head, and gossamer strands escaped from her braid to tumble over her china-doll face. She couldn't hide her worry, not from him. He read it in her posture, in the tight line of her fine-boned jaw and the tiny sigh that escaped her.

Something was still wrong, something he hadn't been able to fix. He wanted to. "Tell me," he urged gently.

"My brother lost his job." She shrugged one slim shoulder, as if it were nothing to worry about. "He will be home again, and that is the good news. Pa and I have missed Rupert terribly. There is always a silver lining."

He realized she hadn't answered his question. An answer of sorts. "You are an optimistic woman."

"It's new. I've made up my mind. No more visions of doom."

"That's a good philosophy. Are you able to follow it?" He reached out, uncertain if he should touch her, if she was ready for that.

"I don't know, as today is the first day I'm using it." Her eyes widened at his touch. She took a sharp intake of breath as if she was surprised, but she didn't move away.

"How is it going so far?"

"B-better than expected."

"That's how my day has been, too." Hope was a powerful thing, and the moment his fingertips grazed her cheek, wishes came to life within him. He wanted to be the man she turned to, the man who could right all the wrongs in her life, the one man she could count on forever.

If she didn't move away with her family. If his parents accepted her. Tension knotted him up, and he willed it away. He wouldn't worry about the future, just this moment.

Her cheek was as soft as ivory silk. Her hair felt as luxurious as liquid platinum and tickled the backs of his knuckles when he brushed away those flyaway tendrils. Five kinds of tenderness roared to life within him. Please, he silently pleaded, please feel for me what I do for you.

Her gaze searched his, and in that moment of connection, he felt a click in his heart, like a lock turning. He folded those gossamer locks behind her ear, but the sensation remained, as if another room had opened within him and there was more space to fill with love for Ruby.

What would she do if she knew?

"You cook, you sew, you crochet." The words sounded strained, and there was no way to hide it. At least she couldn't tell his pulse galloped like a startled jackrabbit. "Do you sing?"

"Very badly, at least that's my fear. I hum at home while I'm doing housework, to spare my father the sound of my voice."

"Surely he hears you humming?"

"I'm very quiet, and he's been gracious enough not to complain. So far. Who knows what would happen if I were to break out in song." She picked up her needle and thread so she would have something to do besides falling into his incredible eyes. "My singing might cause Pa to go deaf, break every glass on the kitchen shelves and draw rodents in from the fields. All very good reasons for me to stick to humming."

"You're funny, Ruby." His chuckle rumbled richly, and he leaned in closer as if to consider this new side of her.

She had been serious, but if he wanted to think she was humorous she wouldn't argue. She fit the crochet needle into a stitch. She concentrated on tightening the thread around it, not too tight to ruin the gage, but her hands were trembling. Breathless, she tried to forget the lingering tingle on her cheek where Lorenzo had brushed a strand of hair from her eyes. His manly presence made her forget where she was, who she was, why she could not let herself wish.

But if she *could* wish, it would be to have the chance

to lose herself in his eyes. To sit basking in the manly assurance of his presence. To listen to his laughter ring one more time.

Lorenzo was a wonderful dream. But that's all he could be. She thought of the look on her father's face when he'd told her of Rupert's letter.

"Are you joining the caroling group at church?" His velvety baritone rang as private as a whisper. "The first practice is this evening."

"Tempting, but I'm not sure if I will." She thought of her father's discouragement. The last thing she wanted was to leave him alone with his worries. "I thought maybe, but that was before Rupert's news. I should stay home, although my friends are going."

"Any chance they might persuade you?"

"Who knows? Maybe. I have to see how my father is first." She wound her needle around the thread to make a single crochet stitch. "I suppose you will be there?"

"That's my plan. It gets me out of the house."

"Why? You're obviously close to your family." She stopped midstitch. "You must like spending time with them."

"Sure, but this time of year? My mother is preoccupied with her Christmas ball planning. My sister and I barely hear about anything else."

"Sounds truly tragic. How do you survive it?"

"Exactly. She wants to know who I'm escorting this year, so the farther away I can get, the better." Humor polished his striking features. "I take refuge at the church. It's a fun time. You should think about coming."

"I should?" She nearly choked on her words. Why, it almost sounded as if he wanted her to be there, as if he had a personal interest in her. Shock rattled her, the crochet hook tumbled from her hand and clattered to the floor. Lorenzo Davis could not be interested in her. That was simply her fanciful nature carrying her away again.

"Reverend Hadly makes it enjoyable. Mostly it's the old gang from school, so it's good to see everyone and catch up. We head over to the diner during our break for dessert. It's a good time."

"Oh, I'm sure." Was she imagining the glint of hope in his eyes as he waited for an answer to his question? Authentic, patient, solid, he was gilded by the light.

Did Lorenzo Davis like her, even a little? Yes, she realized, accepting it finally. The breath rushed out of her, her lungs seized up and one hiccup squeezed out of her too-tight throat. She watched, dizzy with the possibility as Lorenzo knelt to retrieve her crochet hook.

The thick, sandy brown fall of his hair glinted in the sunlight, the muscles in his shoulders bunched as he rose from the floor, and he held out the needle on his wide palm. Why was her heart beating double time?

As she snared her crochet hook, her fingertips unavoidably bumped his hand. The emotional charge that zinged through her scared her. She cared for him more than she'd realized. She fisted her hand around the crochet hook and bowed her head.

Why now, Lord? She'd lived in Angel Falls since April. For nine months, her life had been fine, uneventful and settled. Until now.

"I imagine you have a lot of chores waiting for you at home after your shift here." Kindness was his best feature. It lit him softly, filling his soulful eyes with caring she could not deny.

"Yes. Pa is helpless in the kitchen. I'll have supper to fix and dishes to do." His caring settled within her, making her shaky, making her want to escape. "So it's not likely I'll be able to go tonight."

"That's too bad. I hope your friends can persuade you."

He rose from the chair, towering over her, and it was his heart she saw. His regard she felt. He jammed his hands in his pockets, squared his mighty shoulders and disappointment resonated in his eyes, darkening the color to a sad, midnight blue. "You work hard, Ruby. You deserve to have a little fun."

"I'm just trying to do what's right for my family."

"I know. I admire it." The sunlight chose that moment to dim as he turned away, his boots plodding crisply on the wood floor. She squeezed her eyes shut, unable to breathe as sorrow set in.

If wishes were pennies, she would be rich. She bowed her head, wrapped the thread around her hook to double crochet but couldn't keep her hand steady.

Don't think what it would be like to be beaued by him, she told herself. Some things in life were not meant to be.

If anyone needs help, Lord, it's Ruby. Lorenzo plucked his coat from the wall peg. Saddened by her situation, he jabbed one arm into the sleeve. He understood the meaning of the word *responsibility.* Family before self. Work before play. He admired Ruby's values.

He didn't know if this would ever work out. His heart kept pulling him toward her. Nothing could stop it.

"Renzo?" Pa's cane tapped in the hallway. "You got a moment? Come talk to me."

"Sure thing." With his coat unbuttoned, he left his muffler and hat on the pegs and bypassed the kitchen door. Could he help that his gaze slid into the room, searching for her? No. She sat hunched over her snowflake, carefully moving the steel needle in and out and through her crochet work, so dear his soul ached at the sight. Aware of his father watching, he tore his attention away, steeled his spine and stepped into the empty dining room. "What do you need, Pa?"

"I heard you were talking with the new kitchen maid." Pa ambled over to the tea service set up on the breakfront and chose a cup. He sounded casual, but something deeper resonated in his tone. Disapproval. "Is that right?"

"Yes." He wondered how Pa had known, and so quickly. Perhaps one of the other maids, or maybe Lucia, who had a sharp eye. "I know Ruby from school."

"So you weren't speaking to her about her work?"

"No, why would I? I didn't know I was banished from the kitchen. What's this about, Pa?"

"I know you're friendly with the girl. I have sympathy for her situation, too. But you know the rules, Renzo." Pa poured a cup of steaming tea and set down the silver pot with a clink and clatter. "No fraternizing with the hired help. It distracts them."

"Yes, but Ruby isn't just the hired help." He straightened his spine, drawing up all the inner strength he possessed. "I saw her during her lunch break so I wouldn't interfere with her work. There's nothing wrong with that."

"You can't have it both ways. She's either a maid or a friend. House rules. That's how it is." Pa dropped a sugar cube into his cup and stirred. "I thought you wanted her to get the job."

"I did. I appreciate that Ma chose her."

"Then what's the problem? It's not like she's part of your circle, anyhow. Are you heading back out to the fields?"

"I want to make sure we solve the water problem today. I don't want to keep packing water when we could be pumping it."

"Don't blame you there." Gerard cradled his cup, unable to hide the yearning in his eyes. "Truth is, I wish I could go with you."

"I'd sure like that, but you know what Ma would say."

"She would be after my hide, that's for sure. That woman has forbidden me to lift a hand on my own land."

"For good reason. You had best keep on Ma's good side." He back trailed out of the room.

"That's the truth. I don't want to stir up that woman's ire." Pa grinned easily. "Holler if you need any supplies from the hardware store. At least I could make myself useful driving to and from town."

"Sorry, I already have what I need. If that changes, I'll let you know."

On his way to the back door, he passed by the kitchen again. Remembering Pa's warning, he didn't look into the room. No way would he cost Ruby her job. But did that stop his wish to see her?

No. Wrestling down his disappointment, he yanked

on his hat and scarf and opened the door. Arctic air cocooned him as tromped down the steps. Something tugged him back, and he spun around. In the golden, lamp-lit window, Ruby was back at work pouring hot water into a wash basin. The steam rose like mist around her. It took all his strength to ignore the twist of affection in his chest. He kept on going until the cold and the storm claimed him.

Chapter Six

"Ruby, you've gotten terribly quiet." Meredith commented from the front seat of her fashionable sleigh. She gave the reins an experienced tug to turn her mare, Miss Bradshaw, off Main Street.

"Is something wrong?" Scarlet brushed red tendrils out of her eyes as she squinted at Ruby. "I couldn't believe how hard we had to argue to get you into the sleigh."

"We practically had to drag you," Lila chimed in, cuddled next to her on the backseat. "You must be tired after your first day at your new job."

"There was a lot to learn." And more she'd left undone at home, but her father had insisted. Ruby tried to bury her worry over that, glad three of her friends had driven out of their way to her home to coax her into going. And Lorenzo? Somehow she had to erase the image of him kneeling before her, holding out her crochet hook, looking so handsome her teeth ached. "Some of the other maids weren't exactly friendly to me today, so it was a little more challenging than I'd anticipated."

"How could they not love you?" Lila asked as she

tucked in the cashmere robes more snugly. "We think you are a dear."

"I am a disaster." She couldn't forget what she'd seen on Lorenzo's face. He cared about her.

"A disaster?" Meredith guided Miss Bradshaw along the snowy lane. "Did something terrible happen at work?"

"Not one thing. Multiple things." She rolled her eyes. "I burned my hand, broke a teacup and spilled beet juice down the front of my white apron. Lucia was very annoyed with me."

"You were nervous, that's all." Scarlet lifted a hand to wave at Earlee on the other side of the street as the sleigh slowed to a stop. "Tomorrow will be better, you'll see."

"Much better. You won't be nearly as nervous," Lila agreed. "Just relax. The Davis family is lucky to have you."

"Thanks. You guys are good to me." Encouraged, she sat straighter on the seat. Her friends were some of her greatest treasures. Footsteps crunched in the snow, drawing nearer as Earlee broke away from the shadowy, newly built, two-story schoolhouse, where she taught the lower grades.

"I hope you all know what you're doing, inviting me along." Happiness drew pink in her cheeks and twinkles in her blue eyes. "I'm a horrible singer."

"Then we can be horrible together." Ruby folded back the driving robe and scooted over to make room for her friend. "I can't carry a tune."

"I can't hold a note." Earlee, adorable in her fur-lined cloak, tucked her lunch pail, schoolbooks and slate onto the floorboards before settling on the cushioned seat. "You all have to be honest with me. If I'm bringing down the quality of the caroling, I will bow out joyfully."

"That goes for me, too." Ruby's head jerked as the sleigh took off. "Why am I seeing disaster?"

"You always see disaster." Lila chuckled.

"I'm trying to keep my spirits up, but it's harder than it looks." Her words made everyone in the sleigh laugh, so the atmosphere was merry as Miss Bradshaw pulled them down the road to the white, steepled church.

"Do you think Lorenzo will be there?" Scarlet asked as the sleigh bumped to a stop.

Yes. Ruby bit her lip to keep in the word. Because if she said she knew that Lorenzo would be coming, think of the questions! How on earth could she explain what had happened over her lunch break?

"He sang in the caroling group last year, remember?" Meredith was the first to climb out into the snow. "It stands to reason he will sing this year, too."

"Ruby, you work for the family." Lila took Meredith's hand and climbed carefully from the front seat. "Did you get a chance to ask him if he's coming tonight?"

"He's coming." Her heart skipped a beat. No questions, she prayed as she stumbled onto the icy ground. Her shoes skidded, and she groped for the side of the sleigh before her feet went out from under her.

"Whoopsy." Scarlet caught her elbow, helping to steady her. "Are you okay?"

"Sure, as long as I don't step on that patch of ice again." She smiled. It seemed as if no one would quiz her about Lorenzo, because her friends started calling out to Kate, who gave the final buckle of her horse's blanket a tug before trudging their way. Perfect timing.

"Guess who is walking this way? He must have left his horse at the livery." Kate swiped snowflakes out of her eyes. "Did he get extra handsome when we weren't looking?"

"I think so." Scarlet squinted through the downfall where a man's shadow skirted the side of the church. "Every time I look at him, my heart goes thump."

"Unrequited love is rough on a girl." Kate sighed as they watched him stride closer.

"Very," Scarlet agreed. "I feel so sorry for you, Kate. I'm sure he's about to fall in love with me any minute."

"No, because he's about to fall in love with me," Kate argued good-naturedly and they dissolved into muffled laughter. "What about you, Ruby? Aren't you going to pine after Lorenzo with us?"

Good question. Even from a distance, she could feel his presence. Her heart tugged, her spirit stilled. She blinked snowflakes off her lashes, staring down at the patch on her shoe. "Are you kidding? You two have been admiring him much longer than me, so you should get dibs."

"Hey, less competition for me." Scarlet gave Ruby's hand a squeeze. "Look, he's heading into the church. If we time it right, we'll be right ahead of him. He'll have to notice us."

"No, I want to help Meredith with her horse. You two go on." Shame washed over her. It was all she could do to give Scarlet a reassuring smile and a nod to go ahead. Her friends were in love with Lorenzo. How could that enormous fact slip her mind? She watched Kate and

Scarlet scamper arm in arm up the walkway, Lorenzo approaching.

How would they feel if they knew about this afternoon? That Lorenzo hadn't simply been courteous to her, he'd been friendly. No, more than friendly. A horrible feeling clutched her stomach, proof she'd done something wrong. It was like going behind their backs to move in on the man both Kate and Scarlet wanted. It wasn't like that—that wasn't what had happened—but that's how she felt.

She loved her friends so dearly. She couldn't jeopardize their friendship. Ever. That was the most important reason of all for her to keep her eyes down. No more looking at Lorenzo and wishing.

She heard his boots crunch in the snow. His gait stopped. Her face heated, but she did not look up. She knew he was looking her way. Nervous, she spun around and spied the horse blanket tucked under the front seat.

"Thanks for picking me up, Meredith." She unwedged the folded wool from beneath the springs. "But you can't go out of your way for every practice."

"Hopefully, we won't have to drag you to those. And if we do, my term is done in a few more weeks. No more teaching, so I'll have plenty of time to talk you into loving caroling practice." Meredith gave the knot she'd tied at the tether post a tug to test it and satisfied, circled around to take charge of the blanket.

"Great." Ruby rolled her eyes. It was nice being wanted. "So, do you mean done with teaching? Or done as in the term is over?"

"This will be my last term. At least for now."

"But teaching is so important to you. I thought you

loved it." She hated being aware of the crackle of a man's boots in the snow. Lorenzo. Had he been standing still watching all this time? Dismay seized her stomach.

"I love my work, but I love Shane more." She shook out the warm horse blanket. Happiness lit her up. Being engaged and in love with Shane looked good on her. "I can't wait any longer to start our life together. I can't stand being apart from him."

"Does this mean you've set a wedding date?" *Just forget Lorenzo,* she told herself. *Don't listen to him walking away.* "How soon will you get married?"

"After the new year, but don't tell anyone. I planned to announce it tonight when we took a break." Beaming, Meredith settled the blanket over the mare's broad back. "Shane has bought the Beckham place."

"That big ranch that was for sale? Oh, this means you and Fiona will be neighbors. How wonderful!" She gave Meredith a hug. She thanked God how beautifully her friend's life was coming together. Her teeth started chattering.

"It's cold out here. Go in, get out of this weather." Meredith knelt to fasten the blanket. "Don't look at me like that, I can get the buckles myself. Go on with you. Teacher's orders."

"All right, if you are sure."

"I'm sure. No reason both of us should get colder." Meredith knelt to secure the first buckle. Miss Bradshaw waited patiently, twitching her tail as the snow gathered on her mane.

Lorenzo. She hadn't taken two steps before he stopped on the path ahead of her, stopped and glanced over his wide shoulder. Their gazes collided. For one instant she forgot everything—her job, her family, her duty, her friends. The dreams buried in her soul surfaced. What would it be like to be beaued by him? To see the caring in his eyes shine only for her?

Footsteps padded behind her, fast and hurried, petticoats rustled as someone rushed up the path in a hurry. Not Meredith, she realized too late.

"What are you doing here, Rags?" Narcissa Bell circled around her as if she were avoiding a rodent in her path. "Don't tell me you're singing tonight?"

No need to answer. She held her chin steadily, refusing to let her head drop. Why Narcissa? Why now?

"Well, that's the trouble with church." She dropped her voice so only Ruby could hear. "They let in just any poor trash. Lorenzo, wait for me! Lorenzo?"

She tried to keep her chin up, she really did, but it bobbed down of its own accord. Narcissa ran away on her beautiful, perfect, brand-new shoes, racing to catch up to Lorenzo.

"Are you okay, Ruby?" Meredith took her hand. "I could bring her down a peg. In fact, maybe I will do just that."

"Please, don't. I'm fine."

"I heard what she said to you. It was just plain mean."

"I would rather forget it. Turn the other cheek." Not only was it her faith, but she could not risk Lorenzo overhearing. She was embarrassed enough. No doubt he was wondering why she hadn't spoken to him, why she hadn't smiled, when he'd expressed interest in her being here tonight. Her heart twisted with raw pain, and it wasn't because of Narcissa.

The instant she stepped into the church, the low, pleasant rumble of his voice rose above all the others. She shrugged out of her coat, hardly aware of hanging it on a peg, and followed Meredith into the sanctuary.

Maybe if she didn't meet his gaze, he would simply stop liking her. Things could go back to the way they used to be before she accepted her first ride in his sleigh.

"Gather 'round!" Reverend Hadly clapped, pitching his voice above the merry chatter of the carolers. "Grab a music book on your way up here. What a big group we have this year."

Lorenzo. She could feel the tug of his gaze, like gravity pulling her. Melted snow glistened in his thick, brown hair. Was it her imagination, or did he seem even taller, his shoulders mountain-strong, his presence more riveting?

He'd become more handsome since she'd seen him last. Kate was right.

It's better if you stopped liking him, Ruby. Just find a way to turn your feelings off. A book was shoved in her hands. She blinked against the overly bright lamplight. "Thanks, Meredith."

"Ruby? You're a soprano like Kate. Come this way." Meredith's voice came as if from miles away.

Dimly, she followed her friend, accepted a place next to Kate at the far end of the group.

The reverend's pitch pipe blared, rising above the group's chatter. Silence fell.

"Let's warm up our voices. Sopranos." The minister turned his attention to her section and held the note. "Ahhh."

"Ahhs" erupted around her. Kate's sweet soprano

rang in her right ear. Scarlet, on her left, cozied up to whisper. "Sing, Ruby. You have a lovely voice."

She wanted to argue—hers was by far the worst in the group—but that wasn't the reason she didn't sing. Lorenzo's gaze found hers across the crowd of people and rising voices, silence amid the noise. Voices faded, the music dimmed until there was only the hint of his smile. Something deep within her heart leaped. How tempting to let herself sink into the feeling and into the caring in his eyes. How easy it would be to just let herself fall.

"Did you see?" Scarlet leaned in to whisper. "I think Lorenzo is looking at me."

"No, he's looking at me," Kate murmured, eyes merry. "Do you see the look on his face?"

"One of pure love." Scarlet sounded a little dreamy.

"Definitely," Kate agreed. "You know what that means? He's falling for one of us."

"Finally." Scarlet gave an endearing sigh. "Wishes really do come true."

She wanted those wishes to be for Scarlet or Kate. They deserved them. They deserved Lorenzo. She tucked away her feelings, clenched the songbook more tightly and forced her gaze from his. There could be no more moments like this, no wondering what could be. Yes, this would definitely be much easier if she didn't like him so much.

"Altos! Join in." Reverend Hadly turned to the next group and offered them a lower pitch with his pipe. "Ahhhs" broke out in a chorus, a few voices off-key so he blew the pipe again.

Father, please give Kate or Scarlet a chance with

Lorenzo. They both deserve great happiness. She hoped one of them would win Lorenzo's heart. He was a good man, the very best. Absolutely good enough to marry and give one of her best friends a happily-ever-after.

"Very good!" The reverend praised. "Tenors. Here's your note."

Low-toned voices broke out in a slow, steady pitch. Why could she pick out Lorenzo's voice amid all the others? She tried to close her ears to him. Impossible. She could not close her heart, either.

Ruby wasn't making this easy for him. Lorenzo leaned forward in his chair in the busy diner. Had Pa already spoken to her, the way he'd been warned earlier? Or had Lucia done it? Anger burned in his chest. But what could he do about it? He glanced across the room where she sat at a far table talking with her friends. Not once had she glanced his way. He knew, because he'd been watching her.

"Can you believe some people?" Narcissa leaned against his arm, seated beside him at the table. The clink and clatter of the diner came back into focus and he dragged his attention away from Ruby's table. Narcissa laid her hand on his forearm. "Bringing her own food? To an eating establishment? A slice of pie is a nickel. Honestly. Who can't afford that?"

He winced and shrugged off Narcissa's hold on him. This was a side of Narcissa he didn't like. She didn't capture his attention, she wasn't the one his interest returned to. Five tables away, Ruby nibbled on a cookie she'd packed, while a cup of tea steamed on the table in front of her. He was glad his mother had hired her. He wanted her life's burdens to ease.

Which meant he couldn't risk her job. No way.

"Not everyone is as fortunate as you are, Narcissa." Margaret Roberts stirred honey into her tea. "Remember, it's important to be charitable."

"I *am* charitable." Narcissa gave her ringlets a toss with the hand that wasn't clutching his arm. "I go through my closet twice a year and contribute some very quality frocks to the church donation barrel."

"I meant to feel Christian tolerance." Margaret rolled her eyes. "That's harder to do than to simply donate stuff you no longer want. I give away my used things, too."

Ruby. He shifted in his chair to get a better view of her. Lamplight shone like pale moonlight on her long, silken hair and caressed her ivory complexion. The faint ripple of her laughter at something one of her friends said had to be the dearest sound on earth. Despite her laughter, her eyes held the same reserve he'd seen in the kitchen. Her withdrawal from him was subtle, but he felt it all the way to his soul.

He feared it was his father's doing.

"Can you imagine having to wear secondhand clothes?" Narcissa's high-pitched words sailed over the tops of the other conversations in the diner.

He bit his tongue, not wanting to be unkind to a woman, but he didn't like Narcissa's viewpoint or the fact that, tables away, Ruby stiffened. Pink crept across her endearing face. She had to have overheard.

"Clothes other people have worn? How disgusting." Narcissa continued on. "Ugh. It gives me the shivers."

"Hush." He'd had enough. He pushed away from the table, the chair scraping angrily against the floor. "Stop picking on Ruby. I mean it, Narcissa. Not one more word."

"Who, me?" Innocent eyes batted up at him. "I'm not picking on anyone. It's not against the law to have an opinion."

"Well, I don't like it." He clamped his molars together, so furious that staying silent seemed like the wisest choice. He yanked his jacket off the back of the chair and marched blindly away. And that was the woman his mother wanted him to court?

"You're just jealous because she is the most beautiful girl in the room," he heard Margaret say over the angry knell of his boots.

"Me? Jealous? Over patched rags like that?"

He tugged a fifty-cent piece out of his pocket and caught his buddy's eye, who was still crowded around the table with the rest of the gang. James arched one eyebrow in a question. Lorenzo handed the coin over to their waitress.

"The pie was especially good tonight. Thanks, Teresa. Keep the change." He buttoned up on his way out the door. The snowfall fell in whimsical, artful flakes. They sailed lightly on the wind, spiraling in fairy-tale swirls. They batted his cheek and whirled away on his breath, and when he glanced over his shoulder… Ruby. He could see her through the front window.

She chatted away with her friends, as dear as could be, sipping on her cup of tea. Her fine white-blond hair framed her face in carefree wisps and curls. Her cheeks were still flushed pink from Narcissa's insult, but her

quiet inner dignity shone through as she said something
that made her friends chuckle.

Ruby was a gentle soul. He cared about her. He could
not stop it. He didn't even want to try. He wanted to
spend time getting to know her, sharing stories and feeling the radiance of her smile, but her life was precarious. He feared his parents wouldn't understand.

As if she felt his presence, she looked up. The smile
drained from her mouth, the laughter from her face, as
her gaze found his. In the space of one breath and the
next, it felt as if their hearts connected, beating together
as one. For one unguarded moment, he felt a longing
so strong it buckled his knees. Was she wishing, too?
Thinking she had to choose between keeping her job or
their friendship?

The diner's door swung open, and his friends spilled
out onto the boardwalk.

"Lorenzo!" James rushed over, tying his scarf. Time
lurched forward, and Ruby turned away, but the connection between them remained. "Did you see? Austin
just drove by with his new horses. They are fine!"

"I didn't notice." He reached into his pockets for his
gloves. Ruby's back was to him, standing beside her
table, gathering up her things.

"…patches," Narcissa finished saying with the
haughty disdain he didn't like as she tumbled out the
door. Innocent eyes met his. "Hi, Lorenzo. We were just
talking about your family's Christmas ball. Margaret
and I have already been shopping."

He shook his head, plunged his hands into his gloves

and led the way down the street. Snowflakes flitted ahead and pirouetted around him like lost dreams impossible to catch.

Chapter Seven

Lord, please help me to do the right thing and avoid Lorenzo. Ruby wasn't sure if her prayer was an appropriate one, since surely God was very busy tending to true problems in the world, but she had no one else to turn to. The frigid early morning gleamed black in every direction. Snow crunched beneath Solomon's hooves, and the wind drove in straight from the north. She shivered, clenching her teeth to keep them from chattering.

It would be easier if Lorenzo wasn't in the barn, if he didn't greet her, if she couldn't see the caring in his eyes. Caring she could never have or deserve. She could still hear Kate and Scarlet playfully arguing over him. Worse, she could still picture her father gray with exhaustion when she'd arrived home late. He'd been sick with fatigue, trying to handle the housework on top of the barn work and all day spent walking far and wide looking for work.

Please, let him not be there. She sent one more prayer heavenward for good measure, as the structure loomed overhead.

Knowing shelter from the cold was close, dear old

Solomon nickered low in his throat, as if with relief, and picked up his pace. He had no desire to avoid a certain dashingly handsome man, so he was more than happy to prance into the stable and blow out his breath to get some attention.

"Hello, Miss Ruby." Mateo strode in from the shadows of the stalls. He had the same strapping strength as Lorenzo did, although his features were rougher and his black eyes full of merriment. "It's a cold one this morning. How would Solomon feel about some nice, hot oats along with his rubdown?"

"I'm sure he would like it." She swung down awkwardly, not realizing how numb she'd become. Her feet hit the ground hard enough to rattle her teeth. She couldn't feel her toes.

"You go on in and warm up before your shift starts." Mateo took the gelding's reins, gently rubbing the horse's nose as if they were fast friends.

She patted Solomon goodbye and headed out into the cold, eyes peeled for any sign of Lorenzo. So far, nothing. Maybe he was out in the fields, feeding cattle. A girl could hope. She took off at a fast pace, relieved the coast stayed clear. Her footsteps echoed in the vast, lonely morning, where deep purple clouds tried to blot out the view of the twilit sky. All alone, she skidded on the icy pathway, slid on the steps and stumbled through the door. A broad-shouldered shadow towered over her.

Lorenzo. Not out in the fields, as she'd hoped. She skidded to a stop, gasped in shock and fought the panicked urge to leap back outside.

"Good morning." His baritone rang friendly. A smile beamed across his chiseled features.

She jerked her gaze to the floor, but it was too late. She'd seen the caring in his eyes and felt it like a touch against her cheek as she unbuttoned her coat. "Good morning."

"I noticed you made it to church last night." The warmth in his voice urged her to look up. "Looked like you were having fun."

"I was. I'm not sure I should have spared the time, but Pa talked me into going." She bit her lip and shrugged out of her coat. What was she doing? Talking with him when she ought to be pushing him away. "Then Meredith came by in her sleigh with Scarlet and Lila, and they wouldn't give up until I agreed to go."

"You sound glad that you did." Gentle like a touch, that voice, impossible to ignore.

"I was." Her eyes swept up of their own accord, their gazes connected, and all the words evaporated from her brain. Gone. Vanished. Why couldn't she get her feelings for him under control? Why did they grow with each heartbeat and each breath?

"Let me hang that up for you." He took her coat, a little shabby and patched on one sleeve.

"No, I mean—" Her protest came too late. Her coat already hung from a peg. She couldn't feel more awkward, probably looking like an idiot, standing in the entryway, just standing, struggling to find the right words. Not at all sure how she could tell him what she was honestly feeling. That she would much rather just go back to not knowing him. She was uncomfortable with him liking her.

He should be liking Scarlet or Kate. They deserved

him. Their lives were stable. They weren't fearing they might be homeless before month's end.

"Ruby, do you want to drink a cup of coffee together?" He jammed one iron shoulder against the wall. "I know you have some time. You arrived really early."

"Yes, but I have to change into my maid uniform. I'm sure Cook could use my help. There are some things I need to work at, to get faster." She stumbled away from him, apology in her eyes and gentleness in her voice. "I slowed her down terribly yesterday. I don't want to do that again."

"Sure, I understand." A band of tension cinched around his chest, pulling tight as he watched her scurry away with a swish of her skirts and a flip of her braids. "I know what your job means to you."

"Thanks." She offered him one tentative smile and squeaked away on her worn-out shoes. He hated that hard times had come to her family and that the Ballards had been struggling for so long. He wished there was something he could do. He would start with finding out what his father may have said to her.

"Renzo, to what do I owe this pleasure?" His mother floated into the dining room. "You are always out in the fields this time of morning."

"I finished up with the early-morning fieldwork. Pa and I have papers to go over after breakfast." He gave his coffee another stir with his spoon, pushed away from the sideboard and crossed in front of the hearth, where a cheerful fire chased away the chill from the air. "Now that the water problem is fixed and the cattle are snug in the winter pasture, Pa decided it's time for me to learn about the books."

"A word of warning. Book work vexes your father." Ma poured a cup of tea. "He would much rather be outdoors with the animals. I suppose you're likely to feel the same."

"As it's so cold out, I don't mind staying in where it's warm. For now. I imagine I'll start feeling antsy midway through the day and need to get back out there."

"You are a fine rancher, son, and a hard worker. Your father and I couldn't be more proud of you." She landed a peck of a kiss to his cheek. "Now that I have you all to myself—"

"Sugar?" He interrupted her, sure she was going to bring up the Christmas ball again. The last of the invitations were going out this morning. He plopped two sugar cubes into her cup. Best to distract her. "Are you going to town today?"

"As a matter of fact, I am." Her forehead furrowed as she studied him thoughtfully. "I'm taking your sister in for a dress fitting. Our Christmas ball is fast approaching."

"Yes, I'm aware." Seemed there was no getting around this conversation. He grabbed his cup and headed over to the fireplace to finish thawing out. "I plan to skip it this year."

"What?" His mother dropped her teaspoon. "Don't tease me like that. I almost believed you."

He grinned. As if he could disappoint his mother. "You aren't going to make me get a new suit, are you? Last year's fits just fine."

"You would be more dashing in the latest fashion."

"I don't care about fashion." He took a sip of hot, strong coffee and spotted Ruby. She carried a china teapot so carefully she seemed afraid of dropping it as she stepped into the room.

Ruby. He lowered his cup, captivated as she padded to the table and lowered the pot. Her dove-gray maid's dress and crisp, white apron looked darling on her, but he didn't speak to her, remembering his father's rules.

"Ruby, dear." Ma set her cup on the table. "Could you please move the coffeepot to the table?"

"Of course." She gathered up the coffeepot, not looking his way once. Even when she faced him, her eyes were solely on her work. Not one glance, not one smile.

"Just put that near my husband's chair. Thank you." Anyone could tell by Ma's indulgent smile that she was fond of Ruby. Who wouldn't be? It was impossible not to like her, and he'd passed "like" a long while ago.

"Ma, can we stop at the jeweler's after school, too?" His little sister, Bella, bounded in, her petticoats rustling, looking like a page out of Godey's. Her dark hair shone in the lamplight as brightly as the hope on her face. "I need something really sparkly to go with my new gown."

"We will see." Ma's standard answer when she was likely to say no. "Breakfast, first. Then school. Besides, your fitting may take up all the time we have to spare."

"I know, but I am still going to hope." Bella dropped into her seat and poured a cup of tea.

Ruby moved the sugar and creamer to the table before silently padding from the room. Still, not a single glance his way. He hated how stilted and unnatural it felt as she slipped out of sight.

"Good morning." Pa's cane tapped on the hardwood as he limped into the room. "Renzo, looking forward to cracking the books?"

"Why not? Arithmetic was my favorite subject in school. I might even like it." He took another sip of coffee, upset over Ruby. He really needed to talk to his father, but they weren't alone. And likely Ma would side with Pa.

"For your sake, I hope you do. There's more book work with running a big ranch than anyone wants to think about. And don't you look lovely this morning, Selma." Pa held out his arms.

"The same as always, Gerard." Ma stepped into his embrace and the happy pair cuddled, their love for each other as cozy as the fire blazing in the hearth. "Will you and Renzo need all day for the books? I have hopes of stealing you away this afternoon."

"You do? I wouldn't mind being stolen as long as I'm with you."

"Careful, Pa. I was nearly roped in to try on new clothes. Sounds like she might be trying to trap you next."

"Best stay away from that." Pa laughed as he held out his wife's chair for her. "I'm busy, Selma. All day. Terrible busy. Not a thing I can do about it."

"You men. What am I going to do with you?" Ma's merriment filled the room, but he hardly heard it. His sister rolled her eyes and poured honey into her tea. He plopped down in his chair, debating what to do.

He saw how Ruby's life was. Right now, her job was the only thing supporting her family. If her family's finances didn't improve, she could be moving away. They wouldn't have a chance.

Maybe he should just let his feelings for her go. Perhaps that would be best for her.

Frustrated, he shook his head, hating the roiled-up ball of confusion lodged in his chest.

When she reappeared through the door behind Mae, carrying a tray of oatmeal bowls, tenderness surged through him. She appeared so very serious as she kept the heavy tray balanced and level and convenient for Mae, who served bowls around the table.

Ruby inched closer to him, her gaze down as if absorbed in her task. His adorable Ruby. Emotion knotted him up so tight, all he could see was the platinum-haired beauty doing her best to avoid him.

"Aren't you done with the floor yet?" Cook didn't bother to hide her irritation as she slammed a lid on the soup kettle. "I've got the noon meal to get on the table, and here you are dallying."

"Sorry, ma'am." She inched backward on the floor. She'd been cleaning all morning long. Her arms ached as she scrubbed the brush around and around on the tile. She was doing the best she could, but she'd been too slow, and she was holding up the Davis's midday meal.

"I'm not helping her." An imperial voice rose above the whistle of the tea kettle. Mae swirled around a table. "*I* got my work done on time. Lucia will not be happy to hear about this."

Just keep working, Ruby. Around and around the scrub brush went, making quick progress toward the far side of the room. She was almost there. Her knees protested as she inched backward, still scrubbing. She squeezed the brush tighter and made the last swipes.

There, done. Relieved, she relaxed back on her heels and surveyed her work, breathing hard. The kitchen was huge, far larger than her family's entire shanty.

"At least you were thorough. Very thorough." Cook padded across the wet floor, face pruned as she squinted into corners and beneath the cabinets. She gave Mae a hard stare. "Unlike some people. Ruby, you go throw out that wash water, wash your hands. We have a meal to get on the table."

"Yes, ma'am." She rose to her feet, grateful. She would do better next time. She had to. Pa was counting on her. She gathered the brush and the bucket and hurried toward the door, dodged a frowning Mae and popped outside just long enough to send the wash water sailing in a sparkling arc into the snow at the side of the house. Her breath rose in great gusts and, teeth chattering, she bounded into the hallway. Lorenzo's coat still hung on its peg. She'd been aware of his presence all morning, though she did her best not to notice.

Maybe if she stopped looking at the man, her feelings for him would stop. It was worth a try, right? She stowed the bucket and brush in the closet and hurried toward the basin. She needed to get her hands washed so she could—

Her shoe slipped on the wet tile, skating right out from under her. She went down so hard and fast, she didn't have time to grab anything. She sailed backward through the air, reached out to break her fall and heard something snap. Pain screeched up her left arm as she slammed onto the floor. The back of her head hit and bounced off the tile, only to fall back with a final thud.

Ow. She lay stunned, hardly able to breathe. Spots danced in front of her eyes as she sat up. Her head whirled, and she had to blink hard to keep the room still. Fortunately, she was on the far side of the cook's table and cabinets. Maybe no one saw. Maybe if she could get up fast enough, she could pretend this new humiliation hadn't happened.

Excellent, Ruby. Just perfectly brilliant. Everything ached, but her pride hurt most of all.

She planted the palms of her hands on the wet floor and pushed to sit up. Sharp pain lashed through her left arm, and she bit her lip to keep from crying out. It hurt terribly.

Please, Lord, don't let it be broken. It can't be. Cradling her hurt arm to her chest, she pushed off with her right hand, rose slowly to her feet and headed straight to the wash basin. Her head hurt, her arm hurt. She felt bruised where she'd landed. When she went to grab the bar of soap, it, too, was blurry. She worked the pump handle and it was blurry. Any turn of her head made her skull pound. When she glanced slowly around, the entire kitchen was fuzzy.

"Are you all right, girl?" Cook plunked the lid onto its pot and broke away from the stove. "You hit mighty hard. Sit down and get your bearings."

It was a good idea, because honestly, the spots were getting worse. They had taken to swirling a little, and she was afraid if she sat down even for a minute, she wouldn't be able to get back up. If she couldn't do her job, then she wouldn't get paid. Her family needed her wages.

"I'm fine." She rubbed the bar of soap between her hands, agony shot through her left wrist, and her vision went momentary black. Pure will kept her upright. She rinsed beneath the stream of water from the pump spout. Holding her head very still, she gingerly patted her skin dry. Any movement of her left hand and forearm made her eyesight dim.

"You don't look fine." Cook bustled over. "You hit your head."

"I have a hard head." At least, she hoped that was true.

"You're as pale as a sheet." Cook squinted carefully, assessing. "Your eyes look off. Can you see all right?"

"It's nothing to worry about, truly." She appreciated the older woman's concern, but how could she admit the truth?

"I think we should fetch a doctor." Cook pursed her lips, debating. "I wonder if Mateo can be spared from his work?"

"No. Please." A doctor cost money, and how could she pay him? She thought of the looming mortgage payment, the one her father didn't think he could make. "Bothering Doc Frost is not necessary. My shoes slipped, that's all. It's nothing to worry about."

"All right, but it's against my better judgment. If you begin to feel faint, you sit down right away. Understand, young lady?" Cook's scowl emphasized she was not a woman to be messed with. "Mae, what are you smirking at? Get out the serving tray. I'm ready to dish up the meal."

Somehow she had to help. Ruby willed the spots away and took a careful step. The dots before her eyes did not fade as she opened the cabinet with her good hand and counted out three soup bowls. Her left hand protested, but she bit her bottom lip, did her best not to wince and set the bowls gingerly on the counter for Cook to fill.

"The missus will be eating alone." Cook ladled out dipperfuls of the fragrant chicken-and-dumpling soup. "The men will take their meals in the library. Ruby, you are having trouble moving your left hand."

"I'm fine. See?" She wiggled her fingers to prove it. Okay, they didn't exactly move well, but good enough *if* she ignored the overwhelming pain radiating up her arm.

"Mae, you will serve the meal on your own." Cook appeared mightily displeased as she filled the last soup bowl and set it with a clink on the tray.

Ruby groaned. She wasn't even going to be allowed to carry the tray of food? That was her job. It felt like a disgrace not to do it. Was she being dismissed for the afternoon?

"Take this." Cook shoved a clean dish towel at her. "Fill this with snow. You need to put ice on that wrist. Now go, no arguments."

"It will be as good as new in a minute or two." She took the folded length of soft muslin and headed to the back door, feeling like a failure. Cook was unhappy with her, Mae was sure to be angry over having to do all the serving work, and what if her wrist was truly broken? How could she keep her job?

First things first. She unhooked her coat and tried to slide her left hand into her coat sleeve. More pain. She sighed. Her day *could* be going better. She gritted her teeth. Pain bolted up her arm. It's not broken, she insisted stubbornly.

"Last month, I swear I saw that same pair of shoes sitting on the top of the donation barrel," Mae commented under her breath.

Ruby tumbled out the door, breathing in the sting of bitter cold, thankful to finally be alone. She dropped onto the bottom step, unable to fight any longer. Tears burned behind her eyes but she refused to let them fall. She was stronger than this.

A little help please, Lord. Just a little help.

No answer came on the inclement wind.

Chapter Eight

Lorenzo set down his spoon, his noon meal done. He'd been trying to pay attention to his father's teaching, but his gaze kept drifting to the window where he had a perfect view of the steps off the kitchen door and of Ruby seated there. Alone, shivering in the cold, her head hung down with her left hand covered in a cloth. What had happened to her? Concern tore through him.

"Renzo, you need a break." Pa closed the ledger with a thump.

Startled out of his thoughts, he turned his attention away from the window. How long had he been ignoring his father? Guilt crept in. "Sorry. My mind drifted."

"So I see." Gerard grinned cheerfully. "I get the same way after a while. All those numbers. Then the walls start closing in."

"True." How could he admit that wasn't the reason? Now that they were taking a break might be a good time to bring up his concerns. "We need to talk about Ruby."

"I see you watching the young lady." His father turned serious. "You're unhappy with me. I'm sticking to my word. You're to treat her like any other young lady working for us, with respect and distance."

"I never intended to give Ruby anything less than respect, Pa. You know that."

"I do, but my family had the same rules when I was growing up, and they suited well. You wouldn't want to put Ruby in a difficult situation, feeling she has to be especially nice to you even if she's concerned you are taking her away from her responsibilities to Cook and Lucia."

"That isn't the issue, Pa. Did you speak to her?"

"No, as there hasn't been a need for it. You have been the culprit, not her."

"Ruby has done nothing wrong." She looked sad and despairing, with her head hung. He couldn't just sit here. He wanted to go to her. "We're friends, Pa. You can't expect me to be two-faced. To be friendly when I see her in church, but to ignore her when she's here. Look at her."

"I've never seen anyone who looks like she needs a friend more." Pa nodded once, watching her through the window.

"Don't you fire her." Lorenzo rose from his chair and circled around the desk. "I can't leave her sitting there by herself."

"The staff will help her."

"No, I will." He didn't care if his father guessed the truth. His feelings were honest ones. He adored Ruby. If Pa saw it, then fine. Maybe it was time for his parents, as much as he loved them, to understand he was a man now. He followed their rules out of respect, but he also had to make his own. "It won't cost her a job, all right?"

"Hmm." Gerard said nothing more, clutching his cane.

The shadows clung to her as she transferred the cold cloth to the back of her head. Looked like she'd had a rough morning. Sympathy filled him, sympathy he couldn't stop if a gun was pointed at him. Whether or not he ever won Ruby's heart, he would never leave her out in the cold. He would always need to help her. To do what he could to make her world right.

"I suppose this once." His father called out when Lorenzo reached the door. "And if she's on her own time, not ours."

"I'll agree to that." He hesitated on the threshold, turned back and nodded once. A curious light glinted in Pa's eyes. Maybe he was putting the pieces together.

"You'll want to spend your time with the right kind of young lady." Pa stood and leaned on his cane. "I understand the way crushes work, but you're young. You don't want to settle down before you're ready, son. Best to keep this friendly and nothing more."

Well, at least he knew for sure how his father felt. Troubled, he strode from the room, nearly ramming into one of the downstairs maids.

"Hi, Lorenzo." Mae smiled up at him, eyelashes batting. "Do you need something? I could bring you more tea."

"No. Thank you, though." He circled around her, unable to get the image of Ruby out of his head, sitting on the step, shoulders drooping, wearing that worn-thin coat of hers in such cold weather. She had to be freezing. He pulled an afghan off a chair in the parlor on his way to the back door.

Icy air drove through him, and he was glad he'd taken the time to pull on his coat. He buttoned up as his boots broke the thin sheen of ice on the porch boards. Ruby stiffened at the crackling noise, but she didn't look up. She didn't seem surprised when he eased down on the step beside her.

"You look cold." He shook the folds from the afghan and spread it across her shoulders. The soft wool shivered around her slight form. He liked taking care of her. Very much. "Looks like you had an accident. Are you all right?"

"Oh, it's nothing to worry about." She had the cold cloth on her left hand again. "I tend to be clumsy."

"I've had my moments, too."

"I don't believe that for a second." She twisted away from him so he couldn't read her face.

Did she honestly think that would hide her feelings from him? He could feel her hurt and her embarrassment as if it were his own. Sharp and aching in his heart, where they seemed to be linked.

"It's true. I've had many clumsy moments, too."

"You're just saying that to make me feel better." A trace of a smile warmed her voice.

"You may not know it to look at me, but at one time I was such a disaster with the haying I was ordered away from all haystacks. The first wagon wheel I repaired came off ten minutes later and resulted in a broken leg." He patted his left knee. "When my pa trusted me to take care of my own horse, I forgot to tie Poncho up. When I started cleaning his stall, he took off down the road. We had to pull men out of the fields during calving season to help in the chase."

"Poncho ran away from you? I refuse to accept he could behave so badly."

"He was a barely broken two-year-old and I was ten. It was a long time ago, but it took me years to live it down. That incident was just the start of a very long list." He wasn't going anywhere. He was right where he needed to be. Committed to her, he held out his hands. "Let me take a look at your wrist."

"There is no need." Steel rang in her gentle tone, a strength that made her delicate beauty more lovely, a strength that he admired. She tugged the afghan to her with her good hand. "The swelling is going down, so I'm sure it's not broken."

"Let me be the judge of that." He leaned close enough to breathe in her warm, honeysuckle scent. The vulnerable places within him opened more. Defenseless to her, he peeled away the cloth. Snow tumbled from its folds as he peeked at her hand and arm. Bruising stained her satin, puffy skin. "It looks broken to me."

"No. Don't say that." Distress etched crinkles on her face, drew her rosebud mouth down into a frown of misery. "I have to be fine."

"You will be." He shook all the melting snow out of the cloth. Soft, fragile feelings filled him up and were revealed in his voice. "First we have to get you inside and warmed up. You look so pale. This has to really hurt."

"Not bad." She shook her head slightly and winced. "I only have a few more minutes on my lunch hour before I have to go back to work."

"Then we had better get you inside and thawed." He rolled the dish towel into one long bandage. "You can't be of any use to anyone if you're frozen solid."

"True." The distress on her face eased a notch. He leaned in closer to wind the cloth around her wrist and hand, to give it support. She needed a splint, but it would hold for now. "Does that feel better?"

"Yes, thank you. I think I can work with it like this."

How could anyone so sweet be this stubborn? He rather liked it. She was strong where it mattered most. He rose off the step and offered her his hand. "Come with me."

Her big blue eyes gazed up at him, and in them, he read her protest. "I prefer to do things for myself."

"Sure, but you're injured." He read something else in her honest heart. Encouraged, he caught her free hand with his. Ice cold, it was a wonder she wasn't frostbitten. "It's all right not to be so independent if you sprained your wrist."

"Do you really think it's a sprain?" Hope layered her words as she rose slowly, obviously struggling not to wince.

"No, but it doesn't hurt to pray that it is." He caught her elbow to give her more support as they climbed the few steps together. He knew his father was probably watching from the window, stubbornly dismissing this as a mere crush. He would be wrong.

What he felt for Ruby was amazing. Overwhelming. Peace filled his soul as he propped open the door for her. She tossed him an uncertain smile, cute and wobbling, for she was hiding so much pain. She could deny it, but he knew her. Her skirts rustled, her light step padded on the wood floor and he held on to her as long as he could. Heavenly.

Once in the vestibule, he guided her past the doorway into the kitchen where a twitter of laughter suddenly froze and turned into an uncomfortable silence. Apparently his attention to Ruby hadn't gone unnoticed. He steered her down the hallway, bypassing doorway after doorway until they reached the parlor. A warm fire crackled merrily, heating the room.

"Take my mother's chair. It's the warmest." He lifted the afghan from her shoulders and nudged her gently toward the hearth.

"I don't know what I'm going to say to my pa." She looked up at him with those eyes that could lasso his soul. Trapped, he was helpless to walk away, helpless to deny her anything.

"I'm sure he will understand."

"Understand? Of course he will. He'll be very concerned, but—" She settled into the cushions slowly, wincing, obviously fighting pain. "My job lessens his burden, whether he wants to admit it or not."

"You worry too much." He spread the afghan over her, seeing her problem. Six weeks or so for that bone to heal was a long time to be unable to work and for his mother to go without a maid. She would be forced to replace Ruby, especially with their Christmas ball in the near future. He didn't know what to say to comfort her.

"My brother lost his job and his last two weeks of pay." She lowered her voice, so it would not carry in the cavernous room and be overheard by anyone passing by. "He's coming home on Friday's train. I'm the only one with a job in my family."

"I see. I'm sorry, Ruby." He knelt before her and cradled her hand in his. "Is there anything I can do?"

"No, but thanks for listening."

"Anytime." He loosened the end and unwound the bandage. "I'm pretty sure you cracked a bone. The doctor really should take a look at this."

"Don't you dare fetch him." Her chin went up. "He will tell me not to work, and I can't do that."

"I understand." He chose two short sticks of kindling from the wood box.

The firelight gleamed bronze in his thick hair and caressed the rugged contours of his face. She couldn't help noticing the picture he made with the flames writhing in the background, tossing alternating light and shadows across the powerful plane of his back, the impressive curve of his shoulders and the strength in his muscled arms. He could have been a prince in a fairy tale come to life.

What was she doing? She had vowed to stop being fanciful, to stop wasting her time on storybook wishes that could never come true. Especially now. She squeezed her eyes shut, determined to erase from her mind the image of Lorenzo kneeling at her feet. She couldn't be carried away by her fondness for him. She didn't have the right.

"I should send for Dr. Frost. I should make you go home so you can rest and heal." He laid the kindling sticks on either side of her arm and began binding her wrist. "This is against my better judgment."

"Thank you, Lorenzo. Thank you so much." Gratitude rushed through her with such force she could hardly breathe. "I'm determined to be optimistic. I'm sure this is nothing serious."

"That is incredibly optimistic of you. And stubborn." A slow grin tugged at the corners of his chiseled mouth. "I've met donkeys less headstrong than you."

"It's my best quality." She hardly noticed the pain in her arm as he tightened the bandage. Probably because it took all her willpower not to fall for this man and his midnight blue eyes.

"You have many good qualities."

"Me?" Shy, she tried to drop her gaze but his eyes held hers captive.

The brush of his fingertip as he secured the bandage, the soothing murmur of his words and the unmistakable caring carved into his features made it hard not to fall. It was all she could do to hold herself back.

"You are incomparable, Ruby Ballard."

Her? Hardly. "Are you sure you don't mean odd?"

"Funny. You can try, but you can't use humor to distract me. You are without equal." He turned his attention to checking over her splint to make sure the knot he'd tied in the ends would hold. "That ought to get you through the afternoon if you are careful."

"I will be." The mantel clock donged one o'clock. Time to return to work. As she folded up the afghan and stood to hang it over the chair, she didn't know what to say. How to thank Lorenzo for his help. For... Oh, she didn't know how to say what she felt. It was too big and wonderful.

She cared about him much more than she wanted to admit.

"If this starts hurting worse, you have to let me know. Promise?"

"Promise." She brushed at the wrinkles in her apron with her good hand, stealing one last moment to gaze at the man. With his feet braced and hands clasped behind his back, he looked like everything she could ever want in a man. Everything she could not have. "But it won't hurt worse. I'm sure all this fuss is for nothing."

"Not for nothing." His eyes had never been so blue or mesmerizing, inviting her to fall right in.

It was time to go back to work, so she swirled away. Heart stinging, she strolled toward the door and away from his kindness that only made her want him more.

Lorenzo sat up straight in the hard-backed chair and blinked at the scratches on the ledger page. Determining if the ranch ran at a profit or at a loss was more complicated than he'd thought; his head swam with information and his father's words ran together, making no sense at all. The ledger spread out before him began to blur. There he went, thinking of Ruby again.

How was she doing? He tried to imagine her lifting pots, packing wash water, doing whatever other tasks were required of her. Was she taking care of her wrist? Still determined to ignore her pain because her family was in danger of losing what little they had?

He shoved away from the desk, surprising his father. "I'm going for a cup of tea. Do you want one?"

"That's a dangerous question." Pa thoughtfully marked in the ledger. "Maybe you could bring back something sweet to go with that tea. I thought I smelled a cake baking in the oven."

"I'll see what I can do." He strode into the hallway. The house felt lonely without his mother in it. She had gone to town.

"Is there something I can get you, Master Lorenzo?" Lucia set down her dust cloth, her naturally stern voice echoing in the parlor.

"No, I'll get it myself, thanks." He kept going, sure he felt a hint of disapproval from the housekeeper.

A clatter of silverware echoed in the corridor, and he knew it was Ruby before she slipped into view. Her fine hair tumbled down from her up knot in fine gossamer strands to curl around her collar. Her back was to him as she stood before the table, switching around silverware on the table.

"Is that right this time, Mae?" Her question held a note of vulnerability. She must be learning to set the table.

"No. Honestly, don't you know the difference between a soup spoon, a dinner spoon and a teaspoon?" He recognized Mae's voice as she huffed, irritated. "Try it again."

"How about now?"

Poor Ruby.

"No, that's not right either. You have the forks wrong. Don't you know anything?" Mae's dislike rang in her voice. "This is a salad fork."

"Why is there more than one fork? You can only use one at a time."

"Because this isn't a hovel. The Davises can afford more than one fork for everyone."

"Oh." Ruby bent her head to rearrange the silverware.

He caught sight of her left hand, still splinted. She had to be hurting as she rearranged the order of the forks.

"No, that's wrong, too." Mae apparently left Ruby to guess instead of teaching her. "Get your mind on your job. Lorenzo is not going to marry you and save you from all this."

"I'm sure he wouldn't." Ruby's answer came so small and soft, he could barely hear it.

"He isn't going to marry someone too poor to afford decent shoes."

"I already know that, Mae." Her voice was so little he didn't realize she was still talking. "Besides, I can't think of marrying anyone. I have to help support my family. There. Now, is this right?"

"No. Try again."

Ruby just filled his heart right up. His boot crossed over the threshold before he'd even realized he was moving toward her. She was perfect, absolutely flawless, everything he could ever want. He could have closed his eyes, looked into his soul and dreamed her up. He just wished her life wasn't so hard.

"Mae, please fetch a pot of tea and bring it to the library. My father would also like a slice of whatever cake Cook baked for tonight's dessert." He barely looked at the maid; he only had eyes for Ruby. His precious Ruby. "How's the wrist?"

"Better." Tiny furrows of frustration dug as she stared at the place setting. So determined to do a good job.

"Why don't I believe you?" he asked, resisting the urge to brush gossamer, platinum tendrils out of her eyes. "You're still really pale."

"That's just an illusion, I'm sure. I'm willing my arm better. I've made up my mind so my wrist will have to comply."

"You are a force to be reckoned with."

"I try."

He nudged around a few forks. "That's how it goes. I *think*. I'm no expert. Generally, I grab whatever fork is in front of me and eat with that one."

"Do you usually help the new kitchen maid?"

"Always. Lucia insists."

They laughed together. He had to believe this would work out. That the Good Lord had brought him and Ruby together for a reason.

Boots pounded in the hallway, Mateo's brash and confident gait. "Renzo, there you are. We've got trouble. Thacker spotted a cougar by the horse barn. Ray is doing a head count to make sure we haven't lost any cattle."

"I'll grab my rifle." He had more to say to Ruby, but it would have to wait.

"Be safe." Her gaze found his, and the caring he read there made him feel ten feet tall. Hopeful, he tossed her a wink before he strode away, feeling lighter than air.

Chapter Nine

The long, single note of the train whistle pierced the late afternoon's silence. Earlee Mills looked up from her desk at the head of the classroom. Behind her Charlie Bellamy was writing one hundred times on the blackboard as punishment, "I will never again pull Anna's hair."

Earlee rolled her eyes at his slow progress. *She* may well be the one punished if he didn't hurry up. Judging by the way he was going, school would be dismissed before he finished his final sentence. Unrepentant, he giggled. Two boys in the middle row chuckled in response. Apparently there was some private joke she was missing.

"Quiet, boys." She used her firmest, big-sister tone, the one that kept her eight younger siblings in line whenever necessary. The squirming stopped, and the troublemakers returned to their spelling books. She loaded her pen, tapped off the excess and set the quill tip to the sheet of parchment. She resumed writing a letter to her pen friend, Finn McKaslin.

...so everything on our farm is going well. The animals are snug in the barn, and now that all the long, summer days are passed, and harvest madness is over, I have spare time to work on my latest story. I know, this is the first time that I'm mentioning this—

A commotion overhead snared her attention. It sounded like a herd of buffalo bounding across the ceiling and charging down the stairs. All her students squirmed in their seats, staring at her hard, willing her to ring her hand bell and dismiss school. Remembering what it was like to sit in those desks wishing to be set free, she obliged. She jangled the bell, children exploded out of their seats, and chaos reigned. She turned her chair to deal with Charlie.

"Not so fast, young man." She had to give him credit. He almost looked guilty sneaking away. "You have thirty more lines to write."

"But Miss Mills, I gotta go home. My ma will worry if I'm late."

"You should have thought of that when you were dallying at the blackboard. Your brother can tell her where you are. Right, Tommy?" She addressed the younger Bellamy brother who was straggling up the aisle.

"I guess." Tommy sighed. "I don't like walkin' alone."

"Then hurry and catch up with your friends. Charlie will be staying until he is finished." She reached into her desk drawer to hand the troublemaker a fresh piece of chalk so there would be no more excuses.

"Yes, Miss Mills." Charlie returned to the board while his brother dashed off. Chalk squeaked as he wrote one line after another, remarkably faster than he'd done during class time.

Back to her letter. She reloaded her pen and continued writing.

> ... *My ma says it simply isn't normal, but I can't seem to help myself from writing. Stories just bubble out of my head. I'm probably not very good at it, but it's a lot of fun—*

A knock rapped on the door frame jerking her out of her letter. A tall, broad-shouldered man with light brown hair and Ruby's smile held up one gloved hand in greeting.

"Hullo there, Earlee. Is Ruby around?" Rupert Ballard called out in his friendly, smoky baritone. "I waited for her in front of the school, but she didn't come out. I checked and she's not upstairs in her classroom. Figured maybe she was in here with you."

"Aren't you supposed to be in Wyoming?" She laid down her pen.

"Supposed to be, except for the fact I lost my job." He shrugged those dependable shoulders of his as if it was no big deal, but she knew how precarious the Ballard finances were, since her family also struggled. He straightened up to his full six-foot-plus height. "I just stepped off the train."

"Welcome back." She rose from her chair and glanced over her shoulder to check on Charlie's progress. Amazingly he had only five more lines left. She circled around her desk. "I suppose you haven't heard Ruby's news?"

"Ruby has news?" Puzzled, he crossed his arms over his wide chest. "I can't think of what it would be. No one is courting her, so it can't be an engagement."

"She has a job working for the Davis family. She's no longer in school. I hate to be the one to tell you." She ambled down the aisle, her skirts swishing. "Does your family know you're coming?"

"Sure, but I thought I would swing by, pick up Ruby, and we could walk home together." He scooped a rucksack off the entry floor. "Guess I'll be walking alone. It's good to see you doing so well, Earlee. You make a good teacher."

"I try." She shrugged, aware of the plunk of a chalk stick hitting the wooden holder.

"I'm done, Miss Mills. Can I go now?" Charlie swiped his face with his hand, smearing a streak of chalk dust across his cheek.

"Go on with you." He still had to erase and clean the blackboard, but that could wait until morning. She had floors to sweep and the fire to put out and she wanted to get home. The boy, glad to be freed, dashed down the aisle, his shoes hammering the wood floor as he circled around Rupert and disappeared from sight.

"There's one in every class." He gave his hat brim a tug. "See you around, Earlee."

"Bye, Rupert." There had been a time in her life when she would have given a little, wistful sigh as the handsome man walked away. Roop could make any young lady dream of possibilities and romance. These days, another man held claim to her heart. She spun around, her skirts twirling as her thoughts returned to her letter.

Light already faded from the windows. Sunset was not far away. If she wanted to walk home before dark fell, she would have to finish her letter tomorrow. Not tonight, because she couldn't risk her sisters at home catching a glimpse of Finn's letter. Should her parents find out she was corresponding with a man currently serving time at the territorial prison in Deer Lodge, they would have an apoplexy. No doubt, they would forbid to her to continue writing him. Her heart would shatter into a million pieces if she had to say goodbye to him. Finn didn't appear to return her affections, but she loved him.

She carefully wiped her pen tip and capped the ink bottle. She folded the letter in careful thirds, letting herself dream just a little. Outside the window, snow began to fall in tiny, fragile flakes, dancing like hope on the wind.

"How is the hand, dear?"

Lost in thought, Ruby startled, dropped hold of the mop, and it landed with a smack on the floor. The sound echoed off the vestibule walls as she spun around. Mrs. Davis stood in the hallway, striking in a fashionable, yellow gown, a dress sporting beautiful ruffles, silk ribbons and pearl buttons. At least, she suspected those were pearls, since she'd never seen real ones before.

"Lucia said Cook finally admitted that you were injured." Selma Davis didn't mind the wet floor as she swept closer. "I ought to step foot inside the kitchen more often, but cooking is not my specialty. Otherwise, I would have noticed your splint sooner."

"It's nothing." She knelt to rescue the mop from the floor, using her good hand. "I'm practically fine already."

"I'm relieved to hear that, but I insist on taking a look."

"That's not necessary." She stepped back, accidentally bumping into the door handle. She knew with one look at her wrist, Mrs. Davis would send her home. "It's nothing to fuss about."

"I say differently, and I am your employer." Selma Davis knelt to set the wash-water pail against the wall, out of her path. "You will listen to me."

"Yes, ma'am." It was all over. She had spent the last few days hiding the searing agony every time she hefted a bucket of water or drained the boiling potatoes for Cook. She had improvised peeling carrots and mopping floors and carrying stacks of dirty dishes from the dining room. But no more.

"Follow me." Mrs. Davis plucked the mop out of Ruby's grip and leaned it against the wall. "I think you could use a bit of fussing over. Cook, could you fetch two cups of tea?"

"Right away, Missus." Inside the kitchen, Cook hopped to work. The tea kettle clanked onto the stove, the only sound Ruby could hear over the rushing in her ears.

She was about to lose her job. She would have to go home and explain to Pa why she could no longer help support the family. She felt like a failure. Her father had always been there for her. How could she let him down? Blindly, she tapped after Mrs. Davis.

Never had any hallway seemed so long. As she passed the dining room, she caught sight of Mae dusting. Her smug look said it all. She was probably the one who had spilled the beans to Mrs. Davis.

"Please sit, dear." Her employer gestured to the sofa, the same one Ruby had sat on for her interview.

There was one positive note—at least, her shoes weren't wet and squeaking. She eased onto the cushion, ignoring her crushing disappointment. She took a deep breath, praying for guidance. *Help me to handle this well, Lord. Any guidance would be much appreciated.*

"Let me get a good look." Mrs. Davis settled onto the cushion beside her. She deftly folded back Ruby's sleeve, took a decorative pillow from the corner of the sofa and laid the injured arm on top of it. With a motherly air, she untied the ends of the bandage and carefully unwound it. "You've splinted it carefully."

"Yes, ma'am." That was Lorenzo's doing. How she missed him. She hadn't seen him for days, not in the dining room. One of the stable hands had come for the meals. The men were putting in long days tracking the cougar. Not that she ought to be pining for him. Now it looked as if she wouldn't even be able to say goodbye to him.

"Oh, this is either the worst sprain I've ever seen, or it's broken." Mrs. Davis shook her head sympathetically. "This simply does not look right. Glad I sent out for the doctor."

"The doctor?" Oh, no. She couldn't even think about

what that would cost. Misery clutched her. "I sure wish you hadn't done that, Mrs. Davis."

"Nonsense. You are my employee, Ruby. I won't have this go untreated, and the doctor is my responsibility. You slipped and fell in my kitchen." Her kindness was unexpected. It glittered like a rare gem in her dark and gentle eyes. "I suppose your father knows nothing about this?"

"Only that I told him it's a sprain." She'd taken care to hide every wince of pain as she worked in their shanty. Pa had enough to worry about.

"And he believed you? You poor dear." She leaned in to brush a strand of hair from Ruby's eyes. The softest stroke, just the way she'd always imagined a mother's touch to be. "This looks as if it's been hurting you very much."

"It's not too bad." She shrugged. What she wanted was to have not fallen in the first place.

"Lucia?" Mrs. Davis called over the back of the couch. "I hope you brought some willow bark and a good, hot poultice, but not too hot."

"Of course," came Lucia's no-nonsense answer as she breezed into the room, set down the tray and tapped briskly away with a hard look in Ruby's direction.

Mortified, she slumped in misery. This was causing far too much trouble.

"Cook told me you insisted on doing all your duties." Mrs. Davis smiled sympathetically. "Even the heavy lifting."

"I didn't want to break my promise to you." She took a shaky breath. "I just wanted to do a good job."

"That you certainly did." Mrs. Davis poured two cups

of tea. One smelled particularly bitter. She left them to steep and lifted a bowl from the tray. That smelled even worse. "You will be on light duties next week and, depending on what the doctor says, maybe longer."

"Light duties?" She blinked, not understanding at first. "Does this mean you aren't going to fire me?"

"Goodness, no. Is that what you thought, child?" Mrs. Davis spooned a hot mixture of herbs and who knows what else on Ruby's swollen wrist. "Put that worry out of your mind. Cook speaks highly of you, and she is very hard to please. I'm afraid if I let you go, she would have my hide. Good kitchen maids are hard to find."

"That's not true." She thought of all the women she'd spotted on her way to the interview and the long line of them waiting in the foyer for the chance at this job. "I'm completely replaceable."

"You are indispensible, Ruby, and don't you forget it." Mrs. Davis patted her cheek with a mother's affection. "Give this a few moments to soak in, and you should begin to feel better. I'm afraid this tea is very bitter, but you must drink it. Shall I put in a lot of sugar?"

"Please." Ruby blinked hard, but her vision blurred anyway. Did Mrs. Davis know how much her kindness meant?

"This ought to help." Mrs. Davis stirred in several heaping spoonfuls of sugar before handing over the steaming china cup. "Sip as much of this as you can tolerate."

"I'll try." She didn't want to displease Mrs. Davis, but the odor emanating from that dainty floral teacup was the most horrid thing she'd ever smelled. She cradled it in her right hand and braved a sip. Her tongue curled.

Her mouth puckered, her taste buds cringed, and she choked, coughing it down. It was like drinking kerosene, not that she'd ever tasted kerosene, but surely, even kerosene would taste better.

"That's a good girl, keep drinking." Ms. Davis gently tipped the cup. "At least, one more good swallow."

Sputtering, gasping, another wave of the toxic substance sluiced across her spasming tongue, assaulted her mouth and nearly blinded her as she swallowed. She lowered the cup, swallowed again but the flavor lingered, refusing to budge.

"Now this." Mrs. Davis produced the second cup and saucer of tea, smelling of sweetened chamomile and peach. "It will help wash away that nasty taste. I want you to relax here until the doctor comes."

Two sets of footsteps echoed in the hallway, one gait was as familiar to her as her heartbeat. Lorenzo. His powerful presence shrunk the room. Snow dusted his thick hair, and he brought in the scent of winter and the December wind. The blue flannel shirt he wore emphasized the multiple shades of blue in his irises. The moment his gaze found hers, her knees wobbled.

Good thing she was sitting down because she would have fallen. The cup she held rattled in its saucer, tiny nervous *clink, clinks* that betrayed her. She took a sip, and the sweet, flavorful tea rolled across her tongue, calming it, but nothing could calm her reaction to him.

He affected her. Regardless of how hard she tried to stop it, he dominated her senses, he became the only thing in her world.

"Lorenzo." Mrs. Davis welcomed her son. "I didn't

expect to see you so soon. Come warm yourself by the fire. Does this mean you found the cougar?"

"We tracked him into the foothills far away from us. I'm hoping he stays there." He trailed across the room. Lorenzo smiled at her with dimples that could make a girl swoon six counties away.

Not that she should be swooning.

"The doc is on his way. I saw him riding in when I was on the doorstep knocking the snow off my boots."

The doctor. Ruby flinched, still not sure seeing a medical man was a good idea. He would only advise her to rest her arm, and she couldn't. Not here, not at home. Maybe he will agree that it's a sprain she thought, watching as Lorenzo's gaze found hers. His mouth crooked up again, showing off those arresting dimples.

She had to stop noticing his dimples. And how handsome he was. And how her pulse stilled when he smiled.

"How prompt of Dr. Frost. He is always so busy." Mrs. Davis rose. "Ruby dear, I have an appointment at the dressmaker's, so I must leave you. Lorenzo will look after you in my stead."

Alone with Lorenzo? She set down her cup. She swallowed hard, but her throat was too tight to actually swallow. Tension rolled through her, tightening her up muscle by muscle.

"If your arm hurts too much, someone here will drive you home. I know you have your own horse, but you might not feel much like riding." Mrs. Davis gently patted the side of Ruby's face, a motherly gesture. "If he's free, maybe Lorenzo can take you home."

"Oh, I'm not sure that's a good idea. I don't trust

Lorenzo. He's shifty." The quip hid the tug of emotion in her heart.

An emotion she should not be feeling.

Laughter echoed around her as Mrs. Davis swished away, leaving her and Lorenzo alone. Again.

"I wasn't the one who tattled about your wrist." Lorenzo stalked closer.

"I know that. You might be shifty, but you aren't a promise breaker."

"That's right." Chuckling, he eased onto the cushion next to her, so close the air drained from the room.

She gulped and gasped, barely able to breathe. Whatever she did, no air went into her lungs. Since she was turning red and coughing, Lorenzo was bound to notice.

"Are you all right?" He held out the cup of tea to her, the awful-tasting one.

She shook her head. That tea wasn't going to help. She pointed to the other cup, looking like an idiot. Any other young woman in town would be able to carry on a conversation with the man, but not her. The memory of the last time they were in this room together came alive again. She could feel the tender warmth of his touch and see the caring concern etched on his face as he'd knelt before her.

Her lungs squeezed harder.

"Oh, how about this tea? It smells much better." He handed her the chamomile-and-peach cup, and she slurped it gratefully.

What was wrong with her? Why did she always embarrass herself around Lorenzo? Honestly. He would think something was seriously wrong with her. Miraculously the tea slid down her throat, opened her up, and she swallowed, able to breathe again.

"Better? Good." Larger than life and so incredibly authentic that he shone with the might of it, he took her empty cup. His baritone softened with earnesty. "Even if your wrist is broken, that won't stop you from singing, right? Because tonight is our second caroling practice, and I'd hate for you to miss it."

"No, I reckon I'll be there. I'm sure Pa will insist."

"He loves you."

"That's the rumor." Whatever this emotion was that was fighting to come alive in her heart, she could not acknowledge it. It had to go away. But did it?

No. The wishes she could not hold back overwhelmed her like a blizzard's leading edge, drowning out all sense of direction, blocking out the entire world. Disoriented, she barely heard the knell of another set of boots entering the room.

"Ruby, this is Dr. Hathaway, Doc Frost's new associate."

She couldn't focus on the tall shadow at the room's entrance. Only one man held her attention as he rose from the couch, towering above her. Lorenzo's honesty, his mightiness, his integrity riveted her.

I wish, she thought, gazing up at him. *I so wish.*

Chapter Ten

"What happened to you?" Kate whispered the moment Ruby eased into place with the other sopranos. "Look at your arm."

"It's nothing. Just a little, unimportant crack." Self-conscious, she held her songbook with her good hand. Reverend Hadly shuffled up to the front of the group, everyone quieted, and across the way Lorenzo smiled at her with those dashing dimples, which could make a girl swoon six counties away.

"You mean a cracked *bone?*" Kate nearly dropped her book. "Ruby, that is a big deal. Look at the size of that splint."

"Does it hurt?" Scarlet whispered from her other side. "What about your job? Surely Dr. Frost ordered you to rest."

"I saw the new doctor." Breathless from the effect of Lorenzo's grin, she prayed she sounded normal as she desperately tried to keep her gaze on the minister. But did her eyes obey?

No. They swung to the right until a certain, stunning man filled her view. Why couldn't her eyes stop finding him against her will? Fine, maybe she could admit it. She had a crush on him, but it was just a little one. Nothing serious. Surely it would go away in time, right? All she had to do was to get back in control, keep her eyes from wandering his way and to somehow keep him out of her thoughts.

But how? That was one question she didn't have the answer to.

"Ooh, Dr. Hathaway is to die for." Kate searched through the pages of the book for the carol the reverend announced. "He's almost as handsome as Lorenzo."

"Not even close," Scarlet disagreed good-naturedly. "And I've really looked. No man can compare to Lorenzo."

"Dreamy Lorenzo," Kate whispered.

Scarlet simply sighed, and in that single wistful sound, Ruby heard shades of true caring, not the superficial fondness of a schoolgirl crush. Anguish crinkled in the corners of Scarlet's eyes as she watched Lorenzo, bowed over his songbook. His dark hair tumbled over his forehead, and a cowlick poked up at the back of his head in a thick whirl.

"Rags, what are you looking at?" Narcissa Bell crowded into place directly behind her.

Oh, no. Ruby snapped her gaze away, feeling heat scorch her face. She'd been caught red-handed, and there was no use denying it. She bit her bottom lip, miserable, hoping beyond hope Narcissa wasn't about to announce it to the entire group—and to her friends.

"He's not interested in you. Why would he be? There isn't a single man who would look twice at your patches. You aren't holding out hope, are you?"

Her tongue tied up. She tried to think up something witty and appropriate to say, but could she? No. Not a single word came to mind. Just the flood of humiliation and shame, because any minute, Kate or Scarlet would figure out that she was seeing Lorenzo behind their backs.

"Hush up, Narcissa." Scarlet gave a withering sneer.

The minister tooted on his pitch pipe and hummed. "Sopranos." "Aahs" burst out in perfect tone all around her.

Just focus on the music, she thought, steeling her spine. Narcissa might know exactly how to hurt a person, but she was not about to do the same in return.

"Look at that dress." Narcissa pitched her voice to rise above the singing. "Our maid scrubs our kitchen with rags better than that. Of course, I hear you are a kitchen maid, so maybe it's fitting."

Faces turned toward her, and Ruby blushed. Anger built up like steam behind her ribs, but she could not give in to it. She bowed her head, she couldn't help it. Her throat closed up, so all she could do was pretend to sing along with everyone else. She prayed everyone would stop looking at her.

"Ooh, she makes me mad," Kate leaned in to whisper. "Are you all right?"

"Fine." Had Lorenzo heard? She didn't dare peek between her lashes to see if he had noticed. She cringed. How could he not? The reverend's pipe gave another pitch, and the men joined in, the crescendo of the Major C chord booming like a hallelujah in the sanctuary.

"Very good. Now scales. Ready?"

"Aahs" rippled upward, note after note, and she did her best to join in.

Throughout one Christmas carol after another, she kept her gaze fastened on the reverend. At least, she'd finally learned her lesson. No more gazing at Lorenzo. Now she had another problem. Her ears. They seemed to search through the chorus of voices to pick out his smoky baritone. Each note he hit did funny little things to her heart. It turned tingly, as if more alive than ever before.

Not exactly the reaction she was going for. She was supposed to be ignoring him. Falling out of her crush on him. What was she going to do with herself?

"Ruby?"

She felt a tug on her sleeve. Kate, getting her attention. Her mind had wandered. Again. "Sorry." She shook her head, realizing everyone else was filing down the aisle, merry conversations bouncing off the walls and high ceiling of the sanctuary. Lamplight shone off the stained-glass windows and trailed Narcissa as she huffed away with a clear snort of disapproval.

"I couldn't believe she said that to you." Lila tumbled over with the rest of the gang in her wake. "She did it so everyone would hear, to embarrass you intentionally."

"That's nothing new." Ruby deposited the songbook on a nearby pew with the others. She didn't need to glance around to know Lorenzo had already left with his friends. Without him near, the shadows felt darker, the light less bright. That was the way she would always be without him.

"You need to stand up to her." Meredith smiled at

the reverend on her way down the aisle. "She won't stop picking on you until you do."

"I don't know what to do." Ruby kept her voice low, so it wouldn't carry to the reverend behind them or anyone in the vestibule ahead of them. "What is the right thing?"

"I say give her a taste of her own medicine," Scarlet advised.

"Yes, put her in her place," Meredith agreed. "She has no right making fun of you."

"Her bullying needs to stop," Lila agreed. "I would be happy to do it for you, but what will you do when we're not around?"

"I'll help," Earlee offered. "We outnumber her and her group."

Her friends' solidarity made her feel warm all over. Snug and loved, she wanted to give each one a hug, but she was shy and held back. "Thank you for your offers, but I don't want to sink to her level. This isn't about her behavior, it's about mine."

"Hello, Ruby." A man's pleasant tenor said her name with familiar warmth, as if he knew her well, but she didn't immediately recognize it. She should have, but it wasn't until she'd stepped into the vestibule that she recognized the man hanging his coat in the closet.

"Dr. Hathaway." She had liked the new doctor. He'd been gentle when he tended her wrist and proved easy to talk to. "What are you doing here?"

"After you told me about the caroling group, I decided to come join in." Dark eyes twinkled. "I would have been on time, but I had a patient call."

"Reverend Hadly will be ecstatic you're here." She

was aware of Scarlet nudging her and Kate's veiled smile. "I will see you after the break."

"See you soon, Ruby." He went to tip his hat to her, but then must have realized he wasn't wearing his hat and blushed. His square shoulders didn't waver, however, as he strode away with a confident step.

"Wow," Lila breathed. "You could have told us."

"Told you what?" She spotted her coat piled on the table pushed against the vestibule wall and reached for it.

"No need to deny it with us." Meredith unhooked her coat from the pegs in the closet. "You like him."

"I do?" That was news to her.

"I saw the look he gave you." Scarlet shrugged into her coat. "He likes you. Really likes you."

"No, that's not true." She hadn't noticed anything. She shoved one arm into her coat sleeve. "He was just being nice."

"Nice? No, I saw the sparkle in his eyes." Kate wrapped her scarf around her neck. "He's taken a shine to you. You might have a suitor and soon."

"Dr. Hathaway? You couldn't be more wrong." Regret twisted inside her chest, and she hid the wince as she fit her splinted arm into her other sleeve. Even if there was only one man she wished for, she couldn't have him. Her family came first and so did her friends.

"I saw it, too. If I were penning the story, I would—" Earlee stopped in mid-sentence as she pulled on her mittens. "Ruby, what's wrong with your coat?"

It did feel funny. She shrugged the garment over her shoulders, and it didn't sit right at all. Something pulled down the left side like weight. Her pocket bulged noticeably so she reached into it. "I don't know. Why, it's a package."

"I'll say." Earlee clasped her hands with excitement.

"What is it?" Kate whispered, moving closer.

"Open it," Scarlet urged.

"I can guess what it might be." Lila smiled in her confident way. "Go ahead, unwrap it."

She stared at the brown-wrapped parcel. What could it be? Who had put it there? With trembling fingers she folded back the paper. A beautiful, china-handled crochet hook glinted in the lamplight, and with it was a large skein of quality, heavy-weight thread perfect for making snowflakes.

"The hook is beautiful. I've never seen one like it," Meredith murmured in awe.

"Me, either." Scarlet's eyes had gone wide. "This isn't a small token. Ruby, this is a serious gift."

"I know. I'm stunned." There was only one logical explanation. Lorenzo. But could she say it out loud? Could she even think it? No. Because if she admitted it, then what would her friends think? Oh, this was so much worse than she'd thought. "Someone must have put this in the wrong coat pocket by accident."

"Oh, I don't think so. Your coat is, well, distinct," Kate kindly settled on the word. "It's not a mistake."

"Someone is fond of you." Lila beamed as if she knew a secret.

"Dr. Hathaway was in this vestibule a moment ago and all alone," Earlee surmised.

"He would have had plenty of opportunity to slip that into your coat pocket." Meredith donned her beautiful, knit hat. "I have a feeling Ruby will be the next one of us to find true love."

"Impossible, since I'm doomed to become a spinster." What would they think if they knew? *Wretched,* she ran a fingertip across the thread. Best to put this back in her pocket. "I think being an old maid will give me a certain flair."

"You, an old maid?" Scarlet laughed lovingly. "Not a chance of that. Now, are we going to the diner? We had best get moving."

"No, not me." She longed to go with them and share the sure-to-be-fun moments over tea and pie, but she had something to attend to. "You all go ahead."

"Not without you. What are you going to do?" Earlee asked so sincerely and sweetly it was impossible to deny her the truth.

"I need to sort through the church barrel. I need better shoes." She shrugged, quite as if her pride didn't sting one bit. "I can't risk slipping and sliding around the Davis's kitchen. I'm not that good of a skater."

"Then we shall come with you," Kate declared. "We are like the Musketeers. All for one and one for all."

"Yes, we are," Scarlet agreed as they linked arms. "The church basement, here we come."

The night was crisp and bitter. The raw air burned their faces and the insides of their noses as they plowed through the snow. Their laughter echoed in the empty churchyard, and several horses tied at the hitching post threw disapproving looks their way. Ruby watched Scarlet peel off from the group and duck to fill her mitten with snow.

"Don't you dare!" Meredith squealed, leaping to

make a snowball of her own. Too late, an icy orb hit square on her back. "You are going to pay for that, Scarlet Eudora Fisher!"

"Oh, no!" Laughing, Scarlet dashed behind Ruby and used her for a shield. "You wouldn't risk hitting sweet, little Ruby, would you?"

"Not if she ducks." Meredith wound up and let the ball fly. Ruby, being no dummy, ducked just in time.

Scarlet did not. Snow splatted against her coat and exploded. Her laughter rang merrily. She swiped snow out of her face. "Kate, don't just stand there. Help me!"

Ruby watched the full-scale snowball tactical assault surround her. Kate joined Scarlet, Lila joined Meredith, and Earlee scooped up snow and packed it, casually watching both warring factions as if debating her battle strategy. Squeals of laughter pealed in the dark evening. Ruby laughed too, never happier.

"Ruby." Earlee smiled at her innocently, a second before she launched a snowball through the air.

"Earlee!" With a shriek she tried to duck but the ball of snow thwacked on her shoulder, spraying cold bits into her face.

"Oops, my aim was off. I was aiming higher." Earlee was rewarded by a smack of snow that came out of nowhere. She rubbed the icy chunks out of her eyes, her smile still in place. "Kate, you are going to pay for that."

"Ooh, I'm scared. C'mon, Ruby. Let's get her!"

"Time to get even." Ruby plunged her right hand into the snow, working fast to shape her own weapon. Earlee yelped as Kate launched a second ball at her, she tried to dodge it, and Ruby threw. Her snowball hurtled through the air, walloped Earlee in the back, just as Kate's hit her from the front.

"Look at Ruby, just standing there." Lila swirled around, holding a snowball in each hand. "She's hardly been hit at all."

"That isn't right," Meredith scooped up more snow. "What are we going to do about it, girls?"

"A full-scale war?" Scarlet suggested.

"Sounds good to me." Earlee smiled.

"I'm still on your side, Ruby." Kate, ever loyal, knelt to shape another snowball.

"I adore you for that, but we're outnumbered." Ruby inched her good hand toward the snowy ground, desperately wanting to make some ammunition. Her friendly adversaries were creeping closer.

"I say we can take them all and wi—" Kate's confident remark was interrupted by a pelting snowball.

The battle was on. White projectiles cannoned into the air, sailing in arcs straight toward her. Ruby squeaked, felt her shoes slip on the icy snow—she didn't dare run—so she had to stand her ground. Snowballs rained down all round her. She ignored the twinge in her left wrist, and she packed another weapon. She threw blindly, struck a target, but she was laughing too hard to see who.

The next thing she knew, Earlee was at her side, ignoring the gleeful shouts of "traitor" as she hurriedly packed and threw snow. Ruby laughed, dodging Scarlet's gentle throw and lobbed a return snowball. Joy bubbled through her while she ducked Lila's snowball and returned a volley. Snow walloped against Lila's coat, and laughter rang like bells.

"Truce!" Scarlet called out, waving both hands. "Ruby, you are deadly accurate with a snowball. Who would have guessed it?"

"It's my secret talent." Her left hand smarted, but it was worth it. She joined her friends, swiping the ice and snow residue out of their faces and off their clothes as they tromped toward the basement door. "Rupert taught me. We used to have snowball fights when we were growing up."

"Rupert." Kate said his name with the hint of a sigh. "You have a handsome brother."

"I do?" She sailed through the door Lila held and into the depths of the basement. A single lamp burned on a desk, and heat radiated from the cast-iron stove in the corner. Blessed heat. She headed toward it, realizing she was frozen clear through. "Roop is a good man. He works very hard, and he's incredibly wonderful."

"You aren't sweet on Ruby's brother, are you, Kate?" Earlee asked as she took her place around the stove. The reverend's wife's papers were on a nearby desk. She must have stepped out.

"I'm just saying he's good-looking." Kate shrugged. "A girl has to keep her options open."

"What about Lorenzo?" Scarlet held her hands toward the heat. "I could never give up on Lorenzo."

Lorenzo. Ruby winced. Could she never escape even the mention of the man?

"Let's see if we can find something for Ruby." Lila, the successful manager of the town's finest dress shop, waltzed away from the stove and plucked a very shabby, brown gingham dress from the top of the barrel. "This would be a no."

"Definitely a no." Meredith sidled up to the stove. "Keep going."

"How about this?" Lila plunged her hand inside and withdrew a fine sweater with a hole in the elbow. "It's blue, it's about the right size."

"I could fix that hole," Scarlet spoke up. "I'm a good knitter."

"Then it's a maybe." Lila set it aside and fished inside the barrel. "Ooh, I see something really good."

"I love it!" Scarlet swept up to get a better look at the dress.

A dress? It was practically a gown, in champagne-colored silk. Tiny rows of lace with scalloped edges lined the princess-cut bodice. The ruffled skirt was trimmed in matching velvet. Fine pearls sewn onto the fabric gleamed richly. A careless tear at the collar had been left unattended, so the stitching had come unraveled.

"Who would give that away instead of fixing it?" Kate breathed incredulously.

"I don't know, but it's about your size." Scarlet held up the stunning dress, eyeing Ruby. "It just needs a little taking in."

"And that collar needs to be reset." Lila examined the garment with her expert eye. "I could do it on Monday at the shop. I have the right needles and thread there to do it justice. Ruby, stand up straight."

"Me?" Shock silenced her as Lila held the dress up to her shoulders. The silk rustled luxuriously and was the finest fabric she had ever felt. The gown fell in a flowing, elegant cascade to the floor. Whoever wore this dress would feel like a princess.

"Wow," Kate breathed.

"That color on you—" Scarlet didn't finish her sentence because her jaw had dropped.

"You're beautiful, Ruby," Earlee chimed in.

"Not me." She blushed. Honestly, what was wrong with her friends? Perhaps their normally good judgment was derailed from so much exertion in the bitter cold, which had somehow frozen their brains. She wasn't sure how likely that was, but it was the only explanation she could come up with. She shrugged. "I'm just plain old me."

"You are not plain, Ruby," Meredith argued. "I suspect a certain man doesn't think you are either."

Of course her mind turned straight to Lorenzo. She prayed the soreness in her heart did not show on her face.

"It's settled, then." Lila stepped back to fold up the garment. "The dress is yours."

"But I don't need it. Where would I wear it?" She was a farm girl. It was who she was. Not a young woman who had the need for such finery.

"You never know what God has in store." Kate's words radiated comfort and love and hope. "You have a secret admirer, Ruby. I know you are worried about losing your home, but the Lord's timing is always perfect. Love can happen anytime. Don't give up hope that your life can change for the better. I haven't."

Tears bunched in her throat, making it impossible to speak.

She understood how Kate felt about Lorenzo. She felt the same way.

"Take the dress," Earlee urged. "It will be perfect to wear to the Davis's Christmas ball."

"Yes, there's no telling whose eye you will catch," Scarlet urged. "The new doctor seems taken with you."

It wasn't the doctor she thought of.

"Of course, Lorenzo will be there." Kate sighed.

"Yes, Lorenzo." Scarlet filled up with so much longing, it spilled out, impossible to miss.

You have no right to wish, Ruby Ann Ballard. Seeing the ardent hope in Scarlet's eyes and knowing it was Lorenzo she loved made Ruby bow her head. She was a terrible friend, undeserving of their unconditional love. Miserable, she turned away, pretending to warm her fingers at the stove. Inside, she was ashamed. It felt as if she had betrayed Scarlet.

The memory of her first day at the town school rushed back to her. Of the wobbly feel of her knees when she'd walked through the door, of the echoing sound of conversations and general disarray bouncing off the walls as she peered into the classroom. Her stomach had tied into knots with terror. She had never been around so many people. Where she'd lived before had always been terribly remote, so she hadn't been prepared for such a crowd.

By lunchtime she had friends. Real friends. Scarlet, Lila, Kate, Earlee, Meredith and Fiona had welcomed her with open arms and unconditional kindness, accepting her as she was. She loved them all dearly.

Do the right thing, Ruby. No more wishing for Lorenzo. Not ever again.

"I found them! A pair of good shoes." Lila's triumph echoed in the room. "Ruby, come see."

Chapter Eleven

In three-part harmony, the last note of "O Come All Ye Faithful" ended, and Reverend Hadly congratulated them. "Well done, everyone. Have a safe journey home. We will see you all next time."

Finally. Lorenzo closed his song book, squared his shoulders and searched the crowd. He heard her before he saw her.

"I can't wait to get home." Her dulcet voice somehow lifted quietly to him above all the din in the room. So dear to him, he couldn't think of a more beautiful sound. The tussle of the crowd at the front pew, where the carolers deposited their books, faded into silence as he watched her sweep down the aisle, encircled by her friends.

Did she like the gift he'd left for her? It hadn't been easy to slip it into her coat pocket unnoticed. She had to know that it was from him, but she hadn't glanced at him through the last half of practice. She didn't turn to offer him a smile now.

"I'm worried about Pa," Ruby said. "I hope he

warmed up the supper I left for him. When he's troubled, he tends to forget to eat."

Dazzled, he watched the fall of lamplight as it swept over her, danced in her light hair and worshiped the ivory splendor of her face. He had it bad for her. No use denying it. But at least he knew what stood in his way. Ruby's duty to her family came first. He understood and admired it. His heart tugged him along, taking him forward, toward her. It was as if he had no say.

Not that he minded.

"Lorenzo?" His name came from a far-off distance. He blinked, shook his head, only to see James walking beside him, looking puzzled. "Is everything all right?"

"Sure. Sorry. My mind was somewhere else."

"I can tell."

Ruby might always be at the center of his thoughts, so he would have to learn how to live with it. "What were you saying?"

"Listening to Narcissa talk, you two are going to the ball together. True or not true? I thought you weren't interested in her like that." James grinned, full of trouble. "Hey, don't scowl. I came to warn you."

"Me, too." Luken caught up to them grinning. "I heard it from Narcissa myself."

"I'm not bowing to family pressure this year." It took all his effort to keep from searching for Ruby in the dispersing crowd. Ruby, who'd stolen his heart. "I'm not taking Narcissa. End of story."

"That's what I thought, but it's good to hear." Luken blew out the breath he'd been holding. "I don't want to go after someone you're interested in—"

"I've never been interested in Narcissa."

"Well, I am." Luken grinned again.

"Who are you kidding? You're never going to beau her." James shook his head. "She is out of your reach."

"Still, it wouldn't hurt to try to win her. You never know." Luken squared his shoulders, maybe hiding the pain of unrequited love.

Lorenzo knew exactly how that felt. Needing to see her, he snatched his coat off the wall peg and shrugged into it, heading toward the door. Exceptionally icy air met him as he shouldered outside, buttoning as he went. The instant his gaze found her at one of the hitching posts, the tension coiling within him calmed. Contentment wrapped around his soul like grace.

Love was too weak of a word. He was no longer simply in love with Ruby. He was committed to her. Devoted. Captured one hundred percent.

Departing carolers plowed through the snow on the streets while others untied their horses at the hitching posts. Lanterns flared to life, swinging alongside the dashes of sleighs. But above it all, the music of her presence sang to him. As he trudged along, he noticed every dear thing she did. The brush of her mittened fingertips along her horse's nose, the knot she made worse when she tried to untie the reins with one hand and the crinkle of frustration that furrowed into her forehead.

Cute. He intended to march right over there and help her out, but someone cut in front of him. Another man appeared out of the shadows.

"Here, Miss Ruby, let me." Walt Hathaway took the knotted reins before the young lady could accept or protest. She gazed up at him in shy surprise while her

friends, busy boarding sleighs and untying horses, exchanged knowing looks.

The new doc was interested in Ruby? Lorenzo's feet
froze to the ground. He stared in shock as Walt untan-
gled the knot and presented Ruby with the reins, talking with her warmly.

Unbearable pain hammered into him, radiating
heartbreak through his rib cage like a mortal blow. His
knees buckled, and he blindly reached out. His fingers wrapped around something solid and icy, a hitching post, fighting just to breathe. He watched as Ruby
smiled up at Hathaway, her sweetness beaming.

Something tugged at his hat brim. Poncho nibbled
with his whiskery lips and gave a nicker of comfort.
Chocolate-brown eyes met his, and the horse's caring
was unmistakable. He rubbed the gelding's cheek,
thankful for the friendliness.

"See you later," Luken called out as he headed off
down the street.

"Bye." He waved to James, too, who had mounted up
on his fine buckskin. The wind gusted hard, driving an
arctic chill straight into his bones. It was a brutal night.
Although the snow had stopped, dark clouds blanketed
the sky blotting out all sign of heavenly light. He forced
his attention on loosening the knot that held Poncho to
the post, hands shaking. Out of the corner of his eye, he
watched as Hathaway chuckled, and Ruby's soft laughter joined his.

What if she left with Walt? He swallowed hard, trying
to tamp down the pain that rose in his throat. He stumbled into his sleigh, plopping on the seat. What if Ruby
let the doctor see her home?

I could lose her. He shook out the driving robes, but they were as frigid as the night and offered no relief. His soul felt cold, and he glanced over his shoulder, dreading what he would see. Not that he'd ever really had Ruby. He held no claim on her heart.

It was Ruby's choice, after all, whom she would love. *If* she would love at all. The thought of losing her, of not having the hope of her in his future, crushed him.

"Good night." Ruby's soft farewell drew his attention. As she fit her shoe into Solomon's stirrup, he wanted to be the one who held her elbow to support her into the saddle. He wished to be the one who handed her the reins, to be the recipient of her bashful smile. "I will take better care of my splint. No more snowball fights."

"Not until your wrist is healed." Walt was the fortunate man who waved her off, watching as the horse plodded down the icy street with the *clink, chink* of steel shoes.

Loving Ruby was a perilous thing. He didn't know what dangers lay ahead for his heart. She rode away, a willowy slip of a thing huddled in the saddle. He wasn't the only man who didn't notice the cold, who could not tear his gaze from the woman on her horse. The fringe of her scarf caught on the rising wind, flickering behind her.

Whether or not he eventually won her hand or Walt did, or she decided she wouldn't part from her family, one thing was sure. He would always want her happiness, always fight for it, always pray for it. He would do anything he could to improve her life.

Take what You will from me, Lord, if You can give it to her. His prayer came from the most honest of places in his soul. He thought he felt heaven's hand on his shoulder as he snapped the reins. As Poncho leaped into action, he knew what he had to do.

The night prairie gleamed darkly, as luminous as a black pearl. Rich tones of ebony, onyx and charcoal glossed the miles of snow all around her. Ruby clenched her jaw tight to keep her teeth from chattering. She tipped her head to peer up at the purple-black shadows of the Rocky Mountains standing guard at the edge of the high Montana plains. Darkly velvet clouds tumbled across the sky like unrolled bolts of quilt batting.

So beautiful. She savored the wonder, cherishing the hush of the sleeping landscape, the lonely rush of the wind and the faint scent of wood smoke from some distant chimney. Concentrating on God's handiwork kept her mind off the fact that she was practically frozen solid as Solomon plodded along. The shivery ride home was worth the fun evening. The joy from being with her friends sustained her like a fire on a hearth and she didn't feel the cruel winds overly much as her mind went back over the treasured evening.

Singing alongside Kate and Scarlet, the snowball battle, her friend's cheerful help sorting through the donation barrel. Something that had always hurt her sensibilities had become bearable because of her friends. She was grateful for the nearly new shoes tucked into Solomon's saddlebags along with the winter coat she'd found for Pa—a perfect Christmas gift. Love for her friends burned like a candle in the dark, chasing away all her sorrows.

Thank You, Father, for this time with them. It would

not last much longer, she feared. She fought the rending in her heart at the thought of being separated from her dear friends. And from Lorenzo, she realized, gasping at the anguish slicing through her like the frigid wind.

Even if she could no longer wish for him, her heart still wanted him.

Solomon stumbled in the thick snow, jerking her out of her thoughts. She gasped, fearful for him, but he kept going, laboring along like a trouper. What a good horse.

"I'm sorry, my friend. I hadn't thought how hard this late evening trip would be on you." She leaned forward in the saddle and wrapped her arms as far around his neck as she could. He was breathing so hard. He managed a small whicker of reassurance, as if to say he didn't mind. She did. What a good old friend he was.

Somewhere behind her, a soft chime rose above the prairie's quiet and became the ring of steeled horse hooves. Alone and in the dark, she twisted in the saddle to glance along the long, lonely stretch of road. There was nothing but a faint blur of movement, as shadowed as the landscape, nothing more substantial than a dream. Slowly the dream took on shape and substance as it loomed closer.

A big, dark horse broke out of the night. Poncho neighed a cheerful greeting as he picked up his pace. *Chink, chink!* went his hooves as he pranced closer. Nervousness kicked through her veins. Where Poncho went, his master followed.

"Hey, Ruby." Lorenzo pulled up alongside Solomon, his words rising in great clouds of fog in the frigid air. Tucked in the vehicle behind several layers of warm robes, he was nearly lost in the darkness.

"What are you doing here?" She stared at him, not quite believing. "You live in the opposite direction."

"Yes, I reined Poncho toward home, but he ignored me completely, took charge of the bit and brought me here. He tends to have a mind of his own."

"He ran away with you?" As if she believed that. "If he was a runaway, he is going awfully slow. I would expect a madcap dash at the very least."

"It's the weather. The ice slows him down." He shifted on the seat so she could see the hook of a grin at the corners of his mouth.

"Yes, I can see the danger you've been in." She eyed the gelding plodding along, a few paces ahead of Solomon, ears swiveling as if to take in every word being said. "I'm relieved you've been able to seize control again."

"Me, too. It was a near thing. I may have to punish him. Maybe a whipping."

Poncho blew out his breath, rattling his lips scornfully.

"Yes, I'm sure that will happen." She suspected there wasn't a more pampered horse in the entire territory.

"It's pretty cold to be on the back of a saddle, isn't it?"

"It *is* a bit chilly. I don't mind."

"Your teeth are chattering."

"Only because I have to unclench them to talk with you." She drew Solomon to a stop. "What are you doing here?"

"I told you. It was Poncho's idea. He must be concerned about you and Solomon and wants to offer you a ride."

"*Poncho* does?" She knew the truth, thinking of the gift she'd also tucked in a saddlebag. She couldn't help the sweet longing lifting through her. Lorenzo had come to see her safely home. She knew what it was like to sit on that cushioned seat snug beneath those warm blankets with the steel of Lorenzo's arm pressed to hers. Scarlet's face flashed before her eyes, she imagined her father alone and homeless, and those images stopped her.

She'd given up on those dreams. She straightened her spine, determined to keep things light. It would be easier to send him on his way, easier on her heart. "So, Poncho came all this way in the harsh weather simply because of concern for me?"

"He's stubborn like that. Once you are Poncho's friend, you're a friend for life. He watches out for you."

"I suppose he doesn't like taking no for an answer."

"This terror? I try never to say no to him. There's no telling what he would do."

"Yes, I would live in fear." She laughed; she couldn't help it. Poncho arched his neck proudly, as if enjoying his reputation.

"It must be hard for Solomon to break a path through this new accumulation. Or maybe it's the cold." Lorenzo climbed out and tucked the robes back into place to hold in the heat. "He looks pretty winded."

"I know. I'm worried about him. He's not as young as he used to be." Solomon quivered in the bitter wind. Poor fella. She patted his neck, wishing she could do more. "I didn't realize it would get so cold tonight. I better keep moving. I don't want him to get chilled."

"He's shaking harder." He placed his hand on the

gelding's flank. "Easy, fella. Hop down, Ruby, and let me take a look at him."

Her hand caught his and peace descended on him like grace. He helped her from the saddle, her weight light and sweet in his arms for one too-brief moment before gravity intervened. Her shoes sank in the deep snow, and he had to let her go.

Did he see a plea in her eyes? It was hard to read her in the inky darkness where secrets were easy to keep. The wind gusted meanly, growing colder by the second. Ruby's teeth chattered, and she spun out of his hold to rub Solomon's graying face.

"My sweet boy." Her expression crinkled with concern. "I should have gone straight home tonight instead of heading to town."

"No one expected the temperature to fall like this. You couldn't know." He worked fast, untying Solomon's heavy winter blanket rolled behind the saddle, removed the saddle before covering the gelding snugly. Solomon shivered harder. Not a good sign.

"We'd best keep him moving." He stowed the saddle in back of the sleigh. "It will be easier going for him in the broken trail behind us."

Ruby nodded anxiously, taking her horse by the bits and gently turning him around. Solomon nibbled her hat with affection, his sweet gaze full of trust. That raspy breathing troubled him as he tethered the gelding to the tailgate.

"You're a good boy, Solomon." As much as he worried about the gelding, he was concerned about the woman more. "Let's get you in the sleigh, Ruby. You're shivering, too."

"Not too much."

"I call it too much."

"You're cold, too." She shook so hard, she had trouble walking the length of the sleigh. He held the robes back and handed her in.

"I'm used to the cold." He tucked the robes around her. "I'm a rancher. I burn in the summer and freeze in the winter."

"So, that's why you are here tonight. Because you don't mind the weather?"

"I told you. Poncho was worried, and so was I." He held the reins one-handed and settled in beside her. "Friends help each other, don't they?"

"Yes, but this is a lot for you to do."

"Depends on your perspective, I guess." The soft presence of her shoulder against his arm was sweet. It was all he could do not to slip his arm around her shoulder. "Think of it this way. What if you catch cold tonight? You would miss work. I've heard you are already indispensable to Cook. We never want Cook upset, as she's responsible for the quality of our meals."

"You're not fooling me any, Lorenzo Davis."

"It was worth a try."

She said nothing more for a moment, and silence stretched between them.

He felt her gaze on his face and sensed her scrutiny. "Something troubling you?"

"I'm sure you've heard enough of my troubles."

"We're friends, remember?" And he wanted to be a good deal more. "Tell me."

"My father hasn't said for sure, but I have calculated what little we must have in savings. Even with my job, we probably won't be able to make the mortgage." She swallowed hard.

"I'm sorry to hear that, Ruby. I had hoped you would be able to keep your home."

"Me, too. When that happens, we will have to move in with relatives." She breathed in a little squeak of air. "How do I tell your mother? After I promised not to let her down?"

"Giving notice wouldn't be letting her down, Ruby."

"Yes, but she paid for the doctor for me. And now she will have to turn around and train someone in my place. It would feel as if I was breaking my promise to her."

"Maybe your brother will find another job in time." He did not want to give up hope.

"That seems like an unlikely miracle at this point." The darkness hid the sadness in her eyes, but he knew it was there, for he could read it in her heart. Against his arm, her shoulder firmed. "I have to be strong for my pa. I have to trust that God is leading us to a good place, however difficult the road may be."

"I wish your road was easier." Overhead, the thick mantle of clouds began to thin, lessening the cloying dark gripping the prairie. "Is there any chance you might stay and keep your job, even if your family loses your land? You have good friends here. And Poncho."

"Yes, however will I bear to leave Poncho? It will be a great loss, but distance cannot harm true friendship. I can write letters. Well, not necessarily to Poncho, but to my other friends with opposable thumbs so they can open the envelope."

"I have opposable thumbs." He held up his gloved hands, still maintaining command of the reins. "See?"

"Well, I wasn't planning on writing to you, but I guess I could manage a letter or two now and then." She shook her head. The man dazzled her, but at least the darkness hid some of the effect and made it easier to ignore. She couldn't let it affect her. She'd made up her mind. No more wishing. "I was talking about my good friends."

"I am, what, just a fair-weather friend?"

"What you are is yet to be determined. We will see how good of a letter writer you turn out to be."

"A faithful one." Richly spoken, the sincerity of his vow rang in meaningful, steadfast notes. "It would be a shame if you had to go. Is there any possible way your father might accept help with the mortgage?"

"Oh, Lorenzo." She turned toward him, touched by his offer. She saw the man—all he was, who he was— in that one silent moment. Could he truly care so much about her? "Pa is an independent and proud man. I don't think he would."

"I respect him for it." He turned his attention to the road, making it impossible to guess what was on his face.

She thought of the gift he'd put in her coat pocket, the one she couldn't bring herself to speak of. "I wish I could stay. Your mother is so wonderful to me, and I would love to keep working for her."

For one small instant, she let herself imagine what it would be like. She could rent a cozy room at the boarding house. Living in town, she could see her friends often. It would be a brief walk to the dress shop or to Lila's apartment. Scarlet lived on Third Street. Earlee taught at the town school. Fiona lived a short ways north of town, and soon Meredith would be married and moving into her home nearby. What fun they could all have together. Sewing circles, caroling groups and countless, happy hours of talking and shopping. It could be one, long, wonderful eternity.

But that couldn't be her future. She thought of her father, of his worries and his burdens. Of how the failure to keep his farm would affect him. She thought of her uncle's ranch so far away and the tiny shanty, originally a shed, he and Roop had fixed up after Pa's accident. Living so far to the north, with no one to visit, no church nearby, only a general store miles away—that would be her life. "I cannot leave Pa when he needs me. He has struggled so hard all these years to provide for me. He has endured an unfair amount of hardship. I do not know how much more he can take."

"I understand." Empathetic, Lorenzo reined Poncho to a stop. "What about your brother?"

"If Roop needs to move away to find work, then Pa would be alone. I cannot do that to him." She looked up, surprised to see the faint, flickering glow behind the shanty's curtained windows. She was home already? She climbed from the sleigh before Lorenzo could circle around to help her. She could not get used to relying on him. "This place was Pa's dream, which kept him going through all those painfully hard times. It will break his heart to lose it. Honestly, I fear it will break him."

"I understand. Staying with him is the right choice." He untied Solomon. "What about you? What will it do to you?"

"Me?" She plunged through the deep snow, nearly

tripping on her skirts. "This is the only real home I've had since I was five."

"It will crush you, too."

"I will recover." She reached to take the reins, but he did not let go of them, grateful for the brush of her fingertips to his. A connection roared to life within his soul, deeper than before. She jerked her hand away.

The shanty's front door blew open, and two men burst out, dressed for barn work. Jon Ballard closed the door behind him as Ruby's brother bounded into the snow.

"Roop! You made it home." Ruby beamed at her older sibling, lighting up the night.

"Good to see you, little sister. Don't even think about it. I'll get Solomon's saddle, the poor guy. Looks like he's having a hard time." Rupert ambled up, friendly and eager to help. "Lorenzo. It is mighty good of you to see Ruby home in this weather."

"She is my mother's favorite maid," he answered, making everyone laugh, easily hiding the truth. The truth behind the gift he'd left her and his offer to help her father. "Rupert, I'd like to see to Solomon."

"I'd appreciate any help." Rupert led the way, walking slow to accommodate Solomon's gait.

"Good. C'mon, Poncho." Lorenzo chirruped, taking his gelding by the bit. How perfect he seemed, glossed by the faint emerging starlight breaking through the clouds.

He was everything she ever dreamed of and everything she could never have. Nothing on earth could change it.

Chapter Twelve

Ruby dropped another log on the fire, careful of the whoosh of red ashes, which rose from the hearth like fiery bits of torn paper. They flashed and snapped as they drifted upward, fire-hot, before sailing down. One landed on her cardigan, and she brushed it off absently. The shanty echoed around her. Nearly an hour had passed since Lorenzo had disappeared into the barn with Pa and Roop. They were still there. That couldn't bode well for Solomon.

Worry gnawed at her with big, sharp teeth as she rose to rescue the tea kettle from the stove. She had no idea how long it had been whistling. She measured out fragrant tea leaves and left a pot steeping while she shivered into her coat. She grabbed the full tea kettle handle with a hot pad and slipped out the kitchen door. If the men weren't coming in, then she was going to them.

Star shine glowed along the narrow path as she pushed out the kitchen door.

"Ruby." Lorenzo's voice broke out of the dark, nearly scaring her to death. Her grip slipped, but his gloved hands caught the steaming tea kettle by the handle,

YOUR PARTICIPATION IS REQUESTED!

Dear Reader,

Since you are a lover of historical romance fiction – we would like to get to know you!

Inside you will find a short Reader's Survey. Sharing your answers with us will help our editorial staff understand who you are and what activities you enjoy.

To thank you for your participation, we would like to send you 2 books and 2 gifts – **ABSOLUTELY FREE!**

Enjoy your gifts with our appreciation,

Pam Powers

SEE INSIDE FOR READER'S SURVEY

For Your Inspirational Historical Reading Pleasure...

Get 2 FREE BOOKS from the series of historical love stories that promises romance, adventure and faith.

FREE!

We'll send you 2 books and 2 gifts
ABSOLUTELY FREE
just for completing our Reader's Survey!

YOUR READER'S SURVEY
"THANK YOU" FREE GIFTS INCLUDE:
▶ 2 Love Inspired® Historical books
▶ 2 surprise gifts

▶ **DETACH AND MAIL CARD TODAY!** ▶

PLEASE FILL IN THE CIRCLES COMPLETELY TO RESPOND

1) What type of fiction books do you enjoy reading? (Check all that apply)
- ○ Suspense   ○ Inspirational Fiction ○ Modern-day Romances
- ○ Historical Romance ○ Humour   ○ Mysteries

2) What attracted you most to the last fiction book you purchased on impulse?
- ○ The Title   ○ The Cover   ○ The Author   ○ The Story

3) What is usually the greatest influencer when you <u>plan</u> to buy a book?
- ○ Advertising   ○ Referral   ○ Book Review

4) How often do you access the internet?
- ○ Daily ○ Weekly ○ Monthly ○ Rarely or never.

5) How many NEW paperback fiction novels have you purchased in the past 3 months?
- ○ 0 - 2   ○ 3 - 6   ○ 7 or more

YES! I have completed the Reader's Survey. Please send me the 2 FREE books and 2 FREE gifts (gifts are worth about $10) for which I qualify. I understand that I am under no obligation to purchase any books, as explained on the back of this card.

102/302 IDL FH62

FIRST NAME	LAST NAME

ADDRESS

APT.#	CITY

STATE/PROV.   ZIP/POSTAL CODE

Offer limited to one per household and not applicable to series that subscriber is currently receiving.
Your Privacy – The Reader Service is committed to protecting your privacy. Our Privacy Policy is available online at www.ReaderService.com or upon request from the Reader Service. We make a portion of our mailing list available to reputable third parties that offer products we believe may interest you. If you prefer that we not exchange your name with third parties, or if you wish to clarify or modify your communication preferences, please visit us at www.ReaderService.com/consumerschoice or write to us at Reader Service Preference Service, P.O. Box 9062, Buffalo, NY 14269. Include your complete name and address.

© 2011 HARLEQUIN ENTERPRISES LIMITED
® and ™ are trademarks owned and used by the trademark owner and/or its licensee. Printed in the U.S.A.

The Reader Service — Here's How It Works:

If offer card is missing write to: The Reader Service, P.O. Box 1867, Buffalo, NY 14240-1867 or visit: www.ReaderService.com

BUSINESS REPLY MAIL
FIRST-CLASS MAIL   PERMIT NO. 717   BUFFALO, NY

POSTAGE WILL BE PAID BY ADDRESSEE

THE READER SERVICE
PO BOX 1341
BUFFALO NY 14240-8571

NO POSTAGE
NECESSARY
IF MAILED
IN THE
UNITED STATES

covering hers. "Could you fetch some old blankets or quilts?"

For Solomon? That definitely sounded serious. "How is he?"

"We're taking precautions is all." His baritone grew tender. "He has caught a serious chill in town."

"He's never been this frail before." Her poor Solomon. "What else can I do?"

"I'll take the tea kettle and fix up a mash for him. Get something warm in his stomach."

Somehow her fingers let go. It felt awkward standing like this, alone together beneath a starry sky, when she knew how he felt for her. When he'd done so much for her already. Now this.

She could feel his caring like the silver glow on the snow, chasing the dark away. A girl dreamed of having a man like Lorenzo care for her and treat her like this. She forced her feet to carry her backward step by step. "I was going to bring tea to help warm the three of you, but I thought hot water for Solomon might be more important."

"You're right. If you want to stack the blankets on the step, I'll come back for them."

"No, I can bring them. I'll hurry." It gave her something to do, something to focus on. So she wouldn't start wanting to wish or dream. She turned the knob and stumbled into the kitchen. Her teeth chattered as she hurried through the shanty, flung open the cabinet and hauled out blankets.

You have to be practical, Ruby Ann Ballard. Keep your expectations reasonable. Even under the best circumstances—if her family wasn't facing homelessness, if her friends didn't deserve him more—wealthy Lorenzo Davis was never going to marry a kitchen maid.

He was never going to marry her.

A north wind had kicked up by the time she scurried down the steps. When she breathed in, the bitter air burned her nose and scorched her lungs. Overhead, the clouds had vanished leaving the velvety sky, which shone so darkly, she could almost see heaven. The stars glittered like millions of diamonds scattered carelessly across the sky, diamonds rich with faint lustrous colors—red, blue, yellow, white. God's great handiwork. Surely He was watching over all of them tonight.

"Ruby." Roop this time, not Lorenzo, rising out of the dark. He opened the barn door for her. "Those blankets are a welcome sight."

"I came as fast as I could." She hurried toward him, careful of her shoes on the ice. She didn't need to fall again. As if Roop was thinking the same, he caught her arm and hauled her through the door.

Lantern light chased away the dark. Clover, the milk cow, poked her nose over her stall gate, her big, bovine eyes worried. The atmosphere in the barn seemed grim as she stumbled forward. She couldn't see anything over the divider between the stalls. Only Solomon, head hung low, sides heaving.

"That's it, big boy. Lie down for me." Lorenzo circled into sight from behind Solomon. With a labored groan, the gelding's front knees sank into the extra-soft bedding, and then his rear went down, as weary as if he'd run twenty miles. Pa rose up to peer over the boards at her. Strain lined his face.

Roop took the blankets from her, but it was Lorenzo who held her attention, Lorenzo who knelt at the horse's side to straighten the blanket Rupert had given him, smoothing out the folds with soothing hands. Solomon closed his eyes, understanding they were all there to help him.

Please, Father, watch over our horse, my friend, she added. She believed God cared about His animals, too. She felt something tug on her scarf. Clover had reached over her gate to nibble on the fringe. Ruby rubbed the cow's poll, watching as Pa and Lorenzo covered the gelding with the bedding. Snug, Solomon stretched his neck out, laid his head on the downy hay and closed his eyes.

"I'll stay the night with him." Roop knelt to stroke the horse's neck. "Make sure he doesn't have any problems."

"We'll know more after he gets some rest. Maybe he'll pull out of this." Lorenzo rose, pulling on his gloves, his movements sure and strong. The lamplight found him and worshiped him, delighting in the manly angles of his face and glinting bronze in his hair.

"That's what I hope, too." Roop settled on the hay next to Solomon. "What about your horse? You don't want him getting too cold."

"I'd better head out, but I'll be back come morning."

"That would be mighty good of you." Pa laid one hand on the stall rail, shoulders up, a proud man. "Ruby is awfully in love with that horse."

"I noticed."

What was her father up to? He didn't accept help from others, but he had welcomed Lorenzo and his blacksmithing tools right from the start. Which could only mean one thing. How did she tell her hopeful father that the young Mr. Davis would never be her beau? Her pa must be hoping for a match.

"Ruby, why don't you see Lorenzo out?" Pa tried to sound nonchalant. It didn't work.

"Allkay." The nonsense word garbled out of her throat when she'd meant to say all right or okay, but neither had come out right. Tongue-tied, heat scorched across her face as she took a hurried step. Lorenzo's hand settled against the small of her back, guiding her lightly. No doubt Pa saw that.

The stars glittered, polishing the night. Worried over Solomon, tangled up inside by the hope on Pa's face, she couldn't notice the beauty surrounding her. Worse, she couldn't think of a thing to say. Maybe Lorenzo hadn't noticed how eager her father was to pair them up.

At their approach, Poncho snorted, shifting in his traces. The harness jangled softly as he blew out a breath and made a great, white cloud.

"I'll come fetch you all for church in the morning." Lorenzo folded back the robes and knocked the snow from his boots. "Even if Solomon recovers, he should rest tomorrow."

"Don't you dare come fetch me." She hiked up her chin. "I am perfectly happy to walk."

"Not in this cold. There will be no argument."

"There has to be. Lorenzo, my family is not your responsibility. We can get to the service on our own."

"I'm just being neighborly."

"You are not our neighbor."

"Not strictly speaking, but we *are* friends. I thought we established that."

"You did. I'm still deliberating."

When his gaze found hers, her pulse leaped at his veiled affection, shining like midnight blue dreams. *Friends,* he said, but she knew he wanted more.

So did her heart.

As if he knew, his fingertips brushed her face. He stroked a few wayward tendrils scattered by the wind from her eyes, but his touch remained on her cheek, the most tender touch she had ever known.

Move, feet, she commanded. But not as much as a toe wiggled. She remained rooted to the ground, unable to escape as Lorenzo smiled into her eyes, chasing all the chill from the night. It was as if she could see into his soul. As if he could see into hers.

"Thank you for helping Solomon. For everything." Surely he could see how grateful she was.

Gratitude was all she could let herself feel.

"I'm always here for you." His gaze slid downward to land on her lips. The wish shone in his eyes, but he didn't move forward. He didn't bend closer. He didn't lean in. "Never forget that. Ever."

"As much as I would want to, that's an offer I can't accept." Think of Scarlet and Kate, she thought. Think of Pa alone in the shed on Uncle's land. Think of the Davis's manor house and the elegant daughter-in-law they would have one day. "I'm just being realistic."

"I see." Hurt crinkled in the corners of his eyes, but his understanding did not dim. Surely he could see all that divided them. "Until tomorrow." He tipped his hat, making her heart twist as he climbed into his sleigh.

Do not wish, Ruby. Not even once. She fisted her hands, trembling with the strain as he snapped Poncho's reins and the horse took off at a fast clip. The sleigh bobbed away, taking Lorenzo with it, growing distant on the beautiful prairie. The stars illuminated the entire landscape, tossing glowing lavender across the miles of radiant snow, across him.

She stood in the dark.

I'm just being realistic. Ruby's confession whispered to him over and over, all the way across the glacial prairie. He stared at the reins in his hands, not that he was really driving. Poncho had taken charge and was heading for home lickety-split. He wasted no time turning up the driveway and trotting up the lane where he'd first spotted Ruby looking for her shoe button. Soft emotions melted in his chest, warming him.

How nervous he'd been that day, and he shook his head, remembering. Wanting to badly to have a chance with her. Just one chance. The wish on her face tonight and the sweet longing for something more had been unmistakable. He'd felt the punch of hope with all the breadth of his spirit before she'd gently, sadly turned him down. That told him something. That she cared about him, but not enough. And he understood why. She couldn't let herself.

Poncho nickered, glad when the lights from the house came into sight. The sprawling, two-story home he'd been born in seemed ostentatious after seeing Ruby's humble shanty. The well-built barns and stables housing a herd of fine horses seemed far too lavish after being inside the Ballard's two-stall, sod barn. He didn't know why his family had been so materially blessed, but he did know that those blessings weren't ones he had earned, only stood to inherit. And that Ruby's circumstances were about as bad as they could get.

Solomon's symptoms troubled him as he climbed out of the sleigh, stiff from the cold. Poncho had stopped all on his own, just inside the main barn, apparently grateful for the shelter from the cold.

"You did good tonight, boy." He rubbed the gelding's nose. "Practically a hero."

Poncho nickered low, content, arching his neck with pride. He nibbled the brim of Lorenzo's hat playfully, as if to say he hadn't minded the cold. Not for Ruby.

Yes, he knew how that was. A great love shimmered within him, as pure as the starlight splashing silver across the land. He gave the reins to Thacker, glad for the boy's help, patted Poncho's neck one last time and headed for the house.

He stomped snow from his boots on the back doorstep, the great void of the night echoing around him. He couldn't feel the doorknob, his hands were so numb. He stumbled into the warmth, leaned against the door to close it. His parents and sister would still be up. He fumbled with his gloves, hat and finally got the buttons undone on his coat. He knew his mother would bring up the ball again. Best to face her and get this over with.

"There you are." Pa turned his newspaper page with a rustle, tucked in his chair near the parlor's hearth. "Your mother was starting to worry, but I told her you're a grown man. You can take care of yourself."

"I've been doing it for a long time." He resisted the urge to roll his eyes, crossing straight to the blazing fire roaring in the grate. Since his feet were a tad numb, he stumbled over the edge of the rug.

"Renzo, look at you. You're half frozen." His mother looked up from her embroidery hoop. Beside her, his sister rolled her eyes and went back to her needlework. "Jerry, what are you going to do about that boy?"

"He's a grown man. Not much I can do at this late date," Gerard joked, eyes sparkling. No doubt his father had a good guess as to what his son had been up to. "They say you reap what you sow. If you wanted him to turn out differently, you should have done something about it long before now, Selma."

"Yes, it's all my fault how he turned out. It's a shame."

His parents' jovial laughter warmed the parlor more mightily than any hearth's flame. Bella pulled her needle through the fabric, fussing with it. He turned around to warm up his backside. If he kept rotating like a cooking spit, he might thaw completely before bedtime.

"You were gone a mighty long time. Was there another problem with the cattle?" Pa's amusement knew no end as he lowered his paper. "Is the cougar back? Or rustlers this time, maybe?"

"You know Poncho and I headed to town." He rotated again to face the fire. No sense giving his folks free reign to read his expression. What he felt for Ruby was private. Sacred.

"That's right." His father nodded. "Didn't you have a church thing?"

"The caroling group." Ma was quick to answer. Hard to mistake the happiness in her voice. "So many nice, quality young women there. It's good for you to get out and socialize, Renzo. Maybe make up your mind about who you are inviting to the ball?"

Yep, he knew that was coming. He shifted his weight from foot to foot, holding his frostbitten hands up to the fire. "I've made up my mind, but I'm not in the mood to tell you."

"Gerard, your son is torturing me." Ma's laughter rang like merry bells.

"My son? Why is he only *my* son when you're displeased with him?"

"It just seems fitting."

"Then take comfort, my dear, in the fact that he was gone long enough to escort a lady home from church and spend time talking with her and her family in their parlor."

"Which lady?" Bella's head popped up. "Is Renzo beauing someone?"

He spun around. His younger sister giggled to herself.

"I'm so pleased." His mother beamed, near to bursting with hope as she carefully threaded her needle. "Do we know this young lady?"

"I'm not inviting her to the dance." Mostly because she would be working as a maid that night. His fingertips tingled, beginning to unthaw. He stood tall, seeing his future begin to unroll before him. Somehow, he would have to convince Ruby that she wasn't alone in wanting to help her family. That she didn't need to choose between her duty and her heart.

"But, why not?" Ma's face crinkled up in dismay. "I simply don't understand this."

"I do. Think about it, my dear. There is one young

lady he's been spending time with." Pa chuckled, turning his newspaper page with a rustle. "I hope you know what you're doing, Renzo."

"It really wasn't my decision, Pa." His heart had done that for him. Affection filled him, steadfast and true. He couldn't wait until morning to see her.

"You and young Mr. Davis have been spending a lot of time together." Seated in his chair near the hearth, Pa's whittling knife flashed in the firelight. "Is there anything you want to tell your old man?"

What was she going to do about her misguided father?

"There is nothing to tell." Honestly. Ruby pulled the flatiron out of the flames with the tongs. "Young Mr. Davis, as you call him, is my employer's son. I'm bound to see him, since I work in his home."

"What about tonight?" Pa turned the slim piece of wood and set his knife's blade to carving. "That man went six miles round trip, out of his way to bring you home in his sleigh. It's freezing out there."

"I hope he's home and warm by now." She wrapped the bed iron carefully in a towel and stacked it on top of the other. Poor Pa. He had such high hopes. "Lorenzo was only being kind. Don't read too much into it."

"Kind? That's true, but he didn't have to stay and help tend Solomon. He's acting like a courting man. At least, that's my opinion." Pa's whittling knife stilled as he shifted in his chair. His hip and leg bothered him especially in cold weather. "He's sweet on you, Ruby Ann."

"He can't be anything more than a friend, and you know it."

"I know no such thing."

"You are stubborn. At least, I know where I get it." She hung the tongs on the hook on the wall. "Mrs. Davis paid me at the end of my shift today."

"What do you plan to do with your earnings?" Pa set down his knife.

"I want it to go in your savings account, for the mortgage payment." She fisted her hands, determined to ask the question she already knew the answer to. "Will it be enough of a difference?"

"No, not without Rupert's job." He hung his head, hiding his expression from her. His sadness hung in the air.

And his failure.

To hear it spoken aloud and to listen to the finality of it hit like a punch. She grasped the edge of the hearth, unsteady, the stones hot against her fingertips. How she wished there could be a different answer. Not for herself, but for Pa.

"Is there anything else I can do?" She wasn't skilled enough with a needle to take in sewing, but maybe she could find a cleaning job on Sundays—

"No, sweetheart. I know you've been hoping to keep this home, and I know this hurts you."

"Don't worry about me, Pa." She gathered the bed irons into her arms, determined to keep her chin up. "Whatever happens, we have each other. The good Lord is watching over us."

"Exactly." Pa's attempt to smile fell short. For a brief moment, devastation flashed in his dark eyes, but just for a moment. His strong jaw firmed. "You are all grown up, Ruby Ann. Your mother, God rest her, would be incredibly proud of you."

"Oh, Pa." Tears burned in her throat at his loving words and at the mention of the mother after whom she'd been named. Life was not fair, and there were so many trials, but love was the purpose. In that way she was vastly rich. "She would be proud of you, too."

"Oh, *pshaw!*" He waved her compliment off bashfully. "I'm done with this clothespin. Is that the last you need, or should I make more?"

"It's enough. Thanks." She hugged her heavy load, grateful for the steady heat seeping through the blankets when she stumbled into the night. The tears in her eyes froze on her lashes as she battled the winds to the barn.

The night came alive beneath the brilliance of the stars, casting a storybook glow across the mantled snow. The familiar land stretched out in gentle rises and falls, full of secrets waiting to be told. The wooden fence line marching along the road wore top hats of snow, slanting haphazardly. More snow flocked the bare arms of the cottonwoods, making them seem lifelike as their limbs rose and fell.

She loved this place. It held some of the best memories of her life. Walking down that road to school every morning, knowing her friends would be there to welcome her, riding up the driveway for the very first time full of hope and joy, unable to fully believe this was their own home, the laughter as she gave Solomon a bath, the fun of planting the garden and the hours she'd spent in the deliciously hot summer sun, coaxing wild jackrabbits and deer away from her growing vegetables. How happy she had been.

This home would be a lot to lose.

She shouldered into the barn where a single lantern gleamed from a support post in the aisle. Rupert crossed through the light to take the heated irons from her.

"Thanks, these will help." They clanked, muffled by the towels, as he shifted them in his arms. The night's chill tried to creep into the unheated dwelling, but the animals' heat and the insulated walls mostly kept it out. "Solomon's sleeping. He's warm and snug. I'm praying he'll be fine."

"I hope so." She followed her brother down the aisle, where Clover drowsed and her beloved Solomon didn't stir in his slumber. Beneath the blankets, his sides heaved with each breath. "I'm to blame. I should have come straight home from work."

"No, you deserve to have a little fun with your friends. I would have done the same." He knelt to tuck both irons into the hay, one beneath Solomon's blanket and another in the bedroll he'd made next to him. "Solomon is nearing the end of his life. God is in charge of that, so don't worry. It wasn't your fault."

It was little comfort. "Do you know about the mortgage payment?"

"We've scraped and saved all we could, but it just isn't meant to be."

She bit her bottom lip to hide her grief. Leaving became real. Not some imagined fear she was desperate to stave off, but an inevitable situation. She fisted her hands, resolved to handle this sensibly, for her father's sake.

"Solomon will get better." Maybe she could will it so. She peered over the rail. All four of his hooves moved slightly beneath the blankets, lost in horsy dreams. Love for her old friend filled her. "I could take shifts with you tonight."

"Forget it. I am not letting you do that in this cold. I'm used to it." He shrugged his brawny shoulders, her big brother, able to do anything. "Now go in the house before you turn into an icicle. Or, in your case, a ruby-cicle."

"Funny." She rolled her eyes. She'd missed Rupert's humor, but she wasn't about to tell him that or the jokes would never stop coming. "I suppose we are stuck with you for a while, so I had better get used to having you back."

"Not for long." Roop leaned against the wall, arms folded across his chest, enveloped by shadow. "I've got a few possibilities. If it's God's will, I may be gone on the next train."

"Another job?" Joy leaped within her. "Oh, that would be good news indeed."

"Yes." He didn't seem happy, just coldly determined. "We must wait and see. In the meantime, get yourself out of here. I don't want you worrying, Ruby-bug."

"I'm glad you're home." Why couldn't she fight the sinking feeling that whatever kind of job Roop was seeking would not be a good situation for him?

She shut the door securely behind her, needing heaven to be closer.

Watch over my brother too, please, Father. She held her prayer close to her heart and with all the strength of her soul.

Chapter Thirteen

The thump of the cookstove's door closing startled Ruby from a sound sleep. Warm and snug in her dreams, she batted her eyes open to the arctic morning. The nail heads in the wall boards froze furry white, and the sheet serving as a curtain to separate her bed from the rest of the main room had also frozen stiff. Not the best of signs. All she wanted to do was to stay tucked in her toasty covers.

"Ruby, time to rise and shine." There was a metallic clink as Pa opened the stove's damper. The crackle of kindling and the whir of new, hungry flames filled the silent shanty. "It's the Lord's day and that means church. If Solomon is strong enough to be left alone, that is."

"I'm praying he is." Weekly church and Sunday school were pleasures she would miss. While she could love the Lord anywhere and study His teachings, irregular services from a traveling minister at the settlement near her uncle's farm simply would not be the same.

She threw back the covers, and the glacial air hit her like an avalanche. Teeth clacking, she chose her Sunday dress and her best cardigan and slipped into both. The back door clicked shut, leaving her alone. She washed up, plaited her hair in one long braid and pulled back the curtain.

"Ruby!" The back door popped open, scattering her thoughts. She grabbed the metal handle of the coffeepot and lifted it from the shelf, guilty she hadn't yet made coffee. The haggard grief on Pa's face stopped her. Devastation darkened the eyes that avoided hers. He didn't have to say a word, she could guess.

"Solomon." The coffeepot slipped from her fingers and clattered to the floor. Horror hit her like a runaway train straight to the chest. "Is he…?"

"Sick. Gravely sick." Pa scrubbed a hand over his face. His shoulders, always so straight and strong, slumped. Defeated, he blew out a ragged breath and said no more, as if he was trying to pull himself together.

"What do we do?" Her voice wobbled. Everything wobbled. She clutched the edge of the table, shaking so hard she rattled that, too.

"You sit down before you fall down, honey." Pa hefted the water bucket onto the stove top. Droplets sizzled and popped on the hot surface. "Let me brew up some coffee. I reckon Roop could use something hot. He's been up since the wee hours."

"No, I can do it." She rescued the pot from the floor and gave it a quick swipe before filling it with water. She felt wooden, no longer real as she measured out fragrant coffee grounds. Pa filled the coffeepot with water. What would they do without Solomon? He was family.

"I know this is hard, Ruby. That horse has lived a good, long life. We have all made sure he was as happy as we could make him." Pa's hand settled on her shoulder, consolation on this harsh morn. "Let's do all we can now to make him comfortable."

"Yes, Pa." Hollow inside, she knelt to grab the ring in the floor. A tug lifted the door and revealed three steps into the cellar below. She breathed in the cold scents of earth and stored vegetables as she dropped into the frigid space. Quickly, she grabbed the butter dish, last night's leftover potatoes and cut bacon strips from the slab. *Oh, Solomon.* Grief made her stagger. First she'd fix a hot breakfast for Pa and Roop, then she would go to him.

Boots plodded on the floorboards above, and a shadow fell over her.

"Ruby." Lorenzo reached down to pluck the bowl of potatoes out of her hands. "Hand up what you've got and fetch me three onions and some mustard seed, will you?"

She blinked, not quite believing her eyes. "You came."

"I promised, didn't I?" He took the bacon and butter from her and disappeared from sight.

"H-have you seen Solomon yet?" She couldn't seem to untie the onion sack. She swallowed hard, willed her fingers to shake less and tried again.

"Yes."

Nothing more. Silence settled in, and she feared what he didn't say. The string gave, and she counted out the onions. Their papery skins crackled as she handed them up.

A dark day's growth clung to Lorenzo's angled jaw, making him look like a western legend as he held out his hand. Her fingers wrapped around his, and he swept her up the steps and into the kitchen. She landed on her feet, not wanting to let go.

She shouldn't be so glad to see him. She shouldn't be wanting to lean on him. How did she stop the emotion in her heart? She didn't know. It glowed like sunlight on winter snow, lyrical and radiant with a life all its own.

"I had to come check on Solomon. I had a feeling he might not bounce back." He knelt at her feet to close the trapdoor.

"Why are you doing this? It can't be for m-me." She choked on the word, afraid to say it out loud. "It shouldn't be."

"It was Poncho's idea. He cares a great deal for you." Loving warmth gentled his deep tone. He wasn't talking about a horse's feelings.

"I care a great deal for Poncho, too." She blushed, not at all comfortable confessing her feelings. She wasn't talking about the horse, either.

"That's good to hear." He rose up to his full height, towering above her, manly and strong and good. He brushed stray tendrils out of her eyes. In his, she saw forever. A future she could not have. Being beaued by him. Being courted. Accepting a proposal and planning a wedding.

All that would happen for another girl. Someone who was free to love him in return. *Let it be Scarlet,* she prayed, as she shuttered her gaze and turned away. *If not Scarlet, then Kate.*

"Slice the onions thinly, cook them into a soft mash in the fry pan and add crushed mustard seed." His boots rang on the hardwood. He set the onion on the table with a mild thunk. "I brought this packet of herbs from home. Mix this in halfway through."

How did she thank him? The words clogged in her throat. She could only gape like a fish out of water, struggling for air. He was doing all this for Solomon. It was impossible to adore him any more than she already did, but her poor heart tumbled even farther. No way to stop it.

"I would fix the poultice myself, but I want to help Rupert. I know he's had a long night." Lorenzo's hand settled against her jaw, the warmth of his palm and the slight abrasion of his calloused fingers felt dearer than anything she'd ever known.

All her willpower was not enough to keep her from pressing into his touch just a little, just the tiniest, ittiest bit.

"Go." She put a shield around her heart, trying to resist, and wished she had the strength to step away from him. "Please help Solomon. I'll be out with the poultice when it's done."

"Bring several dish towels when you do." He moved away, as if reluctant, too. The impact of his unguarded blue gaze felt as physical as his touch had been and went deep into her soul. He broke away and strode out of the shanty, but the sweetness remained.

You are walking on dangerous ground, Ruby Ann. She plucked up the knife, the wooden handle rough against her fingers. The shield around her heart wasn't strong enough. He had gotten around it, gotten in. What was she going to do about it? How was she going to stop it? She had no clue.

She set the blade to the head of the onion and sliced

through papery skin. Juice spilled over her fingertips and stung her eyes as she pried off the outside layers. She heard the faint rumble of men's voices through the walls—Pa and Lorenzo talking as they met on the path to the barn.

Lorenzo. She respected him, she adored him, she felt affection for him. But that was all. She could not go any further. She could not fall in love with Lorenzo. Her feelings were on the brink of the rocky edge of a cliff ready to plummet. She had to resist. She had to be a fortress.

Was she strong enough? She did not know.

She wasn't prepared for the sight of the man seated in the straw with the horse's head in his lap. Did he have to be so wonderful? It was Lorenzo's fault she was falling. Any woman would be defenseless again his kindness.

Poncho, tied in the aisle, moved aside for her to pass and nibbled on the edge of her hood as she squeezed by him. Clover stretched across the rails of her stall, curious to see what was in the fry pan. Pa busily forked soiled straw out of the stall, while Rupert replaced it with fresh clean hay.

"It's ready," she said simply.

"Excellent." Lorenzo gently lifted Solomon's head and slid away. He stopped to draw a handkerchief out of his coat pocket and patted dry the gelding's copiously running nose.

Touched, she drew herself up straight, gathering her willpower. *Don't fall in love him, Ruby Ann. Be completely unaffected by him.*

She uncovered the fry pan. "Is this what you meant?"

"It's just right." He smelled of winter wind and hay and horse, a manly combination as he leaned in to take the handle. Steam rolled between them, ripe with onions and the earthy scent of herbs. He took one glove off with his teeth and touched his fingertips into the mixture. "Good, not too hot. Come with me."

Solomon's heavy breathing rasped painfully. His sides heaved as if every breath of air was an impossible strain. Her poor friend. She knelt near the gelding's belly. When she placed her hand on his flesh, his short coarse coat was damp with fever. He moaned once, aware of her presence and her touch.

"You're such a good boy," she told him in her softest voice. "You are the very best horse."

Pa came to stand at Solomon's haunches. They watched as Lorenzo ladled a big scoop of the strong-smelling mash onto the gelding's side, right behind his front leg.

"Let me help." She leaned forward using her good hand to spread the mixture. Steam rose as they worked together in silence. Facing one another, she shook out a dish towel, a bit scorched from her attempt to warm it on the stove. Lorenzo caught two corners and together they lowered it over the poultice to trap in heat.

Did she dare look up? Did she dare meet his gaze? Her throat closed up. Panic popped through her bloodstream and she didn't know what to do. She didn't know how to fight what was happening to her.

"That's awful clever, young Mr. Davis." Pa broke the silence, sounding pleased and sheepish all at once. "I should have thought to do the same. It's like what my mother, God rest her, used on me when I was young."

"My grandfather said what works for us can work for horses. First we loosen up the mucus in his lungs and see if we can bring it up." Lorenzo gently patted Solomon's neck. The gelding nickered with great effort and coughed hard, a terrible hacking sound. He feared he had come too late to make a difference. For Ruby's sake, he would continue to try. He glanced toward the door, but Rupert hadn't returned yet with a bucket of boiling water.

He circled around to Solomon's nose and knelt there, so close to Ruby he could see the slight intake of her breath at his nearness. Her eyes popped wide, and the ice-blue flecks in her irises dazzled. The boom of his pulse rocked through him, and it took all his discipline to hold his hands steady as he globbed the poultice on Solomon's chest. The animal's nostrils flared in protest. He lifted his head, rocking his big body. He was too weak to get up.

"Easy, big fella," Lorenzo crooned, hand on the horse's sweaty shoulder. "Just trust me. I'll take care of you, boy."

Solomon's big, chocolate, horse eyes met his with desperation. Easy to read the fear and pain there. He knew God gave creatures a feeling heart, so he wanted to offer what care he could. He set the pan in the straw and stroked the gelding's neck with his clean hand, willing all the comfort he could into his touch. The coarse velvet coat, the feel of life beneath his fingertips, the shuddering sigh as Solomon eased his head onto his pillow of hay and closed his eyes. His sides heaved as he struggled to breathe, the ghostly rasp echoing through the small structure.

"He's hurting." Ruby sounded tortured. "What else can I do for him?"

"Comfort him." There was nothing more to do. The tinny taste of dread filled his mouth, and he wiped his hand, sticky from the poultice, on a dish towel. He couldn't look away as Ruby spread her arms wide and hugged as much of the horse, belly to back, as she could. Tears spiked her eyelashes.

"Stay with me," she whispered. "Please."

Surely heaven had to hear that plea. He cleared emotion from his throat, set aside the fry pan and studied the woman clinging to the old horse. The most vulnerable places inside him opened ever wider, leaving him without a single defense. A powerful ache he'd never known before, one of pure emotion and spirit gripped him so hard, he thought his heart failed. Love so keen it hurt roared through him with the strength of a lion and the gentleness of a lamb.

There was no going back. No changing his feelings. The iron-clad commitment binding him to her was unbreakable. Unable to resist, his hand landed on her shoulder. She was as fine-boned as a bird, as delicate as a winter's snowflake, as amazing as a miracle. That was Ruby, *his* Ruby. For the rest of his life, he would remain committed to her, bound to her.

Nothing would change that. Regardless of what happened, whether they were together or forever apart.

Across the top of Ruby's blue, knit cap, Jon Ballard nodded slowly, once. Apparently the older man understood. Heat stretched tight across Lorenzo's cheeks, but it felt good that Jon approved.

Rupert clamored in with two heavy buckets in each

hand. Poncho nickered, curious as to the contents, and Lorenzo turned his efforts once again on the dying horse.

Pay attention, Ruby. She flipped a slice of bacon in the frying pan, wincing at the over-brown meat. Fat sizzled and popped in the pan as she turned the remaining pieces, fearing the worst. No, they didn't appear to be too scorched, at least Rupert and Pa would never complain. But Lorenzo would be sitting down to their breakfast table. He was not used to burned food, since she knew firsthand how exacting Cook was.

Coffee, a little over-boiled, steamed in its pot as she set it on a hot pad near Pa's place at the table. It was hard to concentrate with the knots in her stomach and the worry plaguing her. Solomon fought a high fever. Poultices and steam treatments could only do so much. She tried to imagine life without Solomon's comforting presence, his affectionate nips and snuggles and his faithful friendship. Tears burned in her throat.

The pancakes! She whirled around, realizing she'd forgotten the stove. Again. She snatched up the spatula, winced when she used her injured wrist and flipped the first cake on the griddle. She expected a black surface, but it was still golden brown.

Whew. Relief skittered through her as she flipped the rest of the cakes, one after another and watched them carefully.

"I hear you have coffee in here." Lorenzo blew in with a bracing wind.

"That rumor is true," she confirmed, every thought fleeing at his presence.

What was it about the man that affected her? Why him? Why when it was so impossible? She did not know.

The pancakes! She tightened her grip on the spatula, feeling every inch of Lorenzo's gaze as she shoveled the pancakes off the griddle and onto the platter.

"Jon insisted I come in and thaw out. I didn't want to be rude and argue with him, so I agreed." He swept off his hat, scattering tiny flakes that spiraled through the air. "Solomon seems to be improving."

"He is?" She lost hold of the spatula. It clattered to the stovetop and splashed into the bacon pan. "He's so ill. How can you be sure?"

"I can't be. He could still take a bad turn, but he's breathing easier for now. His fever is still high, but better. We've done all we can do. It is in God's hands."

"As all things are." Relief quivered through her, and she rescued the spatula. The wooden handle was slick with grease, and she rubbed it with a dishcloth.

Lorenzo's socks whispered on the plank floor behind her. "That smells good. You could give Cook competition."

"Hardly. You have to stop telling fibs."

His laughter echoed in the room, a merry note. "I'm complimenting you, Ruby. Sincerely."

"You haven't tasted my cooking yet." She flipped the bacon, fighting as hard as she could not to give in to her adoration. "Oh, the biscuits."

What was wrong with her this morning? Lorenzo, he was also the problem. The man tied up her tongue and her mind, and she grabbed the hot pad and instantly dropped it.

"Let me." He knelt, so close she could feel the cold

radiating off his clothes. A dark swirl of hair formed a cowlick at the back of his head and she wanted to run her fingers through it.

Brilliant, Ruby, just perfectly brilliant. She was supposed to be resisting his charm, not doting on every little thing about the man.

Still, how could she do otherwise? He rose to his six-foot height, towering over her, ten kinds of dashing, as his solemn, midnight gaze found hers. He held her captive with a look, he captured her with his silence. She could feel the honest power of his affection as he opened the oven door and knelt to slide out the baking sheet. The connection between them cinched tighter, more binding than before.

A connection she could not allow.

She plunged a cloth into a serving bowl and spread it out, using a fork to slide the buttermilk biscuits off the baking sheet one by one. They plopped into the bowl, steaming and crumbly good, and she breathed in their sweet, doughy scent.

"Thank you." She covered the biscuits with the corners of the cloth, trapping the heat. When she looked up, Lorenzo stood before her, his gaze intent on hers.

Don't notice the light in his eyes. Don't notice his look of great caring, she told herself. *Be strong, Ruby. Don't give in. You can't fall in love with him.*

"I'm glad to help out. I'll stay as long as Solomon needs it." His gaze slid downward to focus on her mouth. More intense this time. Like he was honestly considering leaning in and kissing her.

She gulped. *Must not let him kiss you, Ruby.* Air

wheezed in and out. Panic skittered through her. "I'm sure Solomon will appreciate that very much."

"I'll do everything I can to save him."

"Because you love horses?" A girl had to hope Lorenzo really did care about the horse, that Solomon was the reason he was here.

"Because I love horses." His smile and his eyes said something different.

For one precious moment, the chasm separating them closed. They were no longer divided. Firelight danced over them from the hearth, and sunshine from the window graced them like a blessing.

If only this could be. She saw the same wish in his eyes. The same longing prayer in his soul. Now how was she going to stop falling any harder for him?

Boots stamping off snow echoed in the lean-to, shattering the moment. Lorenzo stepped away as the kitchen door swung open, as Pa stumbled in, shrugging off his coat.

Chapter Fourteen

She'd worried all Sunday long, and this morning turned out to be no different. She wished she could be home, checking on Solomon's recovery. She knew he was safe in Pa's caring hands, but did that stop her from imagining the worst? Trying to think positive didn't help. Ruby balanced the serving tray in both hands, ignoring the twist of pain in her left wrist and hurried out of the kitchen.

She'd never seen such activity. The parlor was a madhouse. Both the upstairs and downstairs maids climbed ladders and handed down the yards upon yards of lace and velvet curtains to be washed, ironed and hung for the approaching ball. Others rolled up the exquisite carpets to be beaten and spot cleaned. The same activities went on in every room throughout the mansion's main floor.

"Ruby, dear." Mrs. Davis granted her a beaming smile, circling furniture and weaving among the busy workers. "You have perfect timing. Please, leave that on the coffee table. I think we could all use a mid-morning break."

"Cook thought you all might like some scones." She slid the tray onto the table, kneeling carefully, just as Cook had taught her. Not a droplet splashed over the teacup rims, and not a single scone slipped off the platter. She was making progress.

"That was very thoughtful of her. My, but you set a very nice tray." Mrs. Davis's compliment meant a lot.

"Thank you." She had worked hard at it, using the fine linen and a pretty lace runner to pretty up the silver tray. She'd folded cloth napkins like swans, and little bowls of cubed sugar, lemon slices and mint sprigs were as artful as she could make them. She took a shaky breath, preparing for what she had to do. "May I have a word with you?"

"Absolutely." The older woman clapped her hands. "You have all worked hard this morning. Take an extra-long break."

Curtains were left piled and carpets unrolled as the half dozen maids broke into conversation and crowded around the tea tray.

"We can speak in the hallway." Mrs. Davis swept toward the arched doorway, her fine skirts rustling. "How is your wrist feeling?"

"Much better, thank you." Self-conscious, she shoved her left hand as far as she could manage into her skirt pocket.

"Lucia tells me you are not exactly following doctor's orders." Selma's rebuke was kindly offered. "You must not work so hard."

"I'm stubborn."

"I've noticed. So what is the trouble, my dear?"

She gulped, unable to say the words. This was even

harder than she'd imagined. Shame filled her, and she had to fight hard to keep her chin up when her head wanted to bob down. "I have to give my notice. I don't want to. I like working here."

"Then what is the problem, child?" Concern softened Selma's face, and she swept to an abrupt stop in the corridor.

Ruby squared her shoulders. She'd rehearsed what to say half of last night, when she'd been too upset to sleep. "My family has to move away. We are about to lose our farm."

"Oh, that's so sad. I'm sorry. I didn't know things at home were so serious." Compassion, not blame, shone in caring, dark eyes. "Do you have someplace to go?"

"My uncle has agreed to let us move onto his land. He lives up near the Canadian border."

"That far?" Selma's distress etched into her face. Her grip tightened as she tugged Ruby into the dining room. "Come sit and tell me about this."

"Oh, there isn't much to tell." She couldn't imagine Selma Davis would want to truly hear about her family's troubles. "My brother left on this morning's train hoping to find work, but it will probably not be in time."

"I see." She drew out a chair for Ruby and motioned for her to sit. "I am sorry to lose you. You are a good employee."

"This is a terrible way to repay your kindness."

"Is there no chance you could stay behind?" The older woman settled in the neighboring chair. "You could lodge in the maids' quarters and send your wages home. I have several other employees who do the same."

That beautiful option shimmered in front of her. She

wanted to reach out and grasp it. *Just think.* She could stay here and see her friends, be here when Fiona's baby was born and for Meredith's wedding, see which house Lila and her new husband settled on buying. Most of all, she would be near Lorenzo. Remembering all he had done for Solomon, affection strengthened into an emotion she could not label.

Then she thought of her father alone in that tiny, little place, how devastated he would be. Both she and Rupert feared for him. He'd had too many hopes shattered in his life, endured tough hardships and losses. No one had worked harder than Jon Ballard to rebuild his life.

How would he take this hard blow? She didn't know, but he did not deserve to be left alone, broken of spirit and void of dreams, struggling to survive.

"I wish," she said simply. "But it cannot be."

"I will be so sorry to see you go. In fact, I am heartbroken. Does Lo—" Mrs. Davis fell silent, her question left unspoken. Genuine sympathy twisted her lovely features, and she sat up straighter, as if coming to a decision. "I will not fill your position until after the new year. That will give you time to reconsider and return if you wish."

"That is incredibly generous. I can't expect you to do that."

"I am your boss, so you will simply have to endure my decisions." Selma leaned in to brush a strand of hair out of Ruby's eyes, as concerned as a mother. "Will you at least be able to stay for the ball? I need every employee I have on staff, it's such a busy evening. Your family could use the extra pay."

"It's my hope to stay here until Christmas, but I don't

know for sure. It depends on the banker. My father is trying to shield me as best he can, so he isn't very forthcoming."

"You be sure and talk to me. Let me know how things are progressing. If you need anything, you can ask me." Such loving words, so honestly spoken.

"I have everything I need." It was so easy to dwell on what was missing, on what one didn't have. Her father lived a life of integrity, and she would, too. "I need to work off the doctor's bill before I go."

"I thought we agreed that was my responsibility." Mrs. Davis drew back in her chair, appraising her carefully. "I noticed you walked to work this morning. Lorenzo told me about your horse. Is he still improving?"

"Yes, thanks to your son." She tried, how hard she tried, to keep any hint of reverence from her voice. "He saved Solomon. He spent his only day off tending our horse."

"Yes, because it was your horse, my dear." Mrs. Davis patted Ruby's hand. "You be sure and take your break. Go on with you and get some tea and scones."

Her employer's words troubled her all the way to the kitchen and through her lunch break. As she crocheted at the table with Cook, who was reading her Bible, she tried not to think about Lorenzo. But did she succeed?

No. Her mind stubbornly boomeranged to the conversation in the dining room. Mrs. Davis could not have been kinder. And to suggest Lorenzo had spent a long day in their little barn for her meant she hadn't hidden her crush on Lorenzo from his mother. Heat blazed across her face, no doubt turning her nose strawberry red. She wrapped thread around her needle and triple crocheted. She was doing a very bad job of keeping control of her heart.

Her hook stilled in the middle of her next triple crochet. She couldn't seem to control her thoughts, either, since they rolled back around to yesterday morning. After Pa had come into the shanty that morning, Lorenzo had joined them for breakfast and pleasant conversation about farming life. He'd stayed in the barn until suppertime, fighting to help save Solomon's life. He'd driven away in twilight shadows, offering her nothing more than a silent wave.

You are in big trouble, Ruby. She shook her head to scatter her thoughts. Determined to try again, she focused on the big window looking out into the backyard. The magnificent Rocky Mountains soared from the prairie floor to the pale blue sky, the rugged peaks wearing capes of pearled snow. No matter what, God's handiwork always managed to soothe her.

A movement caught her eye, a blur of color against the stretching white, shining snow, soaring purple mountains and reaching blue sky. Lorenzo, in his black coat, astride his bay horse, cut across a field. A trail of cattle ambled behind him, ears pricked, noses up, obviously fond of him.

A loud clatter rocketed through the kitchen and shook the table alongside her. She gasped, jarred from her thoughts as Mae scowled down at her.

"You should have fetched the tray, but as you are Mrs. Davis's favorite, I can see I will have to be doing a lot more around here." Her gaze followed Ruby's to the window, and a look of knowing flashed in her narrowed eyes.

Had Mae guessed? She withered. Heat flamed more brightly across her face, making it red enough for everyone to see. Mae knew. Mrs. Davis knew. Who else had figured it out?

"The Christmas ball is coming up." Mae's tone turned speculative and sugary. "I'm sure he will beau someone suitable. Someone as wealthy as he is. He always takes Narcissa Bell. My guess is he will do the same this year. Wouldn't you say, Cook?"

Why did she wince at the sound of Narcissa's name? The mention of the woman made her feel two full inches shorter.

"Don't mind me." Cook didn't look up from the Good Book. "I'm simply studying my Bible, where it says a body should mind her own business and not spread malice or practice jealousy."

"Me? I'm not jealous. I'm just trying to help." Mae gave her braid a toss. "He feels pity for you, Ruby. Nothing more. About to lose your house. How embarrassing. Hey, don't look surprised. The walls have ears around here."

So, her conversation with Mrs. Davis had been overheard. Now every employee in the house would know. The thread she held went fuzzy. She blinked hard, but it didn't help. She listened to Mae's footsteps fade away.

"Don't pay Mae much heed. She's just wishin' the young master paid her such attention." Cook closed her Bible thoughtfully. "I've never seen Master Lorenzo take to any lass the way he has you. Beauty is as beauty does, and to some and to Him, that's what matters."

Across the long span of snowy yard and field, Lorenzo, tall in his saddle, faced her. Although the distance was too great, and there was no way he could see her, her spirit tugged as if he could.

There was no safe way back. She was fooling herself to think there was. That she could control her heart and stop her feelings, to save herself from heartbreak. She gave her thread a tug, thread Lorenzo had given her, and made a wobbly stitch. She had fallen too far, wanting what she could not have. It was her own fault she hurt so much. She had no one but herself to blame. At week's end, she would be packing to leave town and she would never see Lorenzo again.

Earlee Mills swept out of the post office onto the sunny, late afternoon boardwalk, heart tapping with excitement. Joy swooped through her like a sweet spring breeze as she plunked down on the nearest bench, ignored the ice and cold and ran her fingertips across the envelope.

Finn had written her name in his bold, confident script, and she took a moment to simply look at her name written in his hand. Earlee Mills. One day would she be Earlee McKaslin? Her pulse skipped a beat. It was her dearest wish.

If only Finn felt the same way about her. They had been exchanging letters since spring, regular letters, one or more every week. He'd been friendly, he'd been honest, and as time went on, he had been more and more open. But never had he given a single hint that he felt anything more for her than friendship.

Still, she dreamed.

"Hi, Miss Mills!" Tommy Bellamy skipped toward her down the boardwalk, holding his mother's hand. Beside him, his brother Charlie made a funny face.

"Hi there, Tommy and Charlie." She adored her little students, even the troublemakers. "Hello, Mrs. Bellamy."

"Good afternoon, Miss Mills." Clarice Bellamy smiled kindly. "How nice to see you. I trust my boys are behaving themselves better these days?"

"Much. Charlie had to write lines only once so far this week."

"I suppose that's an improvement." The mother shook her head slightly, in good humor, as she herded her sons down the boardwalk.

So it was with a smile on her face that she carefully tore open Finn's envelope and unfolded his letter.

Dear Earlee,
My day is always a bright one when a letter from you arrives.

Why, didn't that make a girl hope? A smile stretched across her face, and she read on.

Life is the same here, work, sleep, work, sleep.
But during the long hours of moving rock in the
quarry, I have a lot of time to think and reflect on
what I should have done differently in my life. Lots
of time to think hard on how I will make better
choices when I'm out. Working for my brother on
his farm sounds like heaven right now. Even in
winter. I miss hearing the prairie winds howling

*over the plains. I can't wait to hear them again.
The winds blow where I am, but it is a different sound that is lonely on the stone walls of the
prison. When I'm in the quarry, the wind has a different tune in the mountains here, rustling through
trees. I miss home and everyone there.*

Her hopes wanted to read more into that last line. He
hadn't written, I miss you, Earlee Elizabeth Mills, she
told herself. So don't pretend that he did.
But she sure wished he had.

*I'm not surprised at all to learn you are a writer.
Your letters have entertained me and made me
feel connected to home, to someone, since I'm so
lonely here.*

He didn't say he felt connected to you, she reminded
herself, although the hope in her heart fluttered more.

*Have you ever thought about trying to publish one
of your stories? I think you should. I believe in
you, Earlee. You have come to be very special
to me.*

Wow! She had to read that last line twice to make
sure she hadn't imagined it. He really cared about her.
She clutched the letter to her heart, unable to keep her
hopes from rising higher and taking all her wishes and
dreams with it.

Tiny flecks hovered in the air, invisible in the night-
fall. They swirled with her breath and dampened her

face and iced on the road at her feet. Ruby prayed the buttons on her old shoes would hold for the mile walk to town and the even longer journey home. Her newer pair of shoes weighed down her bag, where they would stay dry.

She picked her way along the icy ruts. While she'd helped Cook prepare the Davis's supper, talk of rustlers' tracks circulated through the house. Likely Lorenzo would be too busy to go to practice tonight.

That would be a relief. She needed to start easing her heart away from him. He'd never really been hers. She hadn't needed Mae to tell her that. She'd known it all along.

Behind her the faint squeak of approaching sleigh runners on the ice broke the stillness. The *clip* of horseshoes and the bell-like jingle of the harness grew nearer. She veered toward the edge of the road, to let whoever it was pass by. But she didn't need the horse's friendly nicker to know who was driving the sleigh. She felt the mellow glow in her soul crescendo, the way it did when Lorenzo was around.

So, he was coming, after all. She would have to see him. Have to fight the gathering heartbreak threatening to engulf her.

Poncho pulled up alongside her and stopped, his horsy eyes sparkling, glad to see her. He reached out with his whiskery lips to catch the fringe on her scarf with his teeth.

"Hello to you, handsome." She knew Lorenzo watched her as she caught her scarf before his horse could tug it off her. She rubbed that velvety nose and muzzle with her mittened hand. "You look quite dashing. Did your mane get a trim?"

"He's touched that you noticed." Lorenzo held back the robes and offered his hand. "C'mon. Accept a ride. You'll hurt Poncho's feelings if you don't."

"Poncho. What am I going to do with you?" She gave the horse one more pat, the sweet guy, before facing the man who was her real problem. The plea in his dark blue gaze was impossible to turn down. It hooked deep into her, reeling her closer like a fish on a line.

"My mother told me you gave your notice today." His fingers closed around hers to assist her into the sleigh. "How did it go?"

"It was hard, but once I got the words out, your mother was nice about it." She gathered her skirts, settled next to him and extricated her fingers from his grip. "She offered to let me live in the maid quarters."

"Really? That's a good idea." He leaned close to tuck in the robes. "Any chance you will?"

"No." Her apology rang quietly in her words. She looked away from him, staring at the smudge of the town up ahead, dark against the endless, white prairie. "We discussed it last night after you left. This morning, Pa walked Rupert to the train and stopped by the bank on his way home."

"Then it's official." He gave the reins a snap.

"Yes. Pa told them we can't come up with the money." She shrugged her slender shoulders as if she wasn't devastated. "Oh, well." She gave a little sigh.

He wasn't fooled by it. "I really am sorry."

"The hard thing is we were planning on packing the wagon bed and driving north. But now, Solomon is too frail to make the trip north so we have leave him here." Her face crumpled. "I'm worried about what will become of him. Who would buy him in his condition? Probably someone meaning to render him."

"I'm sorry, Ruby." He wanted to reach out to her, but she sat at the far edge of the sleigh, as far away from him as she could get. "You grew up with Solomon."

"I did. He was my only friend as a child. I would make dandelion necklaces, which he would proudly wear, and I'd always share my jelly sandwiches with him."

He tried to imagine Ruby as a child. Petite and lean, with her fine, white-blond hair and winter-sky blue eyes. He reckoned she was probably the cutest thing around. Ruby's daughter one day might look just like that.

Their little girl would have looked just like that. His throat tightened until he could barely speak.

"I have been praying for a good outcome for you and your family. For Solomon, too." He cleared his throat, but the weight of his emotions remained, making him sound gruff. "When exactly will you be leaving?"

"That's up to the banker. I'll find out from Pa when I get home tonight. This is terribly painful for him." Compassion and concern painted her eyes a deeper blue. The lantern light on the dash caressed her, finding ways to adore the curve of her cheekbone or the darling cut of her chin. Her heart-shaped face became even more stunning in the golden light. "I'm hoping I will spend Christmas here, where I have so many friends."

"I hope so, too. I hate to see you go, Ruby." He pulled back on the reins, slowing Poncho on the approach to town.

"You won't miss me one whit when I'm gone." Her Cupid's-bow mouth hooked up at the corners, an attempt at a smile. It couldn't hide the sadness in her eyes.

The sadness at leaving him? That was his hope. "I wasn't kidding. I intend to write. I might be boring, I might be dull, all I do these days is work on the ranch, but I will write."

"Then I suppose I would have to answer." Snowflakes glimmered like diamonds in her hair.

"See that you do. Poncho would be mad if I didn't keep in touch. We could always take a trip up north to visit. Just in case Poncho really gets to missing you."

"What?" She bit her bottom lip, stunned at his offer. Lorenzo wanted to come see her? Anguish swirled within her chest. *No,* she wanted to say. It was what she *had* to say.

"After all, good friends need to keep in touch." His words rumbled with intent, so intimate and respectful, his entire focus seemed to be her. His eyes were full of light, his features soft, his touch gentle as he cupped his hands to her face. Amazing tenderness filled the air, soaring from his heart to hers.

Never had she wanted anything so much. She grasped as hard as she could to her stubborn resolve, but she was not strong enough to resist. How could she be? The powerful forces of her feelings knocked down her last defenses. *I will not love him,* she thought helplessly as he leaned in kissing-close.

Escape. Quick. Now. Those were her last coherent thoughts as his lips slanted over hers, hovering, softening, only a breath could fit between them now. His eyes were as dark as a night sky and full of gently glowing affection. Her pulse galloped crazily, nerves skidded through her. His lips brushed hers as gently as a butter-fly's wing for one brief moment before he hesitated and pulled away.

Pulled away. Her lips tingled with the pure sensation of his kiss, but he had ended it. Disappointment, confusion, embarrassment tore through her, and she tried to make sense of it. Had he had second thoughts, changed his mind or finally realized she was never going to be what he needed? Maybe he'd regained his senses like she had and knew they didn't belong together.

"You are the sweetest thing ever." His baritone rang softly, full of feeling.

"Proof you don't know me very well," she quipped, unable to endure the exquisite tenderness as his gaze caressed hers. She looked away at the street, at the boardwalk, anything but him. She'd done the unthinkable. She'd let him closer when she should be pushing him away.

What was wrong with her? Why had she messed up everything so badly? Her father was counting on her. Her friends—heavens, what would they think about her if they knew how weak she was? How selfish?

"I know everything I need to about you." He caught her chin in his hand and looked within her so deeply, there was no end. Only the sheen of his eyes where love lived.

This cannot be happening. She fisted her hands, trying to wrestle back to reality, but his chiseled lips captured hers again in the most wonderful, the most reverent, the most loving of kisses. Unbearable emotion stole through her as stealthy as the night, pulling at the deepest places of her spirit, cutting like a blade. Love she could not hold back tore through her like a winter's torrent, a million snowflakes blotting out the world.

No kiss had ever been so flawless. She could feel his love for her, and tears prickled behind her eyes. His love, equal to hers. She had never imagined, never dared to dream. But as his lips stroked hers one last, pure time, she caught a glimpse of what could be. A perfect life spent in his arms. A perfect love.

A vision she had to let go of.

"Look where Poncho brought us." His words rumbled against her ear.

She blinked, fighting to bring the real world into focus. A shadowed steeple speared upward as snow began to fall in earnest, airy flakes. The church, she realized as the sleigh stopped. Poncho nickered and arched his neck in pride at his cleverness.

"Ruby!" Earlee waved as she spun on the pathway. "What are you—" Her eyes popped wide in surprise as she recognized Lorenzo in the sleigh. "Oh, maybe I should just keep going."

"No, wait." The moment was over. She had to accept it. She tied up the ribbons of her heart, buried her love for him with all her might and flung back the driving robes. Lorenzo reached to help, but she stopped him with a touch of her mitten to his glove. "Thank you for the ride, but I'll be fine from here."

"Are you sure?" Furrows dug into his forehead, and his gaze searched hers again, but she had to stay closed to him.

She didn't know what to say. Her tongue tied, her thoughts tangled up in knots, making her brain completely useless. She climbed from the sleigh with all the composure she could muster. She gripped her bag tightly. She was an adult, no longer a schoolgirl, and reality could not be wished away. Within days, surely by the end of the week, she would be on a train with her father. She set her chin and walked away.

No matter how many steps she took or how hard she tried, distance did not separate them.

Chapter Fifteen

"What were you doing in Lorenzo's sleigh?" Earlee whispered, clutching Ruby's hand and drawing her up the walkway. "Tell me. Is there something I don't know? What's going on? Is he your beau?"

"No. He can never be that. He came upon me walking on the road. Earlee, I'm begging you. Please don't say anything." Disgrace washed over her. What would Earlee think, knowing how Kate and Scarlet felt about the man? The treasured memory of his kiss burdened her. She hiked her bag higher on her shoulder and blanched at the weight of her guilt.

"But why were you walking in the first place? It's a long way from the Davis ranch to town."

"Solomon is ill."

"Oh, that's why you missed church and yesterday's sewing circle. We worried." Earlee glanced over her shoulder, probably watching Lorenzo tethering Poncho at the hitching post. "Will Solomon be all right?"

"He's improving." Not fast enough. Her worries pulled her down further. Best not to dwell on what she could not change. "I'm only staying tonight for part of the practice. I want to get home and check on him. I shouldn't have come, except I wanted to see you all so badly."

"I'm glad you did. You look as though you need a friend." Earlee wrapped her in a hug. "Is there anything I can do?"

"Or me?" Kate bounded up, breathless and chapped pink from her cold ride from her family's homestead. "I couldn't help but overhear. We all knew it had to be something serious for you to miss both church *and* our meeting."

"Your prayers would sure be a help." She hugged Kate, too. What great friends she was blessed with. The Lord had dealt bountifully with her. She felt full up, no longer alone. "How have you all been?"

"Don't change the subject." Scarlet sauntered up with the rest of the girls, lovely and fashionable in a stunning, gray, tailored coat and hood. "How can you manage while Solomon is recovering?"

"I'll have Shane bring you one of ours to borrow," Meredith offered.

"No, I couldn't, but your offer means a lot." Ruby swept up the steps, miserable over her kiss with Lorenzo, yet so happy to see her friends. "I don't mind walking."

"If you change your mind, let me know." Meredith held the door. "What are we going to do about Christmas? Will you still be here?"

"I don't know."

"Don't worry, we will just have our Christmas early, if we have to. We can't celebrate without you, Ruby." Scarlet leaned in to give her a hug.

She didn't deserve such good friends. Miserable, she tumbled into the vestibule and unbuttoned her coat. Her friends talked, offering their ideas on where to meet for their Christmas party. She was too wretched to utter a single word. They were so good to her. They had no notion what she'd done. How she'd betrayed them. Even if she couldn't help it.

Lila joined the gathering, handed over a wrapped bundle—the mended dress from the church barrel— and added her opinion. Laughter surrounded her as coats were hung or laid on tables, scarves removed and mittens peeled off. For the first time since she'd met them, she didn't feel a part of them. She felt like an outsider. That was her fault, too.

"It is going to be all right." Earlee slipped her hand in hers. "You just have to believe everything will work out. Poor Solomon."

The air changed as someone opened the door and held it. She didn't have to look to know Lorenzo was nearby. He strode into sight on the steps outside, dusted with white, talking over his shoulder with some of his friends. Beside her, Scarlet gave a dreamy sigh and stumbled into the sanctuary, leading the way. Kate gazed longingly as Lorenzo, charged into the vestibule and chuckled at something James Biddle said. When he glanced up, she felt the pull from where she stood.

She let Earlee tug her away. *Squeak,* went her left shoe. *Creak,* went her right. She debated changing into her new ones but decided not to.

This is who she was.

"Do you suppose I could get Lorenzo for Christmas?" Scarlet whispered as they trounced down the aisle. "All wrapped up in a pretty red bow under the tree with a bright shining engagement ring?"

"No, he won't be under your tree, I'm sorry," Kate sympathized. "Because he's going to be under mine."

"What are we going to do about you two?" Lila asked as she scooped up a songbook. "If he walked up to us right now and asked one of you to go to his family's ball, what would you do?"

"As much as I want him, I would tell him to ask Kate." Scarlet's chin went up, her mirth fading.

"I would ask him to take you." Kate slung her arm through Scarlet's, and they leaned together, lifelong friends. "Nothing is more important than our friendship."

"Likewise."

"So neither one of you would go?" Lila asked, doling out books.

Ruby's knees buckled as a book tumbled into her hand. Losing her balance, she seized the back of the bench, bumping her knee against the edge of the wooden seat. Pain cracked through her knee cap, but she hardly noticed it for the guilt blooming through her. It ached like a bleeding wound. She was not as good of a friend—as good of a person—as Kate and Scarlet were.

Not by a long shot.

"I guess that only leaves us right where we are. Dreaming of what cannot be." Keeping her voice low, Scarlet glanced over her shoulder, pure wish telegraphing across her face as Lorenzo shouldered out of the vestibule, flanked by Luken and James.

"He is a very nice dream," Kate agreed. "Hey, I saw

that, Lila. Not every girl can wind up with an amazing Range Rider for a husband."

"True, I'm very blessed. I'm sure God has great loves in store for the rest of you." Lila squinted in her direction. "Ruby, are you all right?"

"Fine. I just banged my knee." Tearing her gaze away before Lorenzo caught her staring, she limped forward on her squeaky shoes.

"First your wrist, then Solomon, now your knee. You must need a hug." Lila wrapped her arms around Ruby. "C'mon, everyone."

"I love you, Ruby," Kate whispered as she joined the hug.

"I love you more," Earlee huddled in.

"No, *I'm* the one who loves her most," Scarlet sidled into the circle.

"No, it's me," Meredith argued, joining in.

"We're so glad you're one of us, Ruby." Lila completed the circle, her loving friends.

Tears burned behind Ruby's eyes, both of gratitude and despair. *I will have to do better,* she vowed. They accepted her just as she was, for all her foibles and faults, and she loved them all dearly. There was nothing she wouldn't do for them, nothing she would not give.

So why had she let her heart carry her away?

Lorenzo took a songbook from the pile, and she felt his gaze on her face, felt his love.

A love she could not have. Determined to be a good friend, a better person, she did not look at him again.

"Sleep in heavenly peace." The last refrain of the beloved carol rang in three-part harmony and faded into silence. The arched ceiling of the sanctuary seemed to hold the memory of the notes as Reverend Hadly smiled. "Wonderful. Just wonderful. I think we are nearly ready for the public. You all take a break. Good work."

Finally. Ruby closed the book, ran her fingertip across the frayed spine and handed it over to Kate. *Do not look over at Lorenzo,* she reminded herself as she exchanged smiles with her friend. It hadn't been easy, but she'd successfully kept her gaze from inching over in search of him.

"Poor Solomon." Kate squeezed her hand. "If he is too weak to bring you next time, I will take the other way into town and pick you up. No arguments."

"Can we talk you into staying for a cup of tea in town with us?" Scarlet took her other hand. "We're not ready to let you go."

"Oh, I wish I could." She hated turning down the chance to spend just a little more time with her friends, but she had another friend waiting for her. She wanted to spend time with him tonight, too.

"Hello, Dr. Hathaway." Meredith plucked the songbook out of Kate's hands and added it neatly to the stack. Trouble danced in her expression as she waved the handsome medical man over. "I'm so glad you've joined the group. Do you have much caroling experience?"

"None, but I'm an optimist. Off tune, but an optimist." He shouldered over, cutting politely but firmly through the departing crowd of singers. His good-natured gaze found hers. "Ruby, how is your wrist?"

"Better. It hardly hurts." Self-conscious, she tucked her left hand into her skirt pocket. In the background, Lorenzo stopped, took notice and kept on going. It was for the best, although it didn't feel that way. "Do you enjoy singing?"

"I do, but I'm not sure anyone enjoys hearing me. Reverend Hadly hasn't asked me to leave yet." Walt Hathaway was innately likeable. Why couldn't she feel something for him? Why did it have to be for Lorenzo?

"The reverend hasn't asked me to leave yet, either." Earlee's contagious smile made everyone grin. "So there's a good chance you are completely safe. No one sings as badly as me."

"I caught you mouthing the words instead of actually singing." Lila rolled her eyes.

"That's how bad I am." Earlee laughed.

"Nice seeing you, ladies. Ruby." The doctor nodded, cast one last look in her direction. Embarrassed by the attention, she bowed her head.

"Ruby," Meredith whispered as the doctor disappeared down the aisle. "He really likes you. I think he's your secret admirer."

"I do, too." Kate's agreement rang like a merry bell. "Let's go get our coats."

"And let's see what he left for Ruby this time," Scarlet finished. "This is so exciting."

"Like a real-life love story," Earlee agreed as she led the way to the vestibule.

Every step she took felt like one of dread. Her shoes were heavy, her knees like stone. Her lips remembered the poignant brand of Lorenzo's kiss, the sweetest thing she'd ever known. The stubborn love in her heart refused to budge. What was she going to do about that?

"Ooh, Ruby's coat looks awfully bulky." Meredith's

delight echoed off the close walls of the vestibule. "Her secret admirer struck again."

"Fitting, since it is the Christmas season," Earlee agreed. "Ruby, I'm dying. Hurry. I want to see what he left you."

"Me, too." Scarlet crowded close.

"Me, three." Kate sidled in.

Her hands trembled as she pulled back the placket of her coat, revealing another wrapped package. She tugged it out of her pocket. A beautiful, white, silk ribbon bound the paper. A simple pull of the bow made the ribbon fall away. As she folded the paper aside, a soul-rending crack tore through her.

"Oh," Meredith breathed.

"Beautiful," Earlee whispered in amazement.

"The best quality I've ever seen," Scarlet added.

"The yarn is perfect. It's the color of your eyes, Ruby," Kate noted.

The skeins of soft wool looked too fine to touch. On top of the fluffy skeins sat a pair of needles carved in a rosebud pattern. She'd never seen such wood, gleaming a rich red-brown that shimmered with a rare luster.

"I sold them in the dress shop," Lila smiled. "My boss, Cora, carries only the very best in her store."

"You know who sent them for sure?" Earlee asked.

"I'm not telling." Lila squeezed Ruby's shoulder. "But I will say, these are gifts of love."

Ruby closed her eyes as the cracking within her broke deeper. How could Lila not condemn her? She ran a finger over the end of one knitting needle, so smooth and lovely it brought tears to her eyes.

"Are you sure you can't join us?" Kate asked as she

opened the door and waltzed out into the snow. "One cup of tea, that's all."

"I need to get going. I have to stop by the depot on my way home and pick up a telegram. Roop promised he would send one today." She took care not to slide on the icy steps. "He left on the morning train hoping to find a job in Butte."

"At the mine?" Earlee looked worried.

"He wouldn't say, but I'm afraid so. It's dangerous work." She tried not to think of it. Shafts caved in, rocks fell from overhead, gases rose up through cracks deep in the ground killing workers. Her stomach went cold. "I will see you all next time?"

"Absolutely," rang a chorus of assurances. After hugs and farewells and laughter, she watched her group of friends trudge along the beaten path toward Main Street, where the rest of the singers had gone. All but one, she noticed, as Poncho blew out a loud breath on the far side of the church. The horse was not alone. A man's silhouette broke away from the shadows pacing toward her, shoulders dependable and straight, powerful enough to carry any burden.

"Let me drive you home." Lorenzo's caring tone rang low. The wind brought his voice to her. "Poncho insists."

"I hate disappointing Poncho, but I have to this time." *You can do this, Ruby. You can be strong. You can say no this time.* She lifted her chin, unwavering, buoyed by the guilt and shame tormenting her. "I prefer to walk."

"Then I will walk with you." He closed the distance between them and held out his hand palm up in a silent offer.

One she could not accept. "No, you should go join your friends at the diner."

"Why?" Only Lorenzo, so wonderful, so perfect, could be as infinitely caring. His hand didn't waver, patiently waiting for her to accept him. "You aren't upset that I kissed you, because I saw you smile afterward. You did smile."

"Did I?" She'd been too dazed to realize it at the time, to overwhelmed to remember it now. "I shouldn't have."

"Your moving away only means we should spend more time together before you go, while we can. Unless you don't intend to answer my letters."

His letters? She squeezed her eyes shut, wincing at the pain burrowing deep. *Lord, what should I do about him wanting to write and visit, about the connection I cannot break?* That connection lived in her like hope and fairy-tale dreams that nothing, not even her will, could diminish.

She had to do the right thing. Resolve twisted through her, stronger than any blizzard, more powerful than any avalanche. But how? How could she reject him? How could she say the words? "I'm trying not to think that far ahead."

"I don't blame you. It has to be painful. I see how close you are to your friends." His hand remained outstretched, steadfastly waiting. Nothing in the world looked more inviting. She knew how safe it would feel to lay her palm against his. To feel his fingers close over hers protectively, devotedly. "It is painful for me, too."

Her fingers crept of their own accord. Oh, she was so weak. Just one more time, she let her palm rest on his. His fingers engulfing hers felt like the most wondrous thing on earth. Caring telegraphed through his touch, through layers of leather and wool. "There can be no more kisses, Lorenzo."

"Why? I know you liked it." His forehead furrowed. "I'm embarrassing you. You're blushing."

Her face blazed warm enough to melt the snow catching on her lashes. Bashful, she dipped her chin, taking one step backward and lifted her hand from his. "It was perfection. Good night."

The dark and the storm separating them was as great as the chasm dividing them. She had duty and loyalties. He had a family ranch to run and all the choices in the world. That was the simple reality. She had to be levelheaded. Her duty and loyalty aside, only in storybooks could a penniless girl find happily-ever-after with a wealthy prince. As she headed into the brunt of the storm, snowflakes hit her cheeks like tears.

Trudging into the yard, she noticed how the shanty's windows were dark and lonely. Yet home never looked so good, iced with a fresh mantle of snow and the curtains she'd made hanging behind the paned glass. The happy memories that lived in that house warmed her as she turned toward the barn. Lantern light faintly crept beneath the door, guiding her through the storm.

"Ruby, is that you?" Pa called from Solomon's stall.

"It's me." She closed the door tight behind her to keep in the warmth.

"What are you doing home so soon?" Hay rustled, and Pa leaned over the rail. "I told you to stay and enjoy time with your friends."

"I did, but I was worried about Solomon." And worried about her father, but she didn't say so. She pulled the telegram out of her coat pocket and handed it to him with snowy mittens. "Besides, I have to get in to work early tomorrow. The Davis's ball is this week. It's a busy time for the kitchen, with so much baking and cooking to do."

"Your job is a blessing, one I don't think you should forsake." Pa held open the gate for her, waiting while she passed into the crisp, crinkling hay.

Solomon lay upright, his hooves tucked under his warm blanket. When he spotted her, his ears went up, his eyes brightened and a weak nicker rumbled in his throat. He rocked up on his knees and rose awkwardly.

"You are my good boy." Such a relief to see him a little stronger. She set down her packages and placed her hands on either side of his long nose, treasuring the sweetness as he leaned his forehead against hers.

Lord, You are generous to spare him. Thank you. She let gratitude fill her heart along with her love for God, Who was good to them in endless ways. She listened to the rattle of paper as Pa unfolded the telegram.

"You are carrying a great deal more than you left home with." He studied her over the top of the page. "What's in those packages? Remember, I said I need no Christmas presents. We can't afford them."

"Lila mended a dress from the church barrel for me." Her tongue tied, and she didn't know how to speak of the gift of yarn and needles, so she said nothing more and stroked Solomon's nose.

"What about the other?" Pa glanced at the message, giving nothing away on his face. The news could not be good. "Did you decide to spend your wages on yourself like I told you?"

"I'm saving my money, just in case there is a chance." She knew her hopes were too high, her one foolish, illogical hope. That Roop would find immediate work in these tough times, that they could scrape together the payment with her earnings. That they could keep their home. Part of her just couldn't let that hope go.

"There will be no 'just in case.' We could sell everything we have, and we still wouldn't make it." Pa folded the telegram and slipped it into his pocket. "Roop says he will be moving on with the morning's train. Maybe he will find work farther west."

"Maybe." She battled overwhelming disappointment. There was no more optimism to have, no more positive thinking that could help. She tucked away her feelings, determined to be what her pa needed, the father who had done his best to be both a ma and a pa, who had always been kind to her. His love for her had never faltered. Hers would not now. "I'm sorry, Pa."

"We have what matters." He shrugged one brawny shoulder, as if the farm and the dream he had worked for was no great loss. His eyes told a different story. He was shattered.

There was no way she could make it better for him. No way to sweep up the pieces of those broken dreams, dust them off and sew them back together again. Solomon sensed their sadness and lifted his head, looking from one to the other, with worry quirking his horsy brows.

"I spoke to the gal who runs one of the boarding-houses in town. Just down the street from your friend

Lila's place." Pa cleared his throat. He laid one hand on Solomon's flank to reassure him. "The boardinghouse gal promised to look after you. She's a motherly sort and has seen you walking to and fro with your friends. I believe she will take care of you, make sure you are eating all your meals and keep you safe for me."

"What are you saying?" She gasped, her hopes rising for one, bright moment. Could it be true? "We are going to stay in town after all?"

"You are." Pa nodded once, a man with his mind made up. "You have a life here, Ruby. A good job. That's no small thing to throw away."

"Pa, you know I can't leave you." That one hope tumbled again and hit the ground hard. "We're a family."

"That we are, but there comes a time when a bird has to fly the coop and take to the sky with her own wings." Pa cleared his throat, but his words grew heavy with emotion and tears he did not shed. "Don't know what I will do without my Ruby-bug, but you need to stay. It isn't every day a man like young Mr. Davis comes courting."

"Lorenzo? He's not courting me." She had to agree to it before he could officially court her. Courting was not a one-sided endeavor. What he was doing was being kind, being interested, being gallant, but he could never be anything more than what-might-have-been. "You have it wrong, Pa."

"That young man is in love with you. How could he not be, my beautiful little girl?" Pa gently laid his gloved hand to her cheek, as he always used to do when she was a child. Memories of a lifetime of kindness and love snapped between them, father and daughter. "Don't let this chance for happiness get away. Chances like this come around rarely in life."

"Pa, it's not like that. I am never going to be the lady of Davis Manor." Could she imagine it? Never. She would picture Kate or Scarlet there instead and pray for it. She wanted Lorenzo's happiness and her friends' more than she wanted her own. "I appreciate the thought, but I cannot stay here. Maybe I can find work in a kitchen or caring for children somewhere up north. There's always the fields come spring."

"I want a good deal more for you, honey." Sorrow stood in his gaze. "You remind me so much of your mother. You are just like her. Sweet and stubborn and good, the light of my life. You deserve to live in a mansion."

"Love makes a home greater than any mansion could ever be. And I'm not changing my mind. You can't make me." She smiled up at him, resolute. "How much longer do we have here?"

"Not long. I'll speak to the banker again tomorrow."

"And what about Solomon?" At his name, her old friend nibbled at her knit cap, stealing it from her head. Her heart broke more, already knowing the answer.

"He would never make the trip north. I don't know what to do, poor fellow. I do not think I can even give him away. He's too sick and old for anyone to want."

Worry choked her.

"The neighbor has offered me fifteen dollars for Clover, when the time comes." Pa's voice cracked, his only show of defeat. "That will be enough for train fare for the two of us."

It was settled. They would be leaving most everything behind. Ruby wrapped her arms around Solomon, swallowing every last tear, refusing to let even one fall. Life was not fair. God had never promised it would be so, only that they would never be alone to face it.

Tucked in the warm stable lost in heartache, heaven felt far away.

So very, very far.

Chapter Sixteen

"Son, surely you are not abandoning me now." Gerard Davis leaned on his cane, his ready grin etched into his lean face. Behind him the manor was a flurry of activity, maids scurrying to and fro with mops and dusters, ordering around stablemen carrying their ladders and who knew what else.

Lorenzo sighed. So far he hadn't been roped into helping, but that was only a matter of time. He shrugged into his coat. "Sorry, duty calls. Some of the cowboys spotted tracks. Rustlers. They came back."

"How many head of cattle are missing?" Pa's good humor vanished, replaced by ashen worry.

"None yet. We've only spotted a downed fence." Last summer's trouble with rustlers had been serious, over a hundred animals had been taken. "Looks as if the rustlers spotted one of the cowboys on his rounds and ran before they took anything. Likely a small gang, maybe an individual, judging by the prints. It was hard to tell. But we want to put an end to this before anyone gets hurt."

"You be careful." Gerard swallowed hard. "I want to go with you, but I can't sit a horse with this leg."

"Ma needs you here." He knew his father carried great guilt over not being able to pull his weight around the ranch. Lorenzo clapped him on the shoulder, son to father, and smiled encouragement into his pa's worried eyes. "Mother needs one of us to order around. It might as well be you."

"That's a fate I'm proud to suffer." A hint of his good humor returned but not strong enough to outshine his worry. "You hurry back and suffer with me, you hear?"

"I hear." He understood what Pa didn't say. He squeezed once before letting go, blessed to have such a father, and grabbed the rifle he'd leaned against the wall. "I'll be back in one piece. Promise."

Pa didn't look reassured, but perhaps that was a father's job. Lorenzo cut in front of the upstairs maid, nearly invisible beneath a mound of lace draperies, and headed toward the kitchen. He intended to drop by and see Ruby. That put a spring in his step. Things had been so busy the last few days, he'd hardly seen more than a glimpse of her. His eyes hungered for the sight of her, searching for her the moment the kitchen doorway came into sight.

She was awe-inspiring. Nothing could be finer than those gossamer, white-blond tendrils curling around her heart-shaped face. Her big, light blue eyes, the cute slope of her nose, the purse of her rosebud mouth as she patted what looked like bread dough into a mound in a big bowl and covered it carefully with a dish towel. Love strengthened within him, too powerful to contain. It spilled over the rim of his heart.

What could he do to make her see it? To make her understand?

When she'd walked away from him again in the churchyard, it had taken every bit of his self-discipline to let her go. She'd said there could be no more kisses. Her circumstances in life must be overwhelming. With every fiber of his being, he wanted the right to fix her problems and to call her his own.

"Master Lorenzo." Cook's knowing look was full of mischief as she spooned flour into a measuring cup. "Your coffee is ready. Ruby, hand it to the young man, will you? My hands are floury."

It was nice to have Cook on his side. Ruby didn't acknowledge his presence. She swept to the counter to rescue a towel-wrapped canteen of coffee. She kept her eyes down, her chin tucked, moving like ten kinds of grace toward him. With every step she took, love arrowed more deeply into him, leaving his heart so consumed it was little good for anything else.

"Here you go." Her soft melody was his most favorite song as she thrust out the jug.

"Thank you, Ruby." What he meant was, *I love you.* What he meant was, *I don't want you to leave.* He could not say the words in front of Cook, and so he took the coffee instead. "This will help keep me warm this morning. You look busy."

"Yes, the ball is in two days, as you well know." A light dusting of flour streaked across her cheek, making her even more adorable. He resisted the urge to brush it away with the pad of his thumb.

"So I've heard." He tucked the canteen into the crook

of his left arm. "I was nearly trampled by a stampede of maids on my way here."

"They are preparing the ballroom."

"I noticed." The memory of their kiss played through him, like music too gentle to endure. Something mightier than tenderness seized him, a power of love he could not describe, but it was more unbreakable than steel. Did she think distance would stop his devotion to her? Is that why she had torn away from him that evening, sure there could be no more kisses?

She swirled away from him now, her duty in bringing him coffee done, but he was not done. Separation could not stop what he felt for her. Nothing could diminish it.

Lord, I pray again for her happiness. I pray for You to show me the best way to give that to her. All that mattered was her. Whether or not God meant for him and Ruby to be together, he intended to do right by her. He opened up to the Lord's leading, not knowing where it would take him. To heartbreak or happiness? There was only one way to find out.

He squared his shoulders, passed through the door and bowed his head against the biting wind. Judging by the angry clouds sailing in from the north, a bad storm was coming.

"You've got a knack for baking." Cook sidled up to inspect the row upon row of butter cookies cooling on racks. "Not a browned one among them. I'm rarely impressed. While they cool, come help me finish the gingerbread men."

"I've never iced anything before." Nervous, she wiped her fingers on a dish towel following Cook around one work table to another one in the corner. It was lined with several different types of cookies in various stages of decoration. Elegant swirls of colorful and lacy icing, sprinkles of cocoa and sugar powder, tiny accents of homemade candies were far too artful for her inexperienced hand.

"Then I shall handle the icing. You may add the buttons." Cook gripped a pastry bag and bent to work, adding smiling, red mouths to a row of cookie men one after another. "Surely you can do that?"

"Yes, ma'am." She harbored a great fondness for the stern lady, who wasn't so intimidating once you got to know her. She would miss working here. Trying not to look ahead to a future she dreaded, she sorted through a dish of small gumdrops choosing three yellow ones and pressed them neatly into the icing placket of a gingerbread man's coat. "I've never seen these kinds of cookies before, but shouldn't they be wearing pants, too?"

"Pants?" Cook roared with laughter. "Why, that hadn't crossed my mind. Surely we cannot have barebottomed cookie men at our ball."

It was pleasant watching Cook add flourishes of pants cuffs and then marking the toes and heels of stockings, for good measure. Amused, Ruby chose gumdrop after gumdrop and after the gingerbread men were fully clothed, added peppermint disks to the top of Christmas tree cookies. It took all her discipline to keep her mind from returning to Lorenzo, but she did it.

"The wind's picking up." Cook straightened and set aside her work. "Time to get that roast in the oven. You may as well get started on the potatoes. I'm planning on baking them tonight."

"Yes ma'am." Ruby tucked the last candy into place, watching as the snow tumbled in a torrent of wind-driven ice. An angry wind struck the house and rattled the glass in the panes. The gray light of afternoon drained from the sky.

"Mercy me, we need more lamps lit. See to it, Ruby." A roasting pot banged against the preparation table. "That is one mean storm blowing in."

She lifted the match tin off the shelf by the stove and lifted the crystal chimney of the wall sconce. One strike, the match sparked to life, and she tipped it against the wick, watching it catch.

The side of the house shook again as a harsh gust collided with it. The window turned white. She could see nothing, not one thing. Lorenzo was somewhere on the prairie in that. Was he all right? Could he find his way?

"That's one mighty blizzard." Gerard Davis ambled in, leaning heavily on his cane. Concern marked his forehead as he glanced at the closed door. Perhaps he had come to check to see if his son had made it home. "No one is coming or going in this. Ruby, looks as if you will be staying here for the night."

"Yes, sir." She replaced the chimney. She thought of Pa alone at home. "My father will worry."

"I'm sure he will miss you, but he has to know I wouldn't let you try to head home in this. You are safe, dear, that's what matters." He gazed out the back window, straining to make out any shapes in the storm, any glimpse of his son returning.

Her stomach twisted tight. What if Lorenzo hadn't made it to shelter in time? The bitter wind swirled, as if with a tornado's hand, and thunder cannoned so hard, it shook every pot and pan in the kitchen. Glasses tinkled. China rattled. Mr. Davis's shoulders sank a hint before he straightened his spine, leaned heavily on his cane and tapped away.

Worry ate at her as she lifted a second glass chimney and struck another match. Had Lorenzo felt the change in the storm and turned back from tracking the rustler? Or was he caught in the blinding blizzard, fighting his way with every step?

"Ruby, best get to those potatoes." Cook's voice drew her back into the kitchen.

"Yes, ma'am." She set the matches down with a clank on the shelf and pulled open the knife drawer to root through it, looking for a paring blade.

The back door burst open and slammed against the wall, caught by the wind. Icy flakes blasted across the threshold, borne on the blizzard's gale. A familiar silhouette broke apart from the deluge. Lorenzo, coated in white. He stumbled stiffly, frozen, as he awkwardly wrestled the door closed.

"Quick, Ruby, help him." Cook abandoned seasoning the roast and grabbed a chair from one of the work tables. Lorenzo stood, nearly board stiff. What she could see of his face behind his muffler was bloodless and caked white.

All the warmth had fled from the kitchen in the force of the wind, and she shivered hard. Ice crackled beneath her shoes. She didn't remember crossing the kitchen, only that she was at his side. "You've looked better."

"I've been warmer." His good humor hadn't been damaged. His midnight blue eyes warmed when he saw her.

Air clogged in her throat, and she blushed at the familiarity of his gaze, oh, so dear. He was a thick layer of ice everywhere. "Where do I begin?"

"The muffler." When he unclenched his jaw, his teeth clattered. "I can't move my hands."

"Don't worry. Let me." Concern rushed through her. Her uncle had lost part of his foot to frostbite. She knew how serious winter weather could be. Hoping Lorenzo would be spared, she broke through the caked snow looking for the end of his muffler.

There it was. Ice tinkled to the floor as she seized it and unwound it in one powerful tug. Aware of Lorenzo's eyes on her, she went up on tiptoes unwrapping the wool fabric from around the back of his neck, exposing his face. White skin, pale blue lips. Panic set in, and she yanked his gloves from his hands.

White. Dangerously white. Poor Lorenzo. Misery resonated in his eyes. He shook so hard, snow tumbled off him like rain. She grabbed his arm, pulling him into the kitchen where the stove's fire seemed defenseless against the encroaching cold. She cupped her hands around his much larger ones, willing warmth into them. Stumbling, she kept walking backward until she reached the stove.

"Sit here." Cook had moved a chair into place and now grabbed a hot pad to open the stove door. "You're frozen clean through. I must be fond of you to let you track so much snow on my clean floor, young man."

"Can't be helped. I'm part snowman." He hated it when Ruby's hand left his. He couldn't feel the floor or his feet. Heat flared from the stove, heat he could barely feel. But he *could* feel it. Relief hit him hard. Something tugged at his collar. Ruby, loosening his coat buttons. The fabric was full of ice, and it had packed around the buttons, making her task harder.

She smelled like ginger cookies and candy. The radiant breeze from the fire whirled fine tendrils against her ivory cheeks. Honest fear for him drew adorable crinkles into her forehead and around her Cupid's-bow mouth. He would never forget their kiss, the sweetness of it, the awe. Like a miracle, it had transformed him. His life would never be the same.

He saw his future in the aquamarine-blue of her eyes, his children in the shape of her porcelain face as she inched so close her hair brushed his jaw and caught on his day's stubble. She eased the frozen jacket off his shoulders, and for one priceless moment, their eyes locked. His spirit brightened, his soul filled and was renewed. He could see within her clearly, see the wrinkle of her brow, the surprise, her will. She moved away to hang up his jacket, unaware of her effect on him. He listened to the pad of her shoes on the floor and the rustle of her skirt as she left his sight.

But not his heart.

"Renzo!" Mother stormed in, a perfect expression of concern, to wrap a warm blanket around his shoulders. Chilblains poked painfully on his fingertips and toes, proof he would be fine. He had been watchful of the conditions and had headed home when the storm looked to be worsening. Ruby had already left the room to sweep up the snow in the entry hall. Each rasp of that broom grated, because he hated the distance between them.

* * *

If only the wind would stop blowing. Ruby saw nothing but her reflection in the smooth, black panels of glass as she settled into the common room in the maid's quarters. A fire snapped comfortingly in the hearth, but it was no match for the extreme cold penetrating the walls and windows.

The mantle clock struck eight times.

"It's time for me to head to my room." Cook's knitting needles made a final click. One by one, the other employees had vanished to their rooms, and now Cook stood, clutching her yarn. "Can you bank the fire when you leave, or do you want me to do it?"

"I can manage." She probably should retire as well, but the room Lucia had shown her to had felt lonely. She had never spent the night by herself before, in a room of her own. "Good night."

"Good night, Ruby dear." The older woman sashayed through the doorway, her no-nonsense gait fading to silence. The fire popped, and a few sparks flew. Was Pa sitting at home watching the flames in the grate, missing her the way she missed him?

"You look lonely sitting there." A familiar baritone startled her, a beloved voice that made her tense. The crochet hook jumped out of her fingers and hit the floor with a metallic chime. Lorenzo leaned one amazingly sculpted shoulder against the door frame. "How about some company?"

Her tongue failed her. Her mind failed her. Every logical thought scattered like smoke in a wind. Apparently, Lorenzo didn't notice. His endlessly blue eyes searched hers, seeing rather than hearing her answer that was both yes and no. Yes, she wanted to see him. No, she should not.

"I'll just stay for a few minutes." He shoved off the door frame and stalked toward her with his confident, easygoing gait, friendly, not threatening at all.

Except to her heart.

"Missing your father?" He eased onto the sofa alongside her. The rustle of the cushion echoed in the vast stillness of the room.

"A little. I wish the storm wasn't so fierce. I had so desperately wanted to go home. I've spent every evening of my life with Pa."

"He must be lonesome for you, too."

"That's what I was just wondering." It seemed as if the entire world had silenced, so that every thud of her pulse, every panicked whoosh of air into her lungs sounded shockingly loud. They were alone, just the two of them, and what was she thinking about?

His kiss. She should forget it. Forget everything. She watched as he bent to retrieve her crochet hook. Embarrassed, she felt heat stretch across her face. "I'm always dropping things."

"It's cute." He held out the hook. Firelight glinted in his dark locks and caressed the side of his lean face. Dimples bracketed a mesmerizing smile, a smile she adored.

Her shaky fingers curled around the hook he offered. *Think of something to say,* she thought desperately. But could she? No. Not one word. Seconds ticked by as his gaze stayed on hers, drawing her soul closer to his. Too close. Panicked, her mind spun. *Think, Ruby.* She bit her bottom lip. *Say something, anything.* "Your hands. How are they?"

"Much better, now I'm adequately thawed." His handsome dimples flashed more deeply. "Hazards of the job. I didn't want to quit when the snow worsened, but for all our effort, Mateo and I lost the trail."

She pictured him out on the plains riding into the teeth of a Montana storm, not knowing what lay in wait ahead of him. Worry gripped her, worry she had no right to. "Where does Mateo stay? He had to be just as frozen as you were."

"At the bunkhouse. Word is he's just fine, too."

"It was just the two of you out there? Aren't rustlers usually armed?"

"I am, too." Apparently danger was of no concern to him. A man like Lorenzo wasn't afraid of a little trouble. "I hated giving up. I wanted to catch 'em before they stole from us or our neighbors."

Don't imagine him on the back of his horse, riding like a hero through the winter snow. Don't do it, she told herself, but did it work?

No, her mind painted the picture of powerful man and undaunted horse, surrounded by snowy sky and reverent prairie. She kept seeing him through the eyes of her heart. How did she stop? Scarlet's face flashed into her mind, a friend who would put her love for a man behind that for a friend. She thought of her pa's face, haunted by worry and failure. Somehow, she had to find a way. Her fingers felt clumsy as she slipped her crochet hook into a loop and drew the thread tight.

"You are still making snowflakes?" He watched her

hook slip through and around, drawing the fine length of thread into a lacy pattern.

"Yes. I'm getting much better at it."

"I'll say. That one is flawless." It was the woman he referred to, not the delicate creation that took shape in her hands, but he was too shy to say it aloud. Yet. "The thread is pretty, too."

"It was a gift." She stopped to run her fingertip across the dainty strand. It shimmered like silk in the light.

"It sounds as if the wind is lessening." His presence made the room shrink. The few feet separating them seemed like inches. "Here's hoping the storm blows itself out overnight."

"I hope so, too, so I can go home. Oh, and because of your mother's ball. After all this preparation, it would be a shame if the weather was so terrible no one could make it." Bashful, she lowered her lashes, crocheting away. Did she feel this, too? So vulnerable, his soul felt exposed, as if all he was and ever would be lay defenseless before her?

"Weather has never stopped one of my mother's balls. Folks say it is the social occasion of the season around here. Ma loves being a hostess, and everyone knows it."

"I've never seen such a fuss. The house has been cleaned from top to bottom, everything is shiny and perfect." Her slender fingers stilled. "And the food. I've never seen so much baked goods in one place. Cook promised me it's just the beginning. We start cooking food for the buffet."

"I know what I'm doing tomorrow. Helping to cut, haul and put up the Christmas tree." It was his favorite part of the holidays, the best part of his mother's party. "Have you seen a Christmas tree before?"

"My friends told me the church has one every year, but I've never seen one. It's not something my family has ever done." She turned dreamy. "I can't wait to see a tree all lit up. Cook says the decorations are from Europe."

"My mother likes imported crystal and baubles." He couldn't wait to see Ruby gazing at the tree. He wanted to experience it through her eyes. He wasn't prepared for the spaces within his heart to open wider, leaving him ever more exposed. It hurt like a wound; it healed like a prayer. He loved this woman more than he could measure. She bit her lip again as her needle came to life. She hooked another stitch, knotted it and cut the thread with a pair of tiny scissors.

"Done." She pressed it flat with her fingertips, the silk in the thread glistened and gleamed. It was lovely, what she had made. She studied it critically and shrugged, hiding secrets in her voice. "Someone gave me the thread."

"Is that right?" He tried to sound casual, but his pulse pounded through him like cannon fire. He smiled, understanding without words how much she'd liked his gift.

"Would you like this one?" She held up the snowflake, perfect with six large points and six smaller ones. Lacy and airy and whimsical, just like the maker.

"I would." Not easy to hide his heart. He didn't even try. "I would like it very much."

"It's yours." She set it on the cushion between them, so reserved she could not place it in his hand. He adored her more as he tucked it into his shirt pocket for safe-keeping.

A knock rapped on the door frame. His mother swept in, not looking surprised at finding him with Ruby. She carried a small bundle tucked in the crook of her arm.

"Renzo, your father's leg is bothering him terribly in this cold weather. Could you go help him up the stairs? Ruby, dear, I've brought you a few things of mine to make your stay overnight a little more comfortable."

"Oh. Thank you." Ruby flushed, apparently surprised at the bundle of clothing topped with a brush and comb his mother set on the sofa table behind them.

"You have a good night, dear. Renzo, hurry. You know how stubborn your father gets." A smile warmed her words as she swept out of the room.

"Good night, Mrs. Davis." Ruby twisted around, but his mother had already gone, her gait tapping away in the corridor.

"Looks like I have to go." He hated the thought of leaving her, but his pa was waiting. He'd searched her out for a reason, so he gathered his courage and whispered in her ear, "Save a dance for me."

"At the ball?" His words startled her. Her eyes widened. She gave a little gasp. Her needle rolled across her lap, and she caught it before it tumbled off her knee.

Cute. He rose, towering over her, his love for her so big, larger than the sky. "Yes, Ruby, at the ball."

He couldn't wait. There he would have the right to hold her in his arms for one dance. It took superhuman effort to break from her side. Any parting felt like a rending loss, even if it was only for the night. As he headed for the door, he told himself it wouldn't be like this forever. One day, he would win her heart, and they need never be apart again. At least, that was his hope.

He glanced over her shoulder one more time just to see her smile. Just to feel the tug on his soul.

Chapter Seventeen

"You look beautiful, Ruby-bug." Pa stomped snow off his boots in the lean-to. "For a moment, I skipped back in time, and it was like looking at your ma when we were courting. I guess this means you might catch yourself a beau tonight."

"Oh, Pa. Really. I'm too sensible to let some man romance me." Love was putting others first above yourself. Love was not self-seeking. She twirled her bangs around her finger and hoped those fine, straight strands would keep a hint of curl. Tonight, Mrs. Davis needed everyone looking their best. What a blessing it was that this dress had been in the church barrel for her to find. "It will be a fabulous night, even if I'm there to carry serving trays."

"It was all I heard about every time I went to town." All week, he had searched newspapers and written in response to job advertisements but without success. While it was too late to save their farm, he'd hoped it might not be too late to avoid life on Uncle's ranch. A new job could change that. It was a hope they would not abandon until the very last. Pa shouldered through the door and drew it shut behind him. "Hear tell, the Davis's ball is quite an event. Maybe I'll get a peek through the windows when I come pick you up tonight."

"Pa, Solomon can't be out in this weather. He's still so terribly weak." She set down her comb, finished with her fussing. "Surely you don't plan on walking with me?"

"It will be well after midnight when your work there is done. Far too late for you to be on the roads alone." Pa cocked his head, listening. "Sounds like someone has driven up. It can't be someone from the Davis ranch come to escort you, can it?"

"No. Mateo lent me a horse from their stable to ride so I could come home and change quickly." She rolled her eyes. Honestly. The lovely velvet skirt shimmered richly as she crossed the shanty. "You have let your hopes get far too high. Lorenzo Davis isn't going to marry the likes of me."

"In that dress, he will likely consider it. Trust me." Pa probably thought he was being kind, but his words tore through her.

A dress did not make a woman. Integrity did. She checked the time—nearly five o'clock. She had best get going. Cook would be needing her soon to help with the last-minute cooking, although they had prepared most of the food ahead. She imagined all the lovely plates, dishes and platters spread across three consecutive cloth-lined tables loaded with delicious things to eat. At least it distracted her from thoughts of Lorenzo.

A knock rapped on the door, and Pa opened it. A middle-aged man in a finely tailored suit stood on the doorstep. Ruby recognized him. He was Meredith's father.

"Mr. Worthington. Good of you to drop by." Pa stepped back, opening the door wide. "Please, sir, come in."

Also the owner of the town's bank, Ruby knew. Cold fear shot like little spikes through her midsection. The important man did not smile. Tension drew lines around his kind eyes and his grim mouth. She knew why he was here. To evict them tonight. Her hands turned to ice. She went numb all over.

"I hate to bring bad news, but I have put it off as long as I can." Robert Worthington looked out of place in their humble home with his expensive clothes. "It's official. I'm foreclosing on this property. I'm sorry, Jon. But it will take some time to get the final papers, so you might as well keep living here through Christmas."

They could stay a while longer? Ruby's throat tightened. She could not believe Mr. Worthington's kindness. That would mean she could spend a little more time at her job and with her friends. They wouldn't be homeless for Christmas. They had more time for Pa and Rupert to find work.

"That's mighty generous of you." Pa looked choked up, too. "It's mighty appreciated."

"You make it easy, Jon. You have been honest with me since your crop failed. I respect that. Ruby, you must be going to Davis's ball tonight."

"Yes, sir. I'll be serving." Her skirts swished as she joined her father, standing at his side.

"Then I shall see you there." Mr. Worthington tipped

his hat, offered a consoling smile and headed out into the evening's dark. "I'll be in touch, Jon."

With a single nod, Pa closed the door. The dignity with which he'd been carrying himself shattered. His strong shoulders slumped, his straight back sank, defeat stole the life from his eyes. His jaw firmed, as if he was fighting hard not to give in to sorrow completely. "Worthington is a decent man. When I saw him, I figured he was coming to evict us. That we would need to leave tonight."

"I thought so, too."

"We have a reprieve, so you go have a good time, honey."

"How can I leave you now?" Torn, she thought of Cook who would be needing help and of her promise to Mrs. Davis not to leave her in a lurch. Her father clearly needed her, too.

"What do you mean? 'Course you gotta go. It will be something to see. All the folks dressed up in their finery. A fancy ballroom. I'm hoping to catch sight of that Christmas tree tonight when I come by. Ought to be one, fine shindig." Pa chucked her chin, just as he used to do when she was young. "You go tonight. You will always regret it if you don't. Think of your responsibility to Mrs. Davis. Don't you worry about your old man."

"You aren't so old, Pa."

"I'm old enough. Now, you go on. Save up every detail so you can tell me about it on our walk home tonight." Love polished his voice and shone in his eyes, chasing away his sorrows.

For now. Ruby gave him a quick hug before pulling

on her coat. It was final. It was real. This home was no longer theirs. They would be leaving this place and this life.

She blinked hard, refusing to give in to despair. It was only a farm they were losing and just a dwelling with four walls. That was all. It helped to remember this earth was not their permanent home, not the place their souls belonged.

Stars glittered overhead as she headed to the barn, gleaming so brightly, so beautifully, they had to be proof of God's word. He was watching and always present. They were not alone even when it felt like it.

There she is. Lorenzo's heart soared, his knees buckled and he had to grab the banister to keep from falling down the stairs. The house shone like a showcase, with every surface polished, wreaths and Christmas decorations and crystal-encased candles hanging everywhere. All of it paled as Ruby swept into sight down the corridor, her beauty outshining everything. He drank her in—soft, blond hair swept up, her precious face aglow, the dress skimming her frame like a princess's gown. She was his dream, everything he could ever wish for.

He could only hope she felt the same way.

He didn't know how he'd gotten so blessed, but he was grateful to the Lord above. Of all His blessings, Ruby was the most cherished. He watched captivated as she sailed out of sight, far down the hall, carrying a platter of sliced ham.

"Renzo." Pa tapped up in his best suit. Pride puffed him up, making him look once again the man he'd been before the rustlers' bullets. "I know that look on your face, since I've seen it on mine."

"What does that mean?"

"It means I looked the same way when I was courting your mother. You are a lost cause, son." Pa's grin widened. "What you feel for that young lady is no passing thing."

"It's forever."

"So I see. I've prayed the woman you fall in love with will be worthy of you."

"Pa." He grimaced, disappointed in his father. "I know you and Ma had hoped I would marry Narcissa or a woman like her, but—"

"No. You misunderstand. We were hoping you would marry *someone*." Pa shook his head, clearly amused. "All this time, you showed no signs of beauing anyone, and I was fine with that. You're young. But your ma is another matter. She thought you needed a nudge in the right direction. All this time, you had your eye on that little gal, didn't you?"

"Yes. I've loved her for a while." For so long, it felt as if he'd always adored her. As if his life hadn't started until she'd walked into it. "Then you and Ma approve of Ruby?"

"Approve of her? Why, she comes from a good family, and she's as sweet as could be. Now, about our house rules."

"I know, I know. I won't bother her while she's working."

"When I said that, I didn't know you were so serious about her. So be sure and get in a dance or two with her before the night ends, all right?" Pa clapped him on the shoulder.

Words failed him. He swallowed hard, unable to say what his father's support meant.

"There are my boys." Mother sailed into sight, resplendent in a deep green gown, radiating with the kind of happiness only hosting a party could bring her. "Don't you both look fine. Our guests are starting to arrive. One of you is going to have to come down here and help me greet them."

"That would be me." When Gerard gazed upon his wife, it was clear that true love existed and happily-ever-afters could come true. He lifted his hand from Lorenzo's shoulder. "Duty calls. And a little advice? Make sure it's a waltz."

Pa winked and tapped down the stairs.

"What are you two muttering about?" His mother planted her bejeweled hands on her hips. "Keeping secrets from me? Not for long. I will worm it out of your father."

"Worm away, darling. A kiss or two might help." Gerard slipped one arm around his wife's waist. Selma laughed as they walked away. That's the kind of happiness he wanted for his future. The kind of love that he felt for a certain kitchen maid who avoided looking his way as she swept through the ballroom doorway and into the corridor, her tray empty.

She hurried toward the kitchen and he watched her go, longing for a happily-ever-after of his own. Somehow, this had to work out between them. Because if it didn't, his heart would never recover.

He would never be whole again.

* * *

So far, so good. Lorenzo was nowhere in sight. She had managed to avoid him. No reason to think avoiding him the rest of the evening would prove any more difficult. She slid a tray of candied sweet potatoes onto the buffet table, readjusted a platter of smoked salmon and swirled on her heel. *There.* She breathed in the aromas of turkey and stuffing, of dumplings dripping with butter. The long tables of shimmering silver and glittering crystal, of ornate china and polished brass, were fit for a king.

"Do you have a moment?" A familiar voice murmured from behind.

Lorenzo. She jumped. She hadn't even heard him approach. He'd been sneaky, she realized, spinning around, glad her tray had been empty. Best to keep her eyes down and avoid the power of his gaze. He would see the sadness in her eyes and ask questions. Questions she didn't want to answer, because that would be confiding in him when she ought to be pushing him away.

You can do this, she told herself, cleared her throat and managed what she hoped was a neutral look. She had to come across as perfectly normal, completely unaffected by his presence. "Did I forget something? Is something wrong with the setting?"

"No, the feast looks wonderful. The guests think so, too. Look." He gestured toward the high, wide-arched entrance where elegant folks she didn't know swept in, sparkling with gems, replete with the finest clothes she'd ever seen. All exclaiming over the beautiful setting.

A lone pianist began to play at the grand piano in the far reaches of the room. Pure, gentle notes of great feeling lifted over the din of the crowd. Ruby fought the urge to pinch herself to be sure she was awake. Being in this grand ballroom with its two-story arched ceiling, Palladian windows and marble floor made her feel as if she'd fallen into a book, someplace far too opulent to exist.

A place where a girl's Cinderella wishes could come true.

"There is something you are needed for." He sounded serious, not that she dared to look up and see for sure. "You had better come with me."

Had she forgotten something? She had been so sure the initial spread had been laid correctly, that nothing had been forgotten. She had to follow Lorenzo through a nearby doorway, heart pounding, wondering what she'd done wrong. Why did he have to be the one to notice?

She kept her gaze trained on the alternating squares of yellow and ivory marble ahead of her toes. Whatever happened, she couldn't look at him. If she didn't see him, she could almost pretend they hadn't kissed or that he didn't care for her. If she didn't gaze into his eyes, she could deny the love staking claim in her heart.

She could never admit that love. She could not give in to storybook wishes. She would be the friend that Scarlet and Kate were. She would be the daughter her father needed. She was a homeless girl with a bleak future.

"This is the solarium." His baritone faintly echoed against the surrounding walls of bowed glass shining as dark as the night. Stars glinted in the panes overhead and cast a silvery glow to compete with the golden chandelier light tumbling in through the doorway.

"I've come to claim my dance." He held out his hand, his callused palm spread wide and waiting. The gentlest question whispered in his eyes and filled the hush in the air between them. "You promised."

"I never answered you."

"Then I heard it in your heart."

She forgot to keep her chin down. Lorenzo filled her vision, strikingly masculine in his black suit. A faint smile eased the chiseled splendor of his high cheekbones as he captured her fingers in his. She had to ignore the comfort, the *rightness* of his touch. She had to step away. Why weren't her feet moving? "I can't. My work. I'm expected to serve."

"I'm sure everyone will understand." His free hand caught her waist, as claiming as a brand. "Do you know how to waltz?"

"No. Which is another reason why you have to let me go."

"Sorry. Not my plan." His shoe nudged hers, forcing her backward in tempo to the piano music spilling into the room. "Just follow me."

His other foot guided hers one step over, one step back. She felt held captive in his arms by a force she could not break. *Dear Lord help me,* she prayed, because she could not help herself. Her heart leaped, and her hopes foolishly took flight. He guided her around the room in one slow swirling turn after another.

Pull away, she told herself. *Stop him.* But how could she? Against her will, her defenses fell, her resistance shattered and love she could not repress lifted her up by the heart. Think of Scarlet and Kate. Think of Pa. Anything but how wondrous it would be to lay her cheek against the dependable plane of his mighty chest.

It was like soaring to the music. His gentle touch at her waist, guiding her, anchored her. Otherwise, she might float away like a lost leaf in a wind. Every brush of her shoes to the marble, every lilting step taken in unison with him made her want to dream. What would it be like to be his?

Like this, she realized as his hand left her waist to settle at the nape of her neck. With infinite tenderness, he guided her cheek to rest on his chest and enfolded her in his arms. Heaven could not be this sweet or eternity this treasured. She let her eyes drift shut. Listening to his heartbeat beneath her ear brought her closer to him in spirit. Every step and every beat of their hearts were in synchrony, in perfect unity.

His chin came to lightly rest on the top of her head, so close, they shared the same breath. She was overwhelmed by the beauty of being held by him. Nothing could be finer, not in all her life to come. Her soul broke into pieces, and every shard of it was his.

I want this so much, but I know it cannot be. Give me strength to end it, she prayed. And in the same prayer, *Never let this end.* Greater love hit her hard enough to bruise, leaving a physical pain that ached in her chest like a wound. She curled her fingers into his jacket, the wool soft beneath her fingertips, wishing she did not have to let go. If only she could hold on forever. But finally, the piano music ended, the last, long note lingering like a memory.

He lifted his chin from her hair but did not move away, did not let go. Heaven could not feel as safe or

secure as being in his sheltering embrace. There were
no worries here, no strife, no hardship. Just the unspoken accord between two kindred spirits. Just his breath
and hers, and the blue of his eyes.

"You have come to mean very much to me, Ruby."
His lips brushed her temple.

She shivered with dread, knowing she should walk
away right now, before there was another loving moment
that had no future. But did her mouth open to protest?
Did her feet carry her away from him?

No, she stood rooted and mute, lacking the will. What
she felt for him was too strong, too great, too mighty.
She was small by comparison, a lone swimmer drowning in a vast sea.

"I pray that I have come to mean the same to you."
He took her hands in his. "I'm in love with you, Ruby."

"L-love?" Shock bolted through her. She'd dreamed
of those words, but to hear them spoken aloud meant
there was no going back, no pretending a romance didn't
exist between them. She squeezed her eyes shut, but that
didn't blot out reality. His hands cradled hers, his breath
fanned her cheek, his presence filled her with a light so
bright she could not deny it. Not anymore.

It was time to do the right thing. The thing she'd been
unable to do. Her heart had pulled her here, although
she'd known better. Scarlet wouldn't have done it. Kate
wouldn't have done it. And as for her father... Self-
reproach filled her. She wasn't the person she wanted
to be. Now was the time to start.

"I am very flattered." She opened her eyes, struggling, still longing for the feeling of waltzing in his
arms. "You know I think very highly of you."

"Just highly? That isn't exactly what I was hoping to hear." Tender, his tone. Always so caring. Hiding the disappointment that crept into his eyes, darkening them. "I was wishing for a good deal more."

"Me, too." She braced her feet, squared her shoulders and slid her hands from his. It destroyed her to do it. Pieces of her soul crumbled apart. This was it. After this, things wouldn't be the same between them. She would lose him forever.

"I know you are worried about your father. I am, too. You don't have to go through this alone, Ruby." His hands fisted, his only show of distress. "I'm here for you. You know that, right?"

"Yes, but I can't accept this." It was like dying inside to watch disappointment slip across his chiseled face. To see his hope became bleak acceptance. Hurt filled his eyes, but it did not chase away the radiant love, his beautiful love. Oh, she so did not want to hurt him. "The banker came by today. We have to leave. Probably right after Christmas. That will give us time to pack what little we can take on the train and to figure out what to do with the rest. With Solomon."

"You've decided. I can't change your mind?"

"No."

"I could still see you. You did promise to write me."

"That was when we were friends. Before—" *you said you loved me.* Heartbreak beat through her, a fresh wound.

"I don't want to lose you, Ruby." His earnestness, his unwavering commitment undid her.

"Neither do I." The truth won. For one instant, she dreamed. Of Lorenzo driving all that way to see her at her uncle's land. Of being beaued by him. Of having the chance to see where their love could lead.

But it wasn't right, and she wasn't free. Tears stood in her eyes because she could not have those dreams. She could not have Lorenzo as her one, true love. She broke away from him, stumbling backward. Staring up into his puzzled, tender gaze, she lifted her chin and gathered her courage.

"We have to be practical, you and I." It was as simple as that. "This is where our lives part. My father's spirit is broken. It's going to take everything my brother and I can do to see him through. I'm not the right one for you. I can't love you. I just do, but I c-can't."

Hot tears blurred her vision, and overwhelmed, breaking apart, she spun around, leaving him while she still could. Everything within her screamed at her to stay with him. To accept him. To follow her heart.

She ran blindly toward the door, listening to the swish of velvet and silk of her dress. Behind her, Lorenzo did not make a sound. She'd rejected him, and she was sorry for it. Was he hurting like this, too? She was doing the right thing, but it didn't feel that way as she stumbled toward the doorway. Now he was free to find someone who belonged in his world, like Scarlet.

"Why, Rags." Narcissa stood in the threshold, her mouth pursed in a brittle smile of triumph.

Had she witnessed the whole thing? Ruby's chin bobbed downward. As if the evening couldn't get any worse. She tried to slip by, but Narcissa refused to move.

"What are you doing in my old dress?" The superior smile turned calculating. "I threw that ratty thing away. It's so last season. Here's a hint. You really ought to stop rooting around in the garbage barrel."

Narcissa's words could not hurt her. They could not humiliate her or make her feel small. But Lorenzo had overheard, and that had been the woman's intent. Maybe now he would see the real Ruby Ballard, a servant in a cast-off dress, instead of through the blinding eyes of his love.

With a laugh, Narcissa stepped aside. Fine, all she wanted to do was to escape. She felt Lorenzo watching her as she slipped into the crowd. The room felt so normal. Everyone surrounding her was having a merry time. Yet, she was shattered. How could everything around her be so festive and merry?

Ruby, you should be working, she reminded herself. Working would help. It would give her something to do, some direction. But how could she focus? Her entire soul was lost. She had never felt more devastated.

"Ruby!" Scarlet sailed over in a gown of evergreen velvet with red, silk trim. "Ooh, it's so good to see you. What's wrong? You're crying."

"No, I'm not." Denial was her only recourse. She swiped her cheek, surprised to find that her fingers came away wet. "It's been a tough night."

"I can't imagine how much work you all put into this, but it's fabulous. You look fabulous." Scarlet gave her red locks a toss and took Ruby by the hand. "You could be a princess in that dress."

"I'm no princess. I'm just me."

"A princess," Scarlet insisted, the good friend that she was. "I know you are working, but come through the buffet line with me so I won't be by myself."

Ruby managed a nod. Somehow, her feet carried her forward. Somehow, she managed to smile and chat as if nothing was wrong, as if she wasn't defeated, as if she hadn't lost the best of all dreams, her one, true love.

There was no way Lorenzo could ever be hers.

Chapter Eighteen

Lorenzo was grateful for the vicious cold, which burned away all feeling, as he headed into a brisk wind. Glad last night was over—he'd barely survived the rest of the ball for his mother's sake—and now he was on the range. Away from every reminder of Ruby. But regardless of how many miles he'd covered with Poncho and his men, his broken heart came with him.

It was a clear morning. The sky, a mild, pearled blue, stretched in all directions over the soundless prairie. Nothing moved, not a leaf in the wind or a single wild creature, as Poncho plowed through a drift, following a trail in the snow.

Right now, he was especially grateful for his work. As long as he concentrated on tracking, he wouldn't have to think. And if he didn't think and if he was too frozen to feel, then he wouldn't have to go over last night again and again, breaking his heart ever more.

Her rejection had been clear, belying the love in her eyes. The love she hadn't vowed to return. He could still see the misery on her face, how torn she was. *I can't love you. I just do, but I c-can't.* The pain he'd felt from her had burrowed into his soul. He didn't understand, so he didn't know what to do. Did he let her go, as she wished? Or did he fight harder for her?

You are doing it again, Renzo. He shook his head, trying to scatter his thoughts. He would be wise to think about the missing cow. Think about his responsibilities. He glanced over his shoulder to check on the cowboys behind him. A gust of wind sliced through his thick layers of wool and flannel, chilling him to the marrow. He welcomed it. He clenched his molars against the pain of the cold, letting it overtake all other pains.

Not even the arctic temperatures could totally stop the torment of being separated from Ruby, from knowing she would never be his to love and care for. Now, when she needed it most. What would become of her and her family? The day after Christmas, he would send Mateo to make an offer on Solomon, so the poor horse would have a comfortable place to spend his final days. That was the only thing left he could think to do for her, to make her life easier.

Poncho's head went up, his nostrils flaring to scent the air. His neck arched, and he nickered. A trained cutting horse, he knew his job and led the way, his pace quicker now. The horses and riders following struggled to catch up. Lorenzo leaned forward in the saddle. What had his horse scented? He had better concentrate on his work and forget the beauty of holding Ruby in his arms. He remembered the image of agony in her eyes as she'd turned away.

Pain threatened to shatter him, but he kept on going. But did his love for her end?

No. His devotion to her went deeper than he'd ever

guessed. It was a force that would not end. Not now. Not ever.

"Poncho was right." Mateo pulled alongside on his pinto and pointed at a small shack tucked between a stand of trees and the snowbound plains. Smoke curled from the stovepipe. A cow, tied to a post, looked over at them curiously, casually chewing her cud. "Someone is squatting in one of the ranch's line shacks. Who's gonna ride for the sheriff?"

A face peeked out from behind a patched curtain. He caught a glimpse of fear and dark curls. "Let's see what we are dealing with first."

With a press of his heels, he urged Poncho toward the shack's front stoop. He had a bad feeling, but not one of danger as the door swung slowly open. In the doorway, a stoop-shouldered man shrugged into a worn, mended wool coat. He looked beaten down, hesitating on the top step. Inside the shack came the muffled sound of a baby's cry and a woman's soothing voice.

"Yer young Mr. Davis, aren't ya?" Head down, unarmed, the rustler closed the door behind him. "I figured ya not might notice one cow missing. Guess I was wrong."

"You don't look like a seasoned criminal, mister." Lorenzo's saddle creaked as he swung down.

"Never stole nuthin' before, and that's the God's truth. My wife and my son were hungry." The man wasn't as old as he'd first appeared, maybe twenty. Maybe younger. It was despair dragging him down and drawing lines into his gaunt face. The stranger looked like he was on the brink of starvation. "Whatever yer gonna do, do it to me. Just make sure Nan and the little ones are okay."

The woman with the dark brown curls reappeared in the window. As she soothed her baby on her shoulder, the sunlight shone on her lean face. He'd never seen anyone look so scared.

"I don't appreciate you stealing my family's cow." Lorenzo trudged closer, aware that Poncho came along with him, his friend and protector.

"Sure, I get that. What I did is wrong. I knew it at the time." Fear rattled through him visibly. "All I can do is apologize. I can't pay ya for the cow. I lost my job a while back. Couldn't get another. We couldn't keep our place, so when I saw this from the road... Why, we're in a hard way, Mr. Davis. I couldn't let my little boy go hungry."

He and the stranger were not so different. They were near the same age. They both had responsibilities and loved ones to provide for. Loved ones they didn't want to disappoint.

A toddler pulled open the door and stood staring out with wide eyes. Tears streaked his face. His mother darted into sight and snatched him back. Lorenzo noticed a dwindling pile of fresh firewood slumped against the side of the shack. An axe was sunk blade first into a downed, half-cut tree.

"Mateo, why don't you take the cow back to the ranch? Have Cook wrap up leftover food from last night's buffet. The Lord above knows we have enough to spare. I'm sure Mother will have a few things of her own to contribute. Put it all on a sled and bring it back here." He didn't turn to see the expression on his cousin's face, but he knew Mateo understood as he rode off to fetch the cow. Standing there, Lorenzo felt his other hired men's curiosity. "The rest of you come help me cut and stack more wood."

"What? You mean, y-ya ain't gonna have me arrested?" The man shook his head, disbelieving.

"Today is Christmas Eve." He watched relief pass across the stranger's face, saw tears spill down the wife's. "Merry Christmas."

Hard times came to everyone. No one was immune from them. He liked to think that if his Ruby were in the same situation someone would show her mercy. The snowflake she'd crocheted felt warm in his shirt pocket, where he kept it close to his heart.

"We'll do what we can to help you," he promised.

"Thank you kindly. I intend to work on yer ranch in payment." The man swiped dampness from his eyes, embarrassed. "You don't know what this means. My family is all I've got. My wife and boys, they are just everything."

"I understand. That's the way I love my family, too." As he wrapped his fingers around the stout handle of the axe's blade, he remembered what Ruby had told him. *We have to be practical, you and I. My father's spirit is broken. It's going to take everything my brother and I can do to see him through.* The full meaning behind her words hit him.

He'd just seen a glimpse of Ruby's past and of Jon Ballard's possible future.

The agony of his broken heart faded. He knew what he had to do. *You work in strange ways, Lord, but good ones. Very, very good ones.* He positioned a chunk of pine, brought the blade down into the wood, and the split pieces fell into the snow at his feet.

Ruby rapped her knuckles on Scarlet's ornately carved front door, more nervous than she could say. How did she tell her friends she would be leaving the day after Christmas, just two days away? How could she endure saying goodbye?

Sorrow gripped her. She straightened her spine and gathered every ounce of her inner strength, but the sadness refused to let go. It held her tight in sharp claws that cut every time she breathed. There had been so many losses and many more were to come. She refused to think Lorenzo's name, because she had to hold it together. This was a celebration, her last and her only Christmas party with her beloved friends.

"Ruby!" The door swung open and Scarlet stepped back in a swish of skirts. "We were waiting for you."

"Sorry I'm so late. I'm still on foot these days."

"I've been keeping your sweet Solomon in my prayers." Scarlet grabbed her by the wrist, lovingly tugging her into a soaring foyer. "Come in, take off your wraps. Meredith was just saying she should have run out with her horse and sleigh to pick you up after work. I was all for that. Handsome men work on that ranch."

"True." Impossible to deny that. She set her bag on a nearby table, tucked her mittens and her cap into her coat pockets. "I hope I didn't miss too much. I've never been to a Christmas party before."

"No, but you've been to a Christmas ball. I was just telling everyone about the tree Mrs. Davis had decorated. Oh, give me that. I'll hang it up." Scarlet cheerfully took the old coat, treating it with care as she hung it in the closet with all the others. "Those soaring little candles and balls of colored glass. Breathtaking. Come on. We didn't want to start without you."

"You waited for me?" Clutching her bag, she stumbled around a maid carrying a tray of empty teacups and trailed Scarlet down a wood-paneled corridor. Open double doors led to a sunny parlor, where familiar faces turned to greet her.

"Ruby!" Everyone chorused, standing to hug her one at a time. First Fiona, with her skirt barely hiding her growing stomach. Then Meredith, alight with the happiness of a woman planning her wedding.

"I hear you looked amazing in that dress." Lila, still wearing a newlywed glow, held her so tight. "I wish I could have seen you in it. Scarlet says you looked like a fairy-tale princess."

"I'm no princess." She blushed. Honestly. This was why she couldn't help adoring her friends. They were good to her. If only she could be as good in return. "You were the one who repaired the dress so expertly. Besides, I think Scarlet was exaggerating. If Earlee had said it, I would have understood, but—"

"Wait! What does that mean?" Earlee wrapped her in a hug next.

"You see everything like a story," Ruby pointed out. "A wonderful, happily ending story."

"I do tend to be a little fanciful, but I can't help it. It's just the way my mind works." Earlee rolled her eyes, adorable with her blond curls and sweetness. She looked particularly cheerful these days, perhaps because her job as a schoolteacher had made such a difference for her family. But that didn't explain the sparkle of quiet joy in her blue eyes, almost as if she were in love. *Interesting.*

"She's been this way as long as we've known her." Kate stepped up next to give Ruby a hug. "I would have loved to have been at that ball so I could have given Narcissa a piece of my mind. Scarlet told us."

"Saying what she did about your dress," Scarlet explained, taking her hand and guiding her to the sofa next to her. "Come sit with me. I've been saving you a place. Narcissa said it loud enough that half the ballroom heard. I nearly lost it, but I remembered just in time that I was a lady."

"You?" Kate quipped. "I've never seen you be ladylike before. Remember when you outran the fastest boy in the fourth grade when he pulled your braids and you took off after him?"

"You tackled him right in front of the reverend who was walking by on the street, and the next Sunday's lecture was about self-control and the importance of restraining one's temper." Lila burst out laughing, joined by everyone else. The merry sound rang in the lovely room like carillon bells chiming, a melody of friendship.

"I remember." Scarlet rolled her eyes. "I had the same urge last night with Narcissa. Can you imagine Sunday's sermon if I had?"

More laughter rang. *How wonderful it is,* Ruby thought, memorizing the sound. She never wanted to forget it. She wanted to hold it close forever.

"Before we get to exchanging presents and dinner—" Earlee started.

"And then on to caroling," Lila added.

"—I copied off the first few pages of my current story." Earlee reached into her bag, pulled out a stack of parchment and handed it to Meredith to pass around. "As you know, I've been penning stories since I was a little girl."

"No kidding. That's not news." Scarlet took two pages and passed the stack to Ruby. "Letting us read one of your stories is. This is exciting."

Ruby glanced down at the first sentence before she passed the last remaining pages to Fiona. Earlee's penmanship flowed flawlessly across the top of the paper. Unable to stop herself, Ruby began to read. *"Ma, when is Da coming back from town?" Fiona O'Rourke threw open the kitchen door, shivering beneath the lean-to's roof.*

"Hey, this is me!" Fiona nearly dropped her pages. "It's me, before I was married."

"It's the story of how you and Ian fell in love," Earlee explained. "Do you hate it?"

"No, I love it." Fiona beamed, reading on. "This is just like Ma and Da, too. Oh, you wrote about the day I met Ian."

"Well, it *is* a romance. I wanted to write about some of the people I love most—my friends. Someone I know thought I should try to publish it. What do you think?"

"Publish it? That's a fantastic idea."

"Fabulous. Does this mean we are all in the story?" Meredith asked.

"Everyone but Ruby, since we hadn't met you yet. Ruby, you make an appearance in Meredith's book."

"I get a book, too?" Meredith clapped her hands, delighted.

"Everyone will. I'm planning a series. It's so fun." Earlee ducked her chin, a little embarrassed as she pulled out carefully wrapped Christmas presents from the depths of her bag and set them one by one on the coffee table between them. "I'm hoping by the time I finish Lila's book, another one of us will be engaged, and there will be a new story to tell."

"Oh, I hope it's me," Scarlet enthused. "I need a tall, dark and handsome man to sweep me off my feet."

"What about Lorenzo?" Kate asked.

His name tore Ruby into shreds. Just when she'd been able to push the misery of losing him into the background, there it was again, stabbing through her as fresh as a new wound. Shattered, she gripped the edge of the couch cushion, holding on. She drew air in through a tight throat and tighter ribs.

"What about him?" Scarlet shrugged.

"Don't you like him anymore?" Kate asked. "What happened? I thought you were head over heels for him."

Just breathe, she told herself. *Relax. Maybe no one will notice.* She wouldn't have to confess what a bad friend she'd been, and they would never know what she'd done. Miserable, she forced herself to draw in air and breathe it out. She couldn't lose her friends, too.

"I was madly in love with him." Scarlet confessed with determined cheer, probably thinking she was hiding her heartbreak. "But I changed my mind."

"Why?" Lila wanted to know. "You've loved him forever."

"He is in love with someone else." This time Scarlet's determined words did not hold a trace of sorrow. "Someone suited to him perfectly."

"Narcissa?" Kate groaned. "Oh, no, not Narcissa. Anyone but her. Poor Lorenzo."

Ruby squeezed her eyes shut, knowing what Scarlet was about to say. It was too late. Scarlet must already know. And if she did, then she knew how Ruby had betrayed her. Grief cinched tight around her. She could not bear to open her eyes and see the disappointment on their faces, the disdain and perhaps the dislike she deserved. A good friend was loyal and true. Things she had not been. She hadn't done it intentionally, but it had happened all the same.

"It's Ruby." Scarlet's tone wasn't accusatory, but it rang with certainty.

"Ruby?" Fiona sounded confused. "Ruby and Lorenzo?"

Here it comes, she thought, bracing herself. Spine straight, shoulders square, she was ready to take the hit. They were going to be angry with her. They weren't going to like her anymore.

"I overheard Narcissa talking to Margaret at the ball," Scarlet explained to an absolutely silent audience. "She told how she saw Ruby dancing in Lorenzo's arms and that he professed his love to her."

"To Ruby?" Earlee blinked, clearly astonished.

No one said anything. She couldn't open her eyes. She couldn't face losing her friends, some of the greatest treasures of her life.

"Ruby, I want you to know how angry I am." Lila said it first, bouncing off the divan with a rustle of skirts and a groan of the cushion, her shoes striking hard against the carpet. She came closer, circling around the coffee table to loom overhead. "Judging by the way everyone looks right now, I'm not alone in my reaction. How could you?"

"It just h-happened." It felt as if the last blessing left to her was being ripped away. "I'm so sorry."

"You should be," Scarlet concurred. "A handsome man has fallen in love with you, and you didn't tell us, your best friends?"

What? Confused, she shook her head. She couldn't be hearing them right. It was her own wishful thinking changing around Scarlet's words. Surely Scarlet was hurt and angry and never wanted to see her again.

"We will forgive you, if you tell us all about it." Lila plopped down on the coffee table in front of her. "What did he say to you? Did you say you loved him, too? Is he your beau, now?"

"No. Because I ended it with him." She opened her eyes, ready to take the consequences. "I know you all h-hate me—"

"Why would we hate you?" Meredith asked.

"Because Scarlet and Kate love him. I tried not to fall for him, I honestly did. But he's so wonderful." She kept her chin up, surprised at the sympathy in Lila's eyes, at the comfort in Scarlet's understanding smile.

"We know how wonderful he is." Scarlet's heartbreak flashed on her face for one brief second before it vanished. "How could you have turned him down?"

"There's something terribly wrong with you, Ruby. Saying no to Lorenzo?" Fiona took Ruby's other hand. "Don't you love him?"

"More than anything." She may as well confess the whole truth. "But it's not right. Scarlet, you said that if Lorenzo asked to beau you, you would say no so Kate could have him. Kate, you said the same thing. I'm not that good of a friend."

"Don't you understand?" Earlee circled the table to kneel close. "You are one of us, our dear friend."

"And I said that about Lorenzo because Kate's happiness means more to me than mine, as yours does to me." Scarlet's eyes brimmed.

"We will always be the best of friends," Lila agreed.

"Which means no one wants your happiness more than we do." A single tear trailed down Scarlet's cheek as she smiled. "Accept him. No one deserves happiness more than you."

Tears blurred her eyes, making the nodding faces and encouraging smiles fuzzy. "Isn't it selfish, though, to put my happiness first?"

"Ruby, you are nothing but loving kindness. You would never hurt anyone for your own gain." Meredith squeezed in to offer a folded handkerchief. "When God gives a person one, rare chance for honest happiness and true love, only a fool would turn it down. A great, grand blessing like that comes around once in a lifetime."

"Just once," Earlee agreed.

"But I'm only me. I'm his family's kitchen maid." For the life of her, she could not imagine living in the Davis home, wearing velvet and silk and greeting fancy guests at next year's Christmas ball. Some dreams were simply too far out of reach for a girl like her. Her family was destitute.

"We are children of God, every last one of us, equal in His eyes." Fiona's fingers tightened around her own reassuringly. "We are all deserving of love, and that means you."

"Say yes to him," Kate urged.

"Accept him," Scarlet insisted. "We love you, Ruby."

"We absolutely adore you," Lila confirmed. "Now, go be happy. That would be the best gift you could give us on this Christmas Eve."

"I adore you all, too." Sobs shook her. She never imagined the friends she loved so much could love her the same way in return. She was the wealthiest person she knew, more blessed than she could say.

Chapter Nineteen

"Lorenzo just drove up." Lila reported as she unwound her scarf in the church's vestibule.

Ruby resisted the need to peer past Scarlet and over Lila's shoulder through the doorway to see him. She thirsted for the sight of his dimpled grin, his carved features and the miraculous bond that snapped between them when their gazes locked. She shrugged out of her coat, laid it on the table, and her palms went damp. It would be hard to see him again, because she knew it was too late.

She'd said no to him. She'd turned down her one chance for real happiness.

"Don't be nervous," Meredith advised in a whisper, for there were others around.

"Nervous? Me? I'm not nervous," she confessed with knocking knees. "I shouldn't have come tonight. It's going to be too hard to see him. There are plenty of sopranos, so I won't be missed. Maybe I'll slip out the back way."

"No, stay. It will be all right," Earlee encouraged.

"Stay and sing with us," Lila urged. "Lorenzo will still want you. You'll see."

She adored her friends, but they were wrong. She thought of her father home right now sorting through their things, deciding what to take and what would become of Solomon. Her life was no fairy tale and it wasn't about to become one. No matter how much she wanted it do. "I'll stay only if I'm hidden in a crowd. You have to help me avoid him."

"I'll do whatever you need." Kate sidled up next to her in the vestibule.

"I still think you just go up to him and tell him how you feel," Scarlet advised, although she squeezed in close, too. "Come on, let's head into the sanctuary. We'll stay with you, Ruby, okay?"

"Okay." She wouldn't have many more chances to spend time with her friends. She took a ragged breath, squared her shoulders and followed Lila through the doorway. She could do this. If she didn't look at Lorenzo not even once, then she would be just fine. It would be like he wasn't even there and she could stay numb. Pretend her heart wasn't decimated.

"Ruby." A man's baritone rang with surprise.

She jumped, pulse racing, before she realized it couldn't be Lorenzo. Dr. Hathaway ambled in her direction. "How's the wrist?"

"Healing. It doesn't hurt anymore."

"Excellent. I'm glad to see you're improving." He glanced at her friends, her protectors, who didn't move from her side. "I've never been caroling before, so this ought to be a fun experience. Is there any chance you might want to walk with me tonight?"

"No, thank you, but that's kind of you to ask." She said the words as gently as she could, realizing he really was interested in her. Bashful, she dipped her chin. "I hope you enjoy the singing, though. Merry Christmas."

"Merry Christmas." He tipped his hat, smiled briefly and ambled away.

"Look at you. Popular. In demand." Earlee squeezed her arm.

"Now we finally know he wasn't the one leaving the gifts," Meredith added as she joined them. "Who thinks Ruby is going to be the next one getting married?"

Ruby rolled her eyes at the numerous "I do's!" that rang around her. Her friends, honestly, they had romance on the brain. Or, maybe they were simply trying to make her feel less hopeless.

Reverend Hadly clapped his hands, pitching his voice over the din in the church. "Time to gather, everyone. Let's get warmed up!"

"Rags." Narcissa stepped in front of her and gave her curls a toss. In an expensive, wool dress, glittering jewelry and the finest shoes, Narcissa should have been a vision, except for the ungracious twist of her mouth and the sour look in her eyes. She said nothing more as she flounced by, but her malice and disdain spoke louder than any words.

Instead of feeling the brunt of it, the meanness bounced right off. Ruby watched her nemesis go, surprised at the pity she felt for the rich girl. Narcissa had everything a person could want—family, friends and a comfortable life full of beautiful things—but no happiness. She would spend the rest of her life putting down others because it made her feel better about herself, but it would never truly work. Unless she changed, Narcissa was doomed to a life filled with misery of her own making. She would never have what mattered most.

"Lorenzo," Scarlet whispered in her ear.

Lorenzo? Ruby fisted her hands, suddenly feeling the need to escape. She couldn't face him. Heartbreak battered her like panic. Before she could hurry out of the aisle, his presence washed over her like a sun break on a stormy day, changing everything. If she hurried, she could put enough distance between them before he came any closer and she wouldn't have to see the hurt in his eyes. She wouldn't have to feel her heartbreak. Why wouldn't her feet move an inch?

"Tell him, Ruby," Kate whispered.

"I can't."

His boots tapped a familiar rhythm up the steps, getting closer, each knelling footfall echoing in the evening's darkness. Her pulse thundered in her ears. She felt her friends leave her one by one, with a squeeze of her hand, a touch to her shoulder, a murmur of encouragement, but they were leaving her. Suddenly, she was alone with Lorenzo striding toward her.

He didn't smile. His gaze had shuttered, his face was stony. His mile-wide shoulders braced. Every shield he had went up. No caring radiated from his heart to hers. Just quiet apology as his eyes met hers.

It *was* too late. He no longer loved her. Fine. That was probably for the best but it hurt, how it hurt. Wretched, she spun on her heels, fleeing for the company of her friends.

Reverend Hadly clapped his hands. "Excellent. Great warm-up. Let's start on the corner of Main, and we won't stop until we've sung to every house on every street in our wonderful town. Now, bundle up and let's go caroling."

Cheers and comments rang out from the group as they broke apart. Somehow Lorenzo was in her peripheral vision, hands in his pockets, head down, already walking away fast, ahead of the crowd. Integrity and dignity radiated from him, unmistakable. A little sigh escaped her; she realized it too late to hide her adoration of the man. Love she could not stop cascaded through her with the force of a mountain avalanche.

Please. She thought she could feel God lean down closer just to listen. *Please take good care of him.* Lorenzo was not hers. He would never be hers to love. But she would always love him.

"Ruby?" Kate looked over her shoulder. "Are you coming?"

"What?" She glanced around, realizing she was still standing in place. Everyone else was leaving. She rushed to Kate's side, and her circle of friends closed around her.

"I couldn't believe it. He barely looked at you," Earlee said sympathetically. "Are you okay?"

She nodded. She would be.

"Maybe it will just take time," Lila agreed. "I think he's very committed to you. You just can't see it because you are afraid."

She hadn't realized how great his love for her felt, how it filled her world, until it was gone.

"We're right here with you," Meredith added.

Tears filled her eyes. Oh, what would she ever do without her friends? She set her chin, determined to handle this the right way. She did not want sadness to mar this wonderful evening of singing and joy. It was Christmas Eve. This night would make a memory she intended to cherish forever.

"Why don't we just have fun," she said, reaching out to take Kate's hand and then Scarlet's. "We are together."

The vestibule was crowded since they were the last of the carolers to amble in. Ruby spotted her coat and snatched it from the table. An envelope stuck out of one pocket with her name on it. In Lorenzo's handwriting.

Her knees turned to jelly. Her hands shook. She stared at it in dread. What could it be? Had he written her a goodbye letter? Agony cut her like a dagger. But what if he had written asking her to stay? It would only be proof he didn't understand. Pain took root, and she couldn't move. She was a mess. Singers filed out into the starry night as she slipped shakily into her coat.

"Hurry, Ruby." Earlee gave a little waving gesture from the doorstep. "We're waiting, but everyone else is leaving without us."

"You all go on. I'll be right behind you." She waited until Earlee was out of sight before tugging the envelope out of her pocket. Her fingers felt wooden, and she had a hard time pulling out the thick piece of paper folded up inside.

It wasn't a letter. It was some official document. It looked like—no, it couldn't be. Denial snapped through her as she straightened out the heavy parchment. The words on the paper were blurry. She blinked, realizing there were tears in her eyes. Tears that streaked down her cheeks and dripped on the hem of her coat and plopped on the toes of her shoes.

It was the deed to her family's farm. Lorenzo. He had done this. She stumbled through the doorway, swiping the wetness from her cheeks with her coat sleeve. In the fading starlight, she clearly read the property number. Lorenzo had bought the land and given it to her.

"I see your secret admirer struck again." His voice broke from the shadows, where his substantial silhouette separated from the darkening night.

"Yes. This is quite a Christmas gift. It's so unbelievable. I don't know how to thank him." She carefully folded the deed into the envelope and slipped it into her pocket. What did she say to thank a man for saving her father's dream? "I'm not sure Pa will accept it. He is a proud man. He doesn't let anyone pay his way."

"Not even his son-in-law?"

"His son-in-law?" Her mind whirled, spinning in place over his words. She sputtered. She couldn't think. She couldn't speak. Did Lorenzo still love her? He couldn't mean to marry her? Could he? She shook her head. No, that simply couldn't be right.

He strode toward her, as mighty as the darkly gleaming mountains at the horizon behind him, as stalwart as the ground at her feet. No man ever had looked as committed as when Lorenzo took her hand. He tugged her gently down the steps until they were face-to-face, hand in hand, alone beneath the dark sky.

"I love you, Ruby." In his voice, in his eyes, in his touch lay the truth. The proof of an infinite love that nothing could defeat—not time, not hardship, not even death. "From the moment I first set eyes on you, I fell hard. It was as if God touched my heart. Your family is my family. Your happiness is my happiness. There isn't one thing in this life that can ever mean more than you. Be my wife, Ruby. Please. You are everything to me."

Could this really be happening to *her*, Ruby Ann Ballard? She blinked, but the moment didn't vanish. It remained, real and true. There had never been a more beautiful night or a more amazing man. She wasn't imagining this, for Lorenzo's hands cradling hers felt real. So did the snow at her feet. Not far away, Poncho nickered, as if urging her to believe. A single snowflake swirled in the air and brushed cold against her cheek.

"You're proposing to me?" It was so hard to accept. She remembered how stony he'd looked in the church, and now she realized why. His hands trembled around her own. This moment was a great risk for him. He was offering her his world, all he was and all he would ever be.

"You are the one for me. The only one. Let me spend my life showing you. I love you so much. Every little thing about you." A muscle tensed along his jaw. His whole, vulnerable heart shone in his eyes. "Please say you love me, too. That you want to be my wife."

This was really happening. God was giving her this great chance at a once-in-a-lifetime love, and she was not going to let it pass her by. This man loved her family and had gone out of his way to show her how much he cared. She was not alone in that cherishing affection. She opened her heart fully, believing in her dreams.

"Yes." Joy lifted her up until she wasn't sure her feet touched the winter ground. All she could see was the matching joy on Lorenzo's face, lighting his eyes, filling his heart. They were connected, soul to soul, and would always be. "I love you more than I know how to say. I want to be your wife more than anything."

"Then I want you to have this." He knelt down in the snow to slip a ring on her finger. The golden band was warm from his pocket, and the gem as big as her thumbnail gleamed without a single light touching it. Snowflakes brushed the faceted surface. Never had she seen anything as stunning as his engagement ring.

"It was my grandmother's," he explained, standing again to tower over her, to shield her from the brunt of the rising wind. "The stone is a ruby."

"A r-ruby?"

"See? We were always meant to be."

Yes, that is just exactly how it felt when his lips met hers. Destined, as if God had led them every step toward each other, toward this perfect moment. In Lorenzo's flawless kiss she saw a glimpse of their future. Loving and happy, raising a family, growing old together, cherishing one another. They would be the wealthiest people she knew, rich in their priceless love for one another.

"I hear singing." Lorenzo broke the kiss, his gaze one of fathomless tenderness. In the distance rang the rise and fall of caroler's voices. "They have started without us."

"Then we had better hurry." *Think of all the happiness to come,* so easy to believe now. They walked down the street, together forever at last, in perfect harmony.

Heaven felt so close as the storm began in earnest. Snowflakes twirled like airy dreams too fragile to touch and floated on gentle breezes. They fell like Christmas

Eve blessings over the happy couple as Lorenzo pulled his snowflake bride into his arms and reverently kissed her one more time.

Epilogue

Christmas Day

"Rupert! You made it." Ruby launched herself across the Davis's toasty parlor, ran past the sparkling Christmas tree and into her brother's arms. Happiness lifted her up as he swept her into a quick hug. Oh, it was good to see him. To have him back where he belonged.

"It's great to be here." He stepped back, grinning wide. "I caught a break and found a job working at a dairy near Helena. The Good Lord provides."

"He surely does." Gerard Davis gripped his cane, limping over with a welcoming smile. "So this is the brother Ruby has gone on about. I'm pleased to meet you, Rupert."

"Good to meet you, sir." He couldn't stop smiling. "I hear congratulations are in order."

"They certainly are." Selma Davis circled around the sofa, sweeping up in her lovely Christmas dress. "Welcome to the family, Rupert. I don't have to tell you how much we already love Ruby."

"That's because they don't know me yet," she spoke

up, blushing. Honestly, she wasn't exactly sure what was wrong with the Davises, but they were easy to love. Already they felt like family.

"Rupert, you look half frozen." Selma took charge, always concerned for others. "Come get warm by the fire. Bella, pour him a cup of hot tea. You're just in time for Christmas dinner."

"Glad you could make it." Lorenzo came up to shake Rupert's hand. "Did you have a chance to check on Solomon on your way here?"

"I did. He's looking stronger. We have many blessings this Christmas."

"Very many," Selma agreed, giving Ruby's hand a squeeze. It was like already having a mother. A real mother. "I'm going to check and see how Cook is coming with dinner. Oh, Lucia. There you are. Is the meal ready?"

"Yes. Please come into the dining room." With a festive smile, Lucia tapped away.

"I hope you're hungry." Lorenzo sidled up to her. "It's the Christmas ball buffet all over again."

"I know, since I helped to cook it." She laughed, feeling light and incredibly hopeful. *Happy* didn't begin to describe it. *Joy?* Even that was too small of a word. Her engagement ring sparkled on her left hand, a symbol of his love. She thought of all the Christmases to come, of family gatherings and of their life ahead. All so wonderful. "Thank you for everything. I love you so much, Lorenzo."

"Not nearly as much as I love you." He kissed her sweetly, her husband-to-be. He noticed her father hanging back. "I'll wait for you in the hall."

"Thanks." She squeezed his hand, loath to let go of him. Her soul felt ripped apart as he left. Yes, God had been incredibly gracious to bring her here, where loved reigned.

"You look happy, Ruby-bug." Pa ambled over, looking bashful, looking proud. "That's the best Christmas present a father could want."

"Thanks for accepting Lorenzo's gift of the farm." She fussed with his collar. It was a little crooked. Then again, maybe it had more to do with her sewing. "I know it was hard on your pride."

"It was his gift for you, Ruby, and so it was easy to accept. I'd do anything for you, sweetheart. Anything at all." He brushed a kiss to her cheek. "Now, go to Lorenzo. He's waiting for you. And be happy. Grab all the happiness you can."

Bliss. That was the word. That described how she felt as she stepped into the hallway and into Lorenzo's loving arms. Some dreams were meant to come true, and this was just the beginning.

* * * * *

Dear Reader,

Welcome back to Angel Falls. *Snowflake Bride* is the fourth book in my Buttons & Bobbins Series. After reading these pages, I hope you felt as if you revisited old friends. I know I did. The Buttons & Bobbins girls are grown up and making their way in the world. Fiona is expecting a baby. Lila is a newlywed. Meredith is planning her wedding. Earlee is teaching school.

As you know, Ruby is the newest member of the Buttons & Bobbins girls. When I first met her in the schoolroom in Meredith's book, I fell in love with her meek and gentle sweetness. Ruby has a good heart, and I hope you came to love her, too, as God led her tenderly and surely toward the true happily-ever-after He intended for her. This Christmas tale reminds me of Cinderella with its Christmas ball, poverty-stricken heroine and a prince worthy of her. I hope Ruby's romance touched you the way it did me. Scarlet's story is next.

Thank you for choosing *Snowflake Bride*.

Wishing you peace, joy and love this holiday season,

Jillian Hart

Questions for Discussion

1. What was your first impression of Ruby? How would you describe her? What do you like most about her character?

2. How would you describe Ruby and Lorenzo's first meeting? Have you ever felt that shy with a handsome man? How did you handle it?

3. Why does Ruby believe Lorenzo would never be interested in her?

4. How would you describe Lorenzo's character? What trait do you like most about him? How has his family contributed to who he is?

5. How would you say Ruby's past has influenced her and made her who she is?

6. What does Ruby fear most?

7. What is the story's predominant imagery? How does it contribute to the meaning of the story? Of the romance?

8. In what ways is Ruby poor? In what ways is she rich? What role does her poverty play?

9. Do you see God at work in this story? Where and how and what meaning do you find there?

10. How would you describe Ruby's faith? Does it change through the course of the book? How would you describe Lorenzo's faith? Does his change through the course of the book?

11. What role does Ruby's friendships play in the story and the romance?

12. What does Ruby learn about herself? About her friends? About Narcissa?

13. What does Lorenzo learn when he finds the homeless family? How does that affect him?

14. What do you think Ruby and Lorenzo have each learned about love?

15. There are many different kinds of love in this story. What are they? What roles do they play in the meaning of the book? In Ruby and Lorenzo's romance?

INSPIRATIONAL

Wholesome romances that touch the heart and soul.

Love Inspired
HISTORICAL

COMING NEXT MONTH
AVAILABLE DECEMBER 6, 2011

MAIL-ORDER CHRISTMAS BRIDES
Jillian Hart and Janet Tronstad

THE CAPTAIN'S CHRISTMAS FAMILY
Glass Slipper Brides
Deborah Hale

THE EARL'S MISTAKEN BRIDE
The Parson's Daughters
Abby Gaines

HER REBEL HEART
Shannon Farrington

LIHCNM1111

REQUEST YOUR FREE BOOKS!

2 FREE INSPIRATIONAL NOVELS
PLUS 2
FREE
MYSTERY GIFTS

Love Inspired
HISTORICAL
INSPIRATIONAL HISTORICAL ROMANCE

YES! Please send me 2 FREE Love Inspired® Historical novels and my 2 FREE mystery gifts (gifts are worth about $10). After receiving them, if I don't wish to receive any more books, I can return the shipping statement marked "cancel". If I don't cancel, I will receive 4 brand-new novels every month and be billed just $4.49 per book in the U.S. or $4.99 per book in Canada. That's a saving of at least 22% off the cover price. It's quite a bargain! Shipping and handling is just 50¢ per book in the U.S. and 75¢ per book in Canada.* I understand that accepting the 2 free books and gifts places me under no obligation to buy anything. I can always return a shipment and cancel at any time. Even if I never buy another book, the two free books and gifts are mine to keep forever.

102/302 IDN FEHF

Name	(PLEASE PRINT)	
Address		Apt. #
City	State/Prov.	Zip/Postal Code

Signature (if under 18, a parent or guardian must sign)

Mail to the **Reader Service:**
IN U.S.A.: P.O. Box 1867, Buffalo, NY 14240-1867
IN CANADA: P.O. Box 609, Fort Erie, Ontario L2A 5X3

Not valid for current subscribers to Love Inspired Historical books.

Want to try two free books from another series?
Call 1-800-873-8635 or visit www.ReaderService.com.

* Terms and prices subject to change without notice. Prices do not include applicable taxes. Sales tax applicable in N.Y. Canadian residents will be charged applicable taxes. Offer not valid in Quebec. This offer is limited to one order per household. All orders subject to credit approval. Credit or debit balances in a customer's account(s) may be offset by any other outstanding balance owed by or to the customer. Please allow 4 to 6 weeks for delivery. Offer available while quantities last.

Your Privacy—The Reader Service is committed to protecting your privacy. Our Privacy Policy is available online at www.ReaderService.com or upon request from the Reader Service.

We make a portion of our mailing list available to reputable third parties that offer products we believe may interest you. If you prefer that we not exchange your name with third parties, or if you wish to clarify or modify your communication preferences, please visit us at www.ReaderService.com/consumerschoice or write to us at Reader Service Preference Service, P.O. Box 9062, Buffalo, NY 14269. Include your complete name and address.

UH11B

When former Amishman Gideon Troyer sees his Amish ex-girlfriend on television at a quilt auction to raise money for surgery to correct her blindness, he's stunned and feels a pull drawing him back to his past.

Read on for a sneak preview of
THE CHRISTMAS QUILT
by Patricia Davids.

Rebecca Beachy pulled the collar of her coat closed against a cold gust of wind and ugly memories. An early storm was on its way, but God had seen fit to hold it off until the quilt auction was over. For that, she was thankful.

When she and her aunt finally reached their seats, Rebecca unbuttoned her coat and removed her heavy bonnet. Many of the people around her greeted her in her native Pennsylvania Dutch. Leaning closer to her aunt, she asked, "Is my *kapp* on straight? Do I look okay?"

"And why wouldn't you look okay?" Vera asked.

"Because I may have egg yolk from breakfast on my dress, or my back may be covered with dust from the buggy seat. I don't know. Just tell me I look presentable." She knew everyone would be staring at her when her quilt was brought up for auction. She didn't like being the center of attention.

"You look lovely." The harsh whisper startled her.

She turned her face toward the sound coming from behind her and caught the scent of a man's spicy aftershave. The voice must belong to an *Englisch* fellow. *"Danki."*

"You're most welcome." He coughed, and she realized he was sick.

"You sound as if you should be abed with that cold."

"So I've been told," he admitted.

"It is a foolish fellow who doesn't follow *goot* advice.

"Some people definitely consider me foolish." His raspy voice held a hint of amusement.

He was poking fun at himself. She liked that. There was something familiar about him, but she couldn't put her finger on what it was. "Have we met?"

*To see if Rebecca and Gideon can let go of the past
and move forward to a future together, pick up
THE CHRISTMAS QUILT by Patricia Davids
Available in December
from Love Inspired Books.*

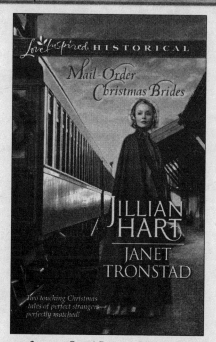

Love Inspired

As a teen, Lucas Clayton vowed never to return to Clayton, Colorado. Now he's back—with a child in tow—and no one is more surprised than Erin Fields, the sweetheart he left behind. But before he can convince Erin he's changed, he has to prove it to a young boy who needs a very special Christmas.

The Prodigal's Christmas Reunion
by Kathryn Springer

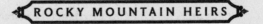

ROCKY MOUNTAIN HEIRS

Available December wherever books are sold.

www.LoveInspiredBooks.com

LI87710